W9-AUI-935

3 9094 01964 1727

WITHDRAWN

MELORA

G·K
Hall
&Co.

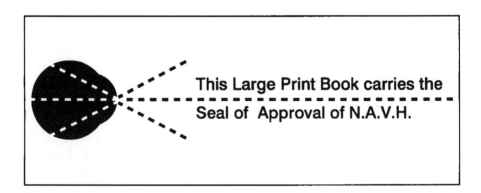

This Large Print Book carries the
Seal of Approval of N.A.V.H.

Melora

Mignon G. Eberhart

G.K. Hall & Co. • Thorndike, Maine

Published in 2000 by arrangement with
Brandt & Brandt Literary Agents, Inc.

G.K. Hall Large Print Romance Series.

The text of this Large Print edition is unabridged.
Other aspects of the book may vary from the original edition.

Set in 16 pt. Plantin by Al Chase.

Printed in the United States on permanent paper.

Library of Congress Cataloging-in-Publication Data
Eberhart, Mignon Good, 1899–
    Melora / Mignon G. Eberhart.
        p.   cm.
    ISBN 0-7838-9150-4 (lg. print : hc : alk. paper)
    1. Remarried people — Fiction.   2. Socialites — Fiction.   3. New
York (N.Y.) — Fiction.   4. Large type books.   I. Title.
PS3509.B453 M45 2000
813'.52—dc21
                                                    00-044835

01964   1727

To Carl E. Brandt,
friend and adviser,
with lasting remembrance

ONE

The night was extremely still, as if the coming storm paused to take wicked counsel with itself and gather its cohorts. It was so still that a sudden squealing of brakes from somewhere on the avenue shrieked like an angry cat, far away. The house was still, too; Anne could hear the rustle of papers from the small study that lay wedged in between her bedroom and Brent's. She could hear the sputter of a match as Brent lighted another cigarette.

She listened and thought of Melora, who had once been Brent's wife.

That afternoon, late, Anne and Cassie had had a difference of opinion. It was too slight to be called a quarrel; it was too nebulous to be called a disagreement, but Anne had opposed Cassie. Cassie was Brent's, and consequently Anne's, sister-in-law, Mrs. Philip Wystan. She had been widowed when Philip was killed during the war but she was still young and very beautiful. She was also very secure in her own and her two teenage children's positions in the Wystan house. Anne had married, in a sense, a ready-made family, in that Brent gave his brother's widow and his brother's children a home.

In contrast to Cassie's well-established standing in the house, Anne herself was still the bride, Mrs. Brent Wystan for only a few months, increasingly aware of her youth and uncertainty, amid the waves and cross-currents of the seas in which Cassie swam so easily.

The occasion for her difference of opinion with Cassie was absurdly trivial. Cassie had accepted an invitation for herself and for Anne and had failed to consult Anne, taking it for granted that Anne would comply. The result was that when Cassie came down the stairs, elegant in her jewels and furs and ready to go, she found Anne in beret and tailored coat about to go for a walk, obviously unprepared to accompany her.

Cassie's jet-black hair shone like satin. Not a strand was out of place beneath the hat which lay like a drifting of blue petals upon it; a spring hat, feminine and chic, although it was then early in January. She had very light, sparkling blue eyes which were exactly the color and brilliance of aquamarines and were set off rather spectacularly by black eyelashes. She eyed Anne, calmly.

"You didn't tell me that you weren't going."

"Going where?" Anne asked, startled and already feeling a premonitory touch of guilt.

"The Ingrams', dear. Cocktails. You've forgotten." Cassie glanced in the mirror, observed the effect of her hat, and added, "Again."

"You didn't tell me — I didn't know anything about it . . ."

"I told you when I accepted." Cassie leaned toward the mirror to scrutinize the crimson lipstick on her lovely mouth. "Darling, there *are* things that are expected of Brent's wife. Re-

8

member, dear, you married Brent Wystan. The wife of a well-known lawyer like Brent should undertake required social duties. You don't want to put a brake on his career, do you?"

"Brent is too good a lawyer to need me or anybody to push his career!"

"People like the Ingrams help."

"You *didn't* tell me about their party today," Anne said.

Cassie gave her a flashing light-blue glance. She opened the door but then, as if at an impulse, turned back. "Darling, when people say that they are only telling you something for your own good usually it isn't true. But this time it is really for your own good." She put her hand on Anne's arm and said gently, "You will believe that, won't you?"

"Why, I — yes, but what?"

"I have done everything possible to help you since you married Brent and came here to live — haven't I, dear?"

"Yes, of course, Cassie. I do thank you. . . ."

"So you will understand that it's my duty to tell you this."

"Tell me what?"

"Darling, Brent has been seeing Melora," Cassie said. "I had to tell you." She patted Anne's cheek lightly and went out in a cloud of perfume and furs.

She left Melora's presence in the house, as if Melora had entered it herself. Now, hours later, Melora was still there, in the house which Anne was sure Melora had graced with such beauty and had governed with such perfection.

Melora had then been Mrs. Brent Wystan. She and Brent had been divorced for over two years, long before Anne had met and fallen in love with Brent.

Anne had never seen a photograph of Melora. If there had been a portrait of her, it had been removed. She had never seen so much as some forgotten snapshot, lying unheeded in a table drawer or the pigeonhole of a desk. No one spoke of Melora. Yet Anne seemed to know exactly what Melora looked like. She had built up her image in her own fancy until it was clear and familiar.

Melora was tall and graceful in every smallest movement. She had dark hair and a rose-and-white skin and dark eyes, which could be arrogant and commanding and also gay and tender. She was elegant. She knew, and carelessly yet efficiently employed, all the extravagant luxuries of living. She was of course beautiful. And she had the assured strength of the conqueror.

It was Melora who had desired the divorce. Brent had told Anne that briefly, before their marriage. At the time it had meant no more to Anne than the fact that Cassie and her two children shared Brent's home and would continue to share it. Nothing that Brent could have said at that time would have penetrated the magic haze that enfolded Anne, nothing except that he had thought he loved Melora but discovered he didn't.

He didn't actually say that, then or at any time since then. Yet something in her marriage and in that house was not quite as Anne had expected it to be. It was a subtle, nebulous something, nothing she could analyze. It nibbled as lightly at her consciousness as a lazy sea nibbles at a rock; yet as powerfully. It was nothing that could be put into words, unless Cassie that afternoon had supplied the key word: Melora.

Brent had come home to dinner that evening, late and hurried. He had suddenly decided to go to France the next day, for a case which had been pending had unexpectedly cleared. He had planned to go to France sometime during the next month to settle the Cadell case, but as it had developed he could get off immediately. The Cadell case had been hanging on for years.

There was a scurry of telephone calls, reservations, packing. Then Brent settled down in his tiny study with a fat brief case full of Cadell papers and told Anne not to wait up for him, to go to sleep, he would be late. So she listened to the occasional rustle of papers in the study, the echoing chime of the great clock in the library on the floor below, and wondered if she could summon the courage to tell Brent that she knew he had been seeing Melora. Perhaps he wouldn't come in to say good night to her at all. She turned on the little bedside lamp so, if he did open the study door, he would see that she was awake.

Melora, she whispered to herself, and said it

11

aloud experimentally: Melora.

It was just a word, three syllables, yet nobody in that house had ever spoken it in Anne's hearing until Cassie had said that afternoon, "Brent has been seeing Melora. I had to tell you."

One o'clock and after a long, long time two o'clock struck. She heard Brent move about in the study and the murmur of the door as he opened it, looked in, and saw her light. He was in pajamas and a dark blue dressing gown and looked very tired. "You should be asleep."

Now was the time, Anne thought. She arranged words: something is wrong between us; if it is Melora, if you want her back — she couldn't say it. Instead she said, "No, I'm awake."

He came into the room. He looked very tall in the tailored, dark dressing gown; his shoulders very broad and yet muscularly compact and hard. His face with its generous width of forehead and chin was fine-drawn with fatigue. His eyes, as always, saw everything and, since he was a lawyer and trained to reticence, gave away nothing unless he desired it. He sat down at the foot of the bed, leaning back against one of the slender bedposts. "Lord, I'm tired."

Now was the time. Get it out, Anne told herself, speak Melora's name.

He was watching her now, struck by something in her face, frowning a little. "Is anything wrong, Anne?"

The tenderness and warmth in his voice, the

12

swift anxiety in his face almost banished Melora's subtle presence. Suddenly Anne saw herself as a jealous, suspicious wife, looking for an attack which didn't exist.

"No, no, nothing is wrong, Brent."

It didn't convince him. "Tell me, Anne."

It was utterly impossible now to speak Melora's name. It was as impossible for her to say now, I don't know what's wrong.

She folded the sheet into pleats, so as to avoid his too perceptive gaze, and as she touched her own initials, A.W., embroidered on the white linen, an ugly little whisper, deep in her mind, asked what Melora, if she returned to the Wystan house, would do with all those evidences of Anne's brief presence.

Brent said, "Dear, is it because I can't take you with me?"

She refolded the little pleats. She did want to go with Brent. She had not until then been separated from him, yet she had known immediately that there was no question of going. There wasn't time; she had no passport; it was merely a quick business trip. His hand came down over her own, warm and hard. "You look like a little girl, afraid of teacher. Look at me."

She looked at him then and he was smiling a little but very gently. "I don't want to leave you at home. I just can't help it. It's for only a few days. You'll be busy."

"No," she said unexpectedly. "I'll not be busy. There's nothing for me to do."

"Why — Anne!"

"Cassie does everything," she said and knew when she said it that she sounded like a sullen child.

"But Anne . . ." He held her hand, straightening out her fingers one at a time, absently. "Dear, why shouldn't she? She knows how things should go. She's lived here ever since she and Philip were married. She knows . . ." He broke off and took her in his arms. His lips moved against her cheek. "I didn't know you felt like this."

Brent was tired, she thought with remorse. "I'm making a fuss about nothing, Brent."

She couldn't guess what he was thinking. She moved her cheek softly against his lips and he kissed her. "It's for only a few days," he said then. "I should be back in ten days — two weeks at the most. . . . Oh, I forgot. I had to take some of the cash from the safe. Everything was so hurried at the office. I took what money old Stevens had there but it wasn't enough and it was too late to get a check cashed. But I've left enough in the safe I think, if you need anything. If it isn't enough, write a check. . . . Now then, I'll try to phone you from Paris, if there's time. I'm not sure yet whether I'll stop there or go straight to Nice. It depends upon reservations."

"Yes, Brent."

"I wish Cassie weren't leaving tomorrow, too. I don't like your being alone."

Melora's image had now completely vanished.

Anne herself was Brent's wife, close in his arms, listening to his husbandly, careful directions. He loved her. Of course, he loved her. She put her arms around his neck. "Alone," she said and laughed, "with the house full of servants! With Aunt Lucy so near!"

His face cleared. Lucy Wystan, Brent's aunt, was as dearly loved as his mother might have been. "Of course. Go to see Aunt Lucy."

"I will. . . . You must get some rest, Brent. It's so late."

He went to see that the window was open at the right height; his tall figure was silhouetted against the red draperies and the white glass curtains. "Going to storm," he said over his shoulder.

He came back, tucked the blankets around her and held her again for a long, close moment. He kissed her again before he turned out the lamp beside her. She watched him move through the little lane of light from the study. He turned back. She couldn't see his face, yet she knew it so well that she seemed to see every feature clearly.

"Good night, dear Anne," he said, and suddenly and vastly yawned again. The door of the study closed. The clock downstairs struck three.

Yet somehow, on the very edge of sleep, Melora seemed to return and stand, framed in the red curtains across the room, watching Anne, half smiling. In her dreams, too, Anne seemed to fight back that smiling image, which wavered and dissolved and yet stubbornly re-

15

turned as if it had an indestructible place in that house.

In the morning there was no time for talk, no time for questions, no time for doubts or uncertainties. Everything was hurried.

It was a complete hegira. Cassie's children, Tod and Daphne, home for the long Christmas holidays, were both going back to school. Cassie was going away for a country week end.

It was a dull, gray morning, threatening snow but still holding off. Just as everybody was leaving, Daphne made a scene. She flung herself upon Brent, locked her arms around his neck and said she wouldn't go back to school.

Brent was intent just then on the time. Cassie had worked it all out. She and Brent would go to Idlewild in the car, leaving Daphne at her school on the way. They would drop Tod somewhere and he would take a taxi to the Pennsylvania Station and thence to the Hamilton Preparatory Academy, not far from Trenton. After Cassie had left Brent at Idlewild, the car and Max, Brent's chauffeur, were to take her to her friends who lived north of Litchfield. Max would then return to the city with the car. It was a neat and efficient timetable, but it allowed for no delay.

Brent gave his watch a quick glance. "What's the matter, kitten?"

"I won't go back," Daphne sobbed. "Don't make me go, Uncle Brent."

"Daff, it isn't like going away from home. The school is only ten minutes away."

"I have to stay there nights," Daphne said and burrowed her dark head into Brent's shoulder.

It was a boarding school. Cassie had decided in favor of that rather than a day school. Anne had heard the long discussions about it. Brent, she thought, secretly had preferred the day school and Daphne's more constant presence at home.

"Now, Daff. Get your coat," Brent said and Daphne wailed, "I'm sick. You wouldn't make me go back to school when I'm sick."

It was of course Cassie's place to deal with Daphne's temperament but in fact, Anne had discovered, it was Brent whom both children respected as the final authority. He loved his brother's children, Anne knew, and she guessed that he tried to supply the fatherly advice and sometimes the discipline they required.

One of Brent's dark eyebrows lifted now indulgently but rather skeptically. "What's the matter?"

"I've got a terrible cold." Daphne's high voice was muffled against his shoulder. "Probably I've got pneumonia."

Brent looked at Anne. "Does she have a temperature?"

Anne put her hand on the child's face and Daphne wriggled to avoid it. Her cheek was warm. Anne got a firm grip on the square little chin and turned Daphne's face toward her. Daphne had light, clear blue eyes, like her mother's. They were bright, no tears in spite of her sobs.

17

Daphne jerked her head away. "Don't touch me! What do *you* know about it?"

"Daff!" Brent said sharply. "Don't talk like that. Apologize to Anne."

Daphne's hands doubled into tight little fists. "I won't apologize! Anne's just a little girl from the Middle West hunting for a job. And she got around you and got you to marry her!"

She stared defiantly at Anne, who wanted to laugh and wanted to slap Daphne in the same instant. Perhaps the impulse to laugh communicated itself to Daphne for she blinked and cried shrilly. "The same way Melora got him . . ." She stopped, put her hand over her mouth and stared at Brent, frightened by her own temerity. The name hovered in the air. Then Brent took Daphne by the shoulders. He was so hard and compactly built that his swiftness of movement was always surprising. Daphne's hand fell away. Her mouth opened in surprise. Brent said, "You're impertinent and insolent."

"I'm telling the truth," Daphne cried. "I won't apologize!"

"You will apologize," Brent said and shook her.

It was a very light shake but it astounded Daphne. Her long, dark hair fell forward over her face.

"Tell Anne you're sorry," Brent said.

Daphne sent one bright, furious glance at Anne. "I'm sorry," she said sulkily.

Brent eyed her for a moment and released her.

18

"I'll settle with you when I get back."

Anne felt a little quiver of amusement. It was the same as the age-old response of a harried parent when there was not time to deal with a naughty child at the moment of naughtiness. And Brent was the only father Daphne and Tod had ever known. While Brent was firm about certain basic standards he was also indulgent. Daphne clearly didn't question his right to punish her; she was only astonished.

Tod, arriving at the top of the stairs at that moment, was surprised, too, and pleased. "For gosh sakes!" he cried. "You shook her! I never thought you'd do it, Uncle Brent."

Daphne flashed a furious look up at her brother. "You'd take anybody's side against me!"

"If you had some beatings you'd be a nicer girl," Tod said nonchalantly and came down the stairs at a loose-jointed, coltish gait. His ears stuck out from his head like two exclamation points. His hair was cut so short that it looked like a dark rug plastered to his bony young skull. He went to the coat closet and yanked out his coat.

The old, tiny elevator, across from the stairway, gave its usual, ill-natured thump and Cassie emerged from it, smiled and said, "The car is waiting, Brent. Where's your coat, Daff?"

"Upstairs," Daphne said and darted up. Brent looked at his watch again and took up his locked brief case. There was a chain attached to it and he fastened the chain around his wrist. Tod, struggling into his coat, came eagerly to watch. "Are you really going to lock it, Uncle Brent?"

"Sure."

"Gosh. Just like the couriers."

"It's only so I'll be sure not to lose it. Here" — Brent gave him the key. "Want to lock it?"

Tod's eyes glistened. He bent over Brent's wrist. Cassie said, "Anne, I'll be back Monday, at the latest Tuesday. I'll phone so you can send the car for me. That is, of course, if you're not going to use it yourself."

"No, that's all right," Anne said, knowing that she would have no particular use for the car and feeling somehow extraordinarily young and awkward. Cassie was perfectly turned out, an elegant lady of fashion, groomed to the last tip of a red fingernail and the last feather of her sleek, black feather cap, which was almost the color of her hair and neatly veiled. She adjusted her fur coat and eyed the baggage that stood beside Brent's bag in the hall. "Oh yes," she said. "Don't forget that dinner party Friday a week. I hope Brent will be back by then."

Brent was talking to Tod and didn't hear her. Anne said, "No, I won't forget."

"The guest list is in the book. I've suggested a menu but of course change anything you like. Cook will know. If you're not certain about place cards I'll do them when I get back. I think you just might send out reminder cards this time. Coming right after the holidays when every-

20

body's been so busy. Yes, I think this time, reminder cards." She made a little mouth of distaste. Cassie felt that anybody lucky enough to be invited to dinner at the Wystan house was not at all likely to forget the date, the time and the honor.

Brent turned from Tod. "Cassie, Daff says she's got a cold. How about giving her another day or two at home?"

Cassie laughed gently. "Daff just doesn't want to go to school."

"Anne could phone the school, watch her. If she's really sick she'd call the doctor."

"You spoil those children, Brent," Cassie said. "Darling, I'm their mother. I love you for it but I'm not going to let Daff get her way too much." She snuggled her arm around Brent's in an impulsive way and hugged it. Brent said, "Well, then tell her to get a move on."

Tod lifted his mother's suitcase and sagged down exaggeratedly. "What have you *got* in this! You're taking enough luggage for three months!"

"Darling, tell Daff to hurry," Cassie said.

Tod quirked a dark eyebrow toward Anne. For just a second he looked like Brent, in his wryly amused expression rather than in his face, although he had the Wystan look of very direct gray eyes and unassailable composure. He went to the foot of the stairs and bellowed, "Daff! Stop looking in the mirror. Everybody's waiting for you."

21

"Don't *yell*," Cassie said sweetly. Brent took up his bag. Cassie sighed and spoke to Anne. "Darling, it's really too bad you're not going with Brent. London, Paris. The Riviera."

Cassie could not have meant to imply that Anne was not welcome on that trip, but Cassie's words did conjure up a flashing vision of Brent at gay dinner parties with distinguished people of the world; lazy, sunny days beside the blue Mediterranean — without Anne.

Brent said, "It's not a pleasure trip." He opened the door. "The car is waiting."

Tod said, "Shall I haul her down by her hair? *Daff, come on!*"

Cassie said, "Well, I'll let you know, Anne, when I want the car. Good-bye, dear." She swept out of the door. Max, the chauffeur, in Oxford-gray uniform, stood at the curb beside the long, luxurious town car. He came hurriedly to take Brent's bag.

Then in a scurry they were leaving. Brent kissed Anne quickly. She said, "Have a good trip," and he said, "Take care of yourself. I'll let you know where I'm staying." He ran down the two steps and across to the car.

"Daff!" Tod bellowed again.

"Don't *yell!*" Daphne said in exactly her mother's voice of gentle distaste. She came down the stairs wearing her blue, school uniform coat and carried the ugly, flat little hat that went with it and that Daphne would not put on her head until she reached the very door of the

22

school. As she passed under the bright light of the chandelier, it struck Anne that the child didn't look well. Her eyes were a little glassy, her cheeks faintly flushed.

Anne said uneasily, "I'd better get the thermometer . . ."

"There's not time." Tod grabbed Daphne's arm. "Come *on!*"

Anne stood in the doorway watching. Max scooped in the luggage, closed the door of the car, got into the front seat. The long car slid smoothly away from the curb, turned the corner and was gone.

The street seemed then very deserted and empty. There were one or two delivery trucks, a few cars parked at the curb. A maid, her white uniform showing below her coat, impatiently walked a dog who had a recalcitrant air and would not be hurried. It was a short street, lined with houses which were wedged together so tightly that cxccpt for an occasional, narrow areaway between them, they made an unbroken line of four stories each, with stately entrances, framed with shrubbery.

Anne could almost feel and taste the coming snow. She closed the door and it made as always a heavy but sedate and decorous jar.

The house then was extremely silent. After a puzzled instant, Anne remembered that it was Thursday, servants' day out. They had left as usual immediately after breakfast had been cleared away and the beds made, probably that morning a little earlier than usual since Cadwallader had known that there would be baggage to carry and had expeditiously removed himself, leaving the task to Max, who was a younger and stronger man.

As with other houses of the same period, there were stairways binding the several floors together — a steep front stairway, going up from the hall, and a still steeper stairway from the entry off the kitchen.

The plan of the house, too, was typical of its period. The kitchen and pantry and dining room were on the first floor. The dining room overlooked a small, fenced-in, city garden. On the second floor the library was at the north, the drawing room at the back and sunny side of the house. Above that were the bedroom floors, only one of which was now in use. There were rooms for maids on the fourth floor and when the house was built they were certainly in use, but times had changed. None of the servants now lived in the house.

She went down the hall to the elevator which somebody, sometime, sensibly had installed. It was small and had been there a long time. Sometimes it wavered upward and sometimes it stuck between floors, until Cadwallader, who understood its whims, contrived to set it on its way again. She closed the door and pressed the button for the third floor. It muttered and grumbled a little and then moved upward.

Her bedroom and Brent's little study had

become a refuge for Anne. They seemed less formal and strange to her than the elegant, vast rooms below, in which every chair, every ash tray was so precisely arranged that she felt that Cadwallader must use a yardstick when he dusted, in order to replace each article in its exact, prescribed position. It was a position which, she was sure, had been prescribed by Melora.

The tiny elevator gave a little lurch and stopped. She opened the door and went into the study.

The white piece of paper which was stuck into the roller of her typewriter caught her eyes at once. She turned on the desk lamp and looked at it.

It was her own letter paper. The words on it were typed in capital letters. I AM GOING TO KILL YOU.

TWO

It was a joke.

But where was the joke?

Who had typed it?

"I am going to kill you."

She stared at the paper in utter, frozen amazement.

Daphne had written it. Daphne, of course, although it was not consistent with Daphne's occasional but precocious sophistication. It was not the kind of joke that Daphne would consider a joke.

But she'd been in a tantrum and Brent had shaken her. It was a light shake but as astounding to Anne as it had been to Daphne and Tod. And Daphne, quite naturally, had turned her anger to Anne. She had gone upstairs for her coat and had been there long enough to stop in the study and furiously type out that childish, yet ugly, little message. It had to be Daphne. It wasn't like her but there was no one else who could have done it, or in fact had the opportunity to type it.

But Anne stood for a long time looking with incredulous eyes at the paper on the typewriter. Finally she took it from the roller with a swift sweep that made the roller clatter, tore it in pieces and dropped it in the wastebasket.

It was a small, trivial and childish thing. But

schoolgirls can be cruel, chiefly perhaps because a child knows nothing of the real nature and power of cruelty. Her thoughts went to the little scene Daphne had made that morning. "Anne's just a little girl from the Middle West hunting for a job. And she got around you and got you to marry her!" Daphne had cried, intending that to hurt, missing her aim, and seizing another weapon: Melora.

And of course Anne *was* a girl from the Middle West, fresh out of school, looking for a job, discovering that jobs were not easy to get but not caring, full of confidence, excited by her first flight from home on her own, excited by the great, glamorous city, excited by all the new sights and sounds and drama of life, when she met Brent. That was at a dinner party at the home of Judge Wallis, an old friend of Anne's father's, in August. In October she and Brent were married.

But she hadn't got around Brent in the sense Daphne meant it, and it seemed an odd thing for Daphne to think of, let alone say. "The same way Melora got him." Children do quote their elders. But nobody would have said just that to Daphne. Certainly not Aunt Lucy, never Aunt Lucy. Cassie then? But Cassie had been friendliness itself.

It didn't matter except that it brought Melora's name, whispering itself over and over, into the silent house.

Anne sat down on the chaise longue. Once the

study had been a dressing room; it was lined with mirrored cupboards. A big writing table for Brent now stood before the window. There were one or two comfortable chairs, a telephone, a small radio and Anne's own typewriter, a remnant of her job-hunting ambition. She had planned to make herself useful and take some of Brent's dictation. It hadn't worked out that way — his office routine was confined to his office — but all the same, the tiny slice of a room was like a haven for Anne.

A few great white snowflakes began to drift past the window. The sky seemed lower and darker. The house was too silent; it seemed to listen and watch Anne warily and a little inimically. The long mirror in the door of a cupboard reflected her coldly in her brown sweater and skirt. It also reflected her own face. She sat up and looked at herself — pale with troubled, drooping lips and blue shadows of sleeplessness below her blue eyes. What a face! she thought, with sharp impatience at her own brooding fancies. All the same, she wanted to escape the house — and Melora.

She went downstairs through the still and watchful house. She took her tailored, tan gabardine coat from the coat room off the hall. She made sure that the house key was in her pocket. She put on a navy blue beret and let herself out of the house. It was snowing a little harder; there was an electric cold in the air.

She turned toward Fifth Avenue, crossed it

and walked briskly along the wide sidewalk which edged the Park.

She walked on and on, passing other pedestrians, already bending their heads away from the snow. She passed nursemaids, scurrying for home, pushing perambulators with sleeping, rosy babies tucked under blankets.

When the great, gray bulk of the Plaza loomed up on the right, its windows twinkling with lights, she crossed Fifth Avenue again to enter a big, lighted coffee shop, where she lunched on coffee and huge, brown doughnuts.

It was snowing harder when she left the coffee shop. She walked home again. By then all the mammoth apartment houses lining the east side of the Avenue had lights which glimmered like jewels through the flying curtains of snow.

Already snow had heaped on the two steps leading to the massive, solemn door of the Wystan house and lay like cotton on the branches of the thick evergreens on either side of the steps. Across the street there were lights in all the houses, too; they looked discreet and dignified, behind curtains. She let herself into the hall and instantly knew that someone was in the house.

Perhaps in her first glimpse of the hall she saw the green scarf lying on the hall table beside the great bowl of crimson roses. There was a coat, too, in a careless huddle on a chair.

She stood for a startled second or two, staring at the fur coat flung so carelessly over the chair.

There was a tap of footsteps across the hall above. A woman came down a few steps of the stairway and leaned over the railing.

"Anne?" she said. "I'm Melora."

She couldn't be Melora!

That was Anne's first thought. The second was that she knew this woman, knew her as familiarly as if for a long time she had studied her face, her every expression, her very pulse beat. The first thought put itself into blunt, surprised words.

"But you can't be Melora!"

The woman only looked at her, soberly for a moment. Then she said in a matter-of-fact way, "Why not?"

"You don't look like Melora! I mean . . ." Anne caught herself. Of course, she didn't look like Melora, because Anne had built and fashioned her own image of Melora and that image was all wrong, a complete fabrication, nothing like the woman who leaned against the railing and looked at her with hazy, light brown eyes.

Anne cried, "But I do know you! I've seen you . . ."

"Oh, I don't think so."

"Yes, I have!" She was confused, yet very certain, too. "*You* must remember. You knew me when I came in!"

"Who else would you be? But we've never seen each other before."

There was no possible reconciliation between the real Melora and the Melora Anne had fancied.

The flesh-and-blood Melora was small, yet she had none of the fine-drawn elegance which Anne had expected. She was instead a little plump, a little shabby and untidy. Her hair was so light that it looked bleached; a pale, pale yellow which was almost white. It was very thick and rather tousled. She wore pink lipstick which had been carelessly applied, a mere smear across her lips, and no other make-up. Her black dress had a mussed, wrinkled look and was too tight for her. The tall, beautiful Melora, whose image Anne had conjured up and lavishly supplied with faultless elegance, was all wrong.

There was, in the same moment, another flashing realization. This Melora, the real Melora, had not chosen and planned the perfection of beauty within the house. This Melora had not decided with exquisite taste that that picture should go near this light, that this little figurine, this ash tray, this lamp should be placed on exactly this table or that case and not a hair's breadth to one side or the other. This Melora had not planned and ordered the household routine with such adroitness and certainty that, even in her absence, it carried on automatically.

And somewhere, sometime she had studied the real Melora so intently that there was a picture printed on her memory. She shut her eyes and tried to recover the whole of that picture. Suddenly it shot into being. "I do remember you! It was — yes, in the Fountain Aganippe restaurant at the Museum. You were with a man.

You sat near me. It was — oh, weeks, a month ago. I do remember. You wore — yes, you wore a black sweater and a — a locket! That was it! On a black ribbon, set with stones of some sort . . . Isn't that right?"

Melora laughed. She had a low, husky voice. "Quite wrong. You're thinking of someone else. You think it strange — I mean, my coming in like this. I rang and nobody answered and — the door was a little open — it does that sometimes, just jars itself open, so I came in."

She said it with perfect simplicity as if it were the most logical thing in the world. The heavy door was not quite closed so she came in — and waited for Anne.

"But — why?" Anne began and stopped, for she thought suddenly, did Brent tell her to see me?

But Brent wouldn't have done that.

Melora looked at Anne with that hazy regard for a second and then without a word turned and went back up the stairs.

Anne followed, trying to conquer the fantastic — and frightening — surmise which had leaped into being. Suppose Melora said, "I've come to tell you that Brent is still in love with me and wants me back, so let's talk it over like two reasonable persons."

Melora was already in the drawing room, turning on a lamp on one of the tables. Light sprang up, bringing color into the room. A great vase of early forsythia, forced in some hothouse, made a golden glow. Melora then sat down. She didn't look at home in the French armchair, with its pale gold and gray satin stripes. She squirmed uneasily. Her cheap, too tight skirt rode up, showing a runner in one thin stocking.

She reached for the box of cigarettes on the table beside her. She didn't look for it; of course, she knew exactly where it was. She took a cigarette and reached for the lighter and lit the cigarette with an unsteady, quick jerk.

Grasp the nettle, Anne thought. Her voice sounded clear and cold, cutting through the silence between them. "Why did you come here?"

Melora's head moved in a kind of undecided gesture. She put her cigarette to her lips and looked all around the room, slowly, taking in every detail of it. "You haven't changed anything. Not a single thing."

Anne couldn't have changed anything. She wouldn't have dared. She had thought that Melora had ordered that perfection. She had felt as if some unwritten but immutable law forbade the slightest change.

Melora's hazy eyes flickered toward Anne and away again.

Anne tried to control her careening thoughts, which she knew were thrusting her too fast and too far and perhaps in the wrong direction. "Brent is gone, as you know." Her voice was harsh with strain. "You can say whatever you want to say."

Melora said finally, "When did he leave?"

"This morning. Didn't you know that?"

With the toe of her shabby pump, Melora traced a rosy ribbon woven into the old, thin Aubusson rug, and said, "I want some money."

It was the last thing Anne expected her to say. "Money!"

"Yes. Please."

"But you *had* money," Anne cried in blank astonishment. She didn't know how much, but she did know that Cassie had once referred to Melora's divorce settlement in a veiled yet perfectly clear way as being far too generous on Brent's part.

"I know." Melora's white eyelids drooped. "I know but — isn't there some money in the house? In the safe?" She dropped an ash on the rug and guiltily scrubbed at it with the toe of her slipper.

"Do you mean that you *need* money?"

Melora nodded.

"But you — Brent wouldn't want you to . . ." Anne stopped. Brent wouldn't let Melora suffer for lack of money. On the other hand, Melora didn't seem to be suffering exactly and, besides, it was Brent's money to give, not Anne's.

Melora's eyelids fluttered. She looked up and down and said softly, "There is some money in the safe. Isn't there?"

"Y-yes."

"How much?"

"Why, I" — Anne caught herself on the verge of confused stammering again — "I'd have to ask Brent."

"You mean before you give me any money?"
Anne nodded.

"No," Melora said after a moment while she looked at Anne with that hazy, thoughtful regard. "No, that won't do. I have to have it now."

"No — I'm sorry — I can't."

Melora leaned forward. "Brent would give it to me," she said softly.

And he would give it to her. "He's a sucker," Cassie had said once, indulgently but half angrily. "Anybody who puts up a hard-luck story . . ."

Melora said, "How long have you been married? Three months — four? How long have you known Brent? Since last fall, isn't it? You don't really know him very well, do you?"

Wherever Melora had been living, whatever she had been doing, she had clearly kept herself informed about Brent. But then, Cassie said she had been seeing Brent.

"He'd give money to me," Melora said with cool certainty.

Anne didn't know whether the truth of it conquered her reluctance, or whether she simply had to get Melora out of the house, give her money, give her anything to get her to leave. "All right," she said shortly and walked out of the room. It was odd that she could walk, for her knees were shaking. She went upstairs; the safe was in Brent's bedroom. She pushed aside the picture which hung over it. Her fingers were unsteady as she twirled the knob; it took two or three attempts. Finally, the heavy door was willing to open. A sheaf of bills lay on the second shelf.

Melora, of course, had known that Brent always kept cash in the house because so frequently he was obliged to make sudden and unexpected trips.

Anne counted the crisp bills quickly. There were exactly five hundred dollars. She debated for a second, then took three hundred, replaced the remaining two hundred, closed the safe and went down to the drawing room.

Melora was standing at the end of the room, behind a chair. Her head was bent closely over something in her hands, which Anne could not see. Her pose suggested reading and near-sightedness. That, of course, would explain the way she looked at Anne. It was a near-sighted, hazy stare, anxious only to see clearly.

Melora heard her. She turned with surprising swiftness, and Anne had been mistaken; she wasn't reading. There was nothing in her hands. She came to meet Anne and passed her, without looking at her, going toward the door. She turned toward the stairs and disappeared and Anne was still standing there, her hand out, but Melora had taken the sheaf of bills.

Anne stared at her own empty hand. Melora had moved so lightly that it was like a trick of legerdemain, but she had taken the money. Anne caught a quick breath and followed Melora down the stairs.

She was already in the hall, near the door, reaching for her coat. She had pushed the money down the tight collar of her dress; it made a bulge just above her collarbone. She slid into the coat and picked up the scarf. The coat was mink and had once been a fine coat. It now had a look of shabbiness and lack of care. The guard hairs were worn down. One cuff had slipped its stitching and had not been repaired and hung down over Melora's hand. The scarf was a green, printed silk. It, too, had once been charming and pretty; it was now spotted and creased.

And suddenly, contradictorily, Anne wanted to put out her hand. She wanted to tell Melora that she would help her. She wanted to assure her of care. There, of course, lay the danger of the real Melora. In a flash of insight Anne recognized the strength of her appeal.

She wasn't beautiful; she wasn't elegant. She had a runner in her stocking and her high heels were worn down. Her obviously ungirdled figure was dumpy; her face a little puffy and too pale under the bright light of the chandelier. But all at once Anne knew that Helen of Troy needn't really have been beautiful; Mary Stuart needed no grace. They needed only to tug at the heart.

She looked up at Anne and said, "I'll go now," and tied the green scarf over her head, her hazy brown eyes fixed on Anne in a long, near-sighted look. Anne thought she was going to say something. She seemed to hesitate and hunt for words. But then she said only, "Thank you," opened the door and went out so quietly, yet so swiftly, that again it was like a magician's trick, an illusion. One instant Melora was there, fixing Anne with a long look in which there seemed to be some somber significance. The next instant she wasn't there at all. The closed door was like a wall. Its dark panels gleamed from polish. It was so sedate and so blank that it denied Melora's presence.

Anne sat down on the lower steps of the stairs. The silent house again watched and waited as if Anne herself were a stranger, an unheralded intruder in that house.

Moments must have passed before she thought suddenly that Melora ought not to go out into the storm like that in those thin stockings, those shabby pumps.

She ran to the door and opened it. Snow drove into her face. There was no plodding figure anywhere along the street. She closed the door again. The huge red roses from the table near by sent up a sweet and heavy fragrance.

The snow, now driving hard with a wind behind it, whispered against the door. Anne went slowly back to the yellow and gray drawing room. Melora's cigarette lay in the ash tray. The yellow and gray satin cushion of the chair where she had sat showed a slight indentation. There was the smudged gray trace of the ashes on the rug which Melora's foot had scrubbed at apologetically. So she had really been there.

If she had come to tell Anne that Brent was still in love with her, that he wanted her back again, then she hadn't.

If that hadn't been her intention in coming to Anne, there was no way to guess what it had been. She had asked for money, yes; but it was a casual request, almost like an afterthought. She had taken the money the same way, with almost startling avidity, yet as simply as if it didn't really matter.

She wouldn't have asked Anne for money if she hadn't needed it desperately.

Anne debated and came to the conclusion that she was wrong about that, too. Melora would have asked for money without the least pause or hesitancy.

It was snowing more and more heavily. Already the snow had muffled street sounds and put its own peculiar silence upon the already silent house, upon the streets, upon the whole city.

The clock in the library struck four times, its measured tone chiming heavily through the house. Anne wondered how long she had been sitting there, looking at the smudge of ashes on the rug, looking at the burned end of Melora's cigarette in the crystal ash tray, looking at nothing.

It was strange that while Melora had been so different from Anne's image of her, that image hadn't in fact vanished at all. A tall woman, with shining black hair and a beautiful face — a woman who could charm and yet rule, sure of her power — still existed. She still dwelt within that house, still eyed Anne with a half-scornful smile.

But instead of velvet dark eyes, which could smile and beckon and flash with anger, she now strangely had ice-blue, sparkling eyes, which Anne knew. It was, of course, Cassie's image, translated by her imagination to a fancied image of Melora.

Anne felt suddenly cold. She rose with a quick, almost frightened movement, crossed the room, and stood at the windows, looking down through veils of snow into the enclosed, small garden below the windows. The marble benches, the burlap-covered shrubs were now covered with snow, which masked their identities.

She wished she could mask as completely that image she had named Melora but which was in fact Cassie. But that was wrong, too; once that image of Melora was revealed in its own identity, she had to analyze it clearly and at once.

It was Cassie, of course, who arranged every detail of the house with such perfection. She knew that now after having seen Melora. It was, of course, Cassie who understood and performed so perfectly all the social chores which were important — Cassie had said they were important — to a man like Brent. Cassie was the authority in the house, a smiling, gracious and efficient authority, and that was perfectly natural. As Mrs. Philip Wystan she had ruled it and ruled it well. That was clear, too.

Certainly she had welcomed Anne. Certainly she had shown every evidence of friendship. She was Brent's sister-in-law but Brent thought of her as a sister, and it was certain, too, that no sister could have been more assiduously devoted to her brother than Cassie was to Brent. So Anne couldn't possibly have deep in her heart, unrevealed until then, a nagging, ugly little resentment about Cassie. If Brent had been in love with Cassie he'd have married her, not Anne!

He had loved his brother, Philip, but Philip had been dead for fifteen years. It was like Brent to care for Philip's widow and his children, but it wasn't like Brent to hug a grief so long or so closely that he would have felt it in any way disloyal to Philip to marry his widow. So he wasn't in love with Cassie.

"You understand," he had said to Anne before their marriage, "that Cassie and the children have shared my home," and Anne had said swiftly that they must continue to share it. She had seen herself making friends with Cassie and Daphne and Tod. The house was big, too big; it wouldn't have occurred to Anne to suggest their leaving. So Cassie had stayed, the children had stayed — and Cassie was mistress of the house as she had always been.

And that was the root of it, Anne thought at last, wryly. Without knowing it, she had been quite simply resentful of Cassie's position as mistress of the house. But she wasn't jealous of

41

Cassie or afraid of her, so she would exorcise that haunting image which had so persistently named itself Melora.

What of Melora, then — what of Melora? She couldn't be jealous of Melora either — and like her and be attracted by her at the same time. That wasn't possible either. And jealousy is a self-destructive poison. Well then, she'd put Melora out of her mind.

Another resolution formed itself quickly. She wouldn't quarrel with Cassie — but somehow, by making small beginnings, she would take her own place as Brent's wife.

She felt instantly more like herself, ready to tackle anything. It was as if she had needed a mental housecleaning and had accomplished it.

She turned from the window. A crumpled piece of paper lay on the floor, behind the chair where Melora had stood, bent closely over something in her hands as if she were reading, near-sightedly — yet in the same instant she had turned and there was nothing at all in her hands.

Anne picked it up. It was another sheet of her own letter paper. The same typed words were dreadfully clear in the gray light. "I am going to kill you."

THREE

She burned it to charred small bits in the ash tray where Melora's cigarette lay. Melora obviously had found it — where? — and read it and disposed of it with swift, almost furtive ease. Anne wondered what Melora had thought of it.

The ugly, acrid smell of burning paper lay in the room, haunting it and the house. She decided to go see Lucy Wystan. Brent had said, go to Aunt Lucy.

Lucy Wystan, Brent's aunt, could banish any dark fancy on Anne's part, merely by being Lucy. She hoped Lucy would ask her to stay to dinner.

As she started downstairs, the telephone rang. Its imperative peal startled her. For a second she thought, perhaps it's Brent. The bad weather just might have delayed his flight; he might be returning home. She ran to the telephone extension in the library.

"Hello, Anne." She knew the voice at once, hearty, warm, a little wheezy. "This is Gary Molloy. Is Brent at home?"

Gary Molloy was a lawyer, too. He was not a partner of Brent's — Brent had no partners — but he was an old family friend.

He sounded worried. "I phoned his office and they said he wasn't there and they couldn't tell me when he was expected."

"He started for Paris this morning."

"To settle the Cadell case?" There was dismay in Gary's rich, if husky voice. "I thought he wasn't going until next month!"

"He finished up another case sooner than he expected. So he had a chance to go now."

"Look here, something's come up about the Cadell case. Brent should know about it. Will he be phoning to you from Paris?"

"Yes, if he has time. What's wrong, Gary?" Dismay touched her, too. The Cadell case had dragged out for years; Brent had expected that his trip to France would at last end it.

"I'd better come around to see you." There was a pause while Gary seemed to consult his desk calendar. "I can't make it until around six, or a little after. Is that all right with you?"

"Yes, of course. I'll be here."

She wouldn't be able to have dinner with Lucy, but a talk with Gary and probably an effort to get in touch with Brent would give her something to do and something which was of importance to Brent.

She had too little to do. She had told Brent that impulsively and unexpectedly the night before, and it was true. She often felt like a guest in the house. But that was going to be different from now on.

In spite of everything Cassie had done, she always had time to make herself even more beautiful than she was. Anne glanced down at her brown skirt and sweater with sudden distaste, went up to her room, got out of the schoolgirlish skirt and sweater, and looked over what seemed to her an inordinate number of dresses. She chose a red dress, a favorite, of thin wool, expertly simple and fine in its dressmaking. She had selected it although aware of Cassie's politely unspoken disapproval.

Cassie herself usually wore custom-made dresses. She had introduced Anne to the great dressmaking establishments, the glamorous names in the world of fashion. Cassie was openly disdainful when Anne bought a dress or a coat or a blouse off the rack; it was Cassie's phrase for describing an ordinary dress. She had lifted her eyebrows at the red dress. "Red?"

"I like it," Anne had said.

"Oh. Take it then, darling."

But Cassie's eyes had traveled up and down and met Anne's eyes in the mirror of the fitting room. The red was becoming to Anne. It brought out the deep blue of her eyes and the curve of her red mouth. Her brown hair mysteriously became darker and seemed to curve more softly about her small head. She became unexpectedly vivid in the red dress, like a bird emerging suddenly with a scarlet coat. But Anne had been shocked by the price tag. She had been constantly shocked by the prices in the stores to which Cassie led her.

"But I've dressed for a year, everything, for less than that," Anne had said with dismay when she learned the price of another, simple blue dress which Cassie had made her buy, saying it would do for "little dinners." Cassie had said, "You weren't Mrs. Brent Wystan then."

She had guided Anne, like that, many times. It was obviously a kindness and a duty Cassie owed to Brent. So Anne had obeyed when Cassie said, buy this, don't buy that; go here, don't go there; be sure to speak to Mrs. Y., *don't* speak to Mrs. X; and never, never accept or refuse an invitation without asking me.

She wondered suddenly whether or not Melora had obeyed Cassie, but she could not envision the two women, so different, in agreement about anything.

The red dress looked bright and gay. Anne put on red lipstick, the same scarlet as the dress. She took out the fur coat Brent had given her. A wry little wave of mirth touched her as she thought of Brent absently signing checks to pay for all those fur coats, Cassie's, her own — and Melora's. There were bills for clothes, too; dresses and hats and slender, pointed slippers, and handbags, which looked so simple and cost so much.

Cassie had money. At least Philip had left her some money — perhaps not much. But if her income didn't keep up to her spending and Brent worked a little harder to make up the difference, certainly Cassie earned her keep. Anne didn't. But she intended to do so from that minute on.

She walked the nine short blocks to Lucy Wystan's apartment. The snow was steady as if settling in for a long performance and certain of its virtuoso power, but it was not yet truly a blizzard. The wide avenue was slushy and slippery. Traffic was slow and punctuated by loud honking. Already some of the cars showed dim parking lights.

There were few pedestrians. She thought of Melora's figure, plowing along through the snow, and wondered where she was by then. Probably she had reached home, some small apartment, tucked away on a side street, certainly untidy. She could almost see Melora plodding up a bare and shabby stairway.

Did Brent know that stairway and that apartment well? She thrust away that unexpected query with sharp impatience. She *wasn't* jealous of Melora. Or Cassie!

She stopped for the red light of a street crossing. Across Fifth Avenue the Metropolitan Museum made a vast gray shape. Workmen bundled up in coats and gloves were shoveling away at the broad steps, trying to clear off the trodden layers of snow. Lights glimmered all along the vast building. She remembered then, like the flash of a picture on a screen, exactly where and when she had seen Melora before that day.

Melora had said Anne was mistaken, but she wasn't mistaken. She *had* seen Melora, and idly, yet attracted and curious, somehow too, had watched Melora so closely that she remembered everything about her.

It had been perhaps a month ago, in December, when Cassie and Anne had gone to see a loan exhibit. Cassie had whisked her through it, pausing only for a brief survey of each picture and a close look at the tiny plaque showing the title of the picture, the artist's name and the name of the owner who had lent the picture. Cassie had worked at it with swift efficiency. When she left she would be able to discuss each picture and its place in the exhibition.

"There, that's done," Cassie had said with a sigh and looked at her watch. "Just in time. I told Max to bring the car to the door at three-thirty promptly."

But at the very door Anne had rebelled. "I'm not going yet."

Cassie had been surprised. "What on earth are you going to do?"

"Look at the pictures," Anne had said with an unusual edge in her voice.

Cassie hadn't heard and had not been even faintly aware of what seemed to Anne almost a dramatic moment of rebellion. "But we looked at the pictures!"

Anne had choked back an unexpected giggle. "I'll walk home," she said.

Cassie had looked at her watch again and smiled indulgently. "Of course, darling. As you please." She had gone down the steps where the car waited for them.

Yet if Cassie and Anne had been put to a memory test concerning that exhibition Cassie would have come out of it with flying colors and an exact catalogue of what they had seen. Anne had gone back up the long flight of steps.

However, in fact, Anne had looked at perhaps five or six pictures altogether; one or two of them for a long, long time from a close view which showed bold brush strokes, slowly back to a longer view from which all those strange brush strokes magically mingled and became light and shadow and depth. She then went to the restaurant. She was tired and took espresso (waiting as the enormous machine hissed) rather than walk the length of the room to the counter where she could get tea. She had found a small table near the pool and sat for some time idly sipping her coffee and surveying the enormous room, which centers about the huge, rectangular pool, where graceful, green figures of the muses ride with abandonment on strange sea creatures which thrust elongated, spouting heads out of the water. She had looked absently, too, at the people near her. Some were visitors to the Museum as she was, resting tired feet and eyes; some, she had thought, were art students. A man at a table near her had been reading a magazine and drinking tea. A woman across from her had been doing nothing.

After a while Anne had discovered that her gaze returned again and again to the woman across from her. She had been wearing black, a tight, black skirt and a black sweater, which came up in a roll around her neck. Her shaggy, very light hair had looked as if it hadn't been brushed. Her only ornament was a very large locket, set with small stones, turquoises and dark red stones, garnets perhaps. It had shown up strongly against the black sweater and the woman had toyed with it, turning and twisting it on its black ribbon. Once or twice the woman had released the locket, lighted a cigarette and smoked it slowly, with a quiet, deadly patient air of waiting for something that she knew was going to happen. Once or twice, too, her eyes had met Anne's in a hazy, half-focused way, which seemed, however, to mark Anne's presence.

Anne had looked away, half embarrassed, caught and staring, but then irresistibly looked again. She had finished her coffee when a man came in and joined the woman opposite. He had cut off her view of the woman's face.

That woman, of course, was Melora. Anne didn't remember anything of the man who had joined her. She had had an impression that he was young, and looked, she had thought vaguely, like a struggling young artist. Anne had left, suddenly sure that Brent was at home and waiting for her, and hoping that she might have a few moments alone with him before Cassie returned and before the relentless routine of the house began to operate in its evening course of cocktails (all together in the library), dinner (all together in the huge dining room where the clatter of a spoon sounded so loud), coffee in the drawing room, which Anne would have to pour.

50

Cassie had insisted on resigning her place at the coffee tray to Anne — and Anne had been sure, every time, that her hand would slip and send a cup crashing to the floor. The cups were Minton, Cassie had warned her, and had belonged to Brent's mother.

Brent hadn't been at home when she got home; there was a telephone message to the effect that he wouldn't be home to dinner at all. She and Cassie had dined alone.

But that *had* been Melora and that was why she had seemed so instantly known to Anne. The recollection evoked new questions. Where had Melora been living? Who were her friends and in what milieu had she spent those years since her divorce from Brent?

Anne was so deeply engrossed in thought that she passed the cross street and the towering apartment house where Lucy Wystan lived, and had to retrace her steps. It was so dark that the lights from the great building seemed to reach up into the sky. The doorman knew her and spoke to her. The elevator man said that Miss Wystan was in. Old Agnes, a cook and maid who had worked for the Wystans since Lucy was a young girl, met her at the door, took her coat and shook off the snow, and said that Miss Lucy was clipping the poodles.

Lucy had been born and lived most of her life in the Wystan house. It was only after Brent's marriage to Melora that Lucy had left there and

51

taken her own apartment. She had never married. Brent's and Philip's mother had died when they were very young and Lucy had stayed on in her brother's house to bring up his two boys. She loved Brent and she had loved Philip as if they were her own children.

She had been a beauty certainly and she still was. She had Brent's direct, dark gray eyes and the firm Wystan chin and strong nose. She had an air of fire and spirit and a keen but kind tongue. Her hair was still dark and brushed up in crisp curls, high on her rather haughty head. She was surprisingly youthful in appearance; she was as slim and erect and as lithe as a girl.

Her apartment was furnished with deep, comfortable chairs and sofas, and odd pieces of heavy old mahogany which had been in the Wystan house before it had been ruthlessly, yet oh, so perfectly redecorated — by Cassie, of course, not Melora. The huge wall desk almost reached the ceiling of the living room. All the furniture was outsize here, for it was a small apartment; a penthouse actually, with tiny rooms and an enormous terrace.

Anne never entered Lucy's apartment that she did not remember in vivid detail the first time Brent had brought her there. It had been a balmy evening in September. They had sat on the terrace before dinner watching the lights of the city and the blue hills of New Jersey. It had grown cold after dinner. Lucy had lighted the fire and they had had coffee before it and Anne made friends with the younger of her two poodles. The older dog, Brummel, was more reserved. When they left, Lucy had put her hands on Anne's cheeks and given her a serious, deep look and then kissed her.

That was only a few weeks before Anne had returned home to help her mother make preparations for her wedding. It was intended to be a small and simple wedding but actually the old gray chapel, with its ivy-laden walls, was crowded to the doors. Lucy had come with Brent. Cassie had had a cold and couldn't come and it had been decided — Anne didn't know by whom — that Tod and Daphne were not to be taken out of school for the journey west.

Within the week Anne's mother and father had left for Melbourne where her father had taken an exchange professorship. Their plans to leave, indeed, had been a clinching argument in favor of a marriage after only two months' acquaintance. Not that Anne — or Brent — needed an argument. Brent and her father had become friends at once. Lucy had stood with charming dignity beside them in the little receiving line after the wedding.

Anne now followed Agnes into the wide, comfortable living room where Lucy sat at a bridge table which was covered with newspapers. More newspapers were spread like a carpet around her. A huge apron was tied over her dress, and she wore gloves and horn-rimmed spectacles. She had an electric clipper in one hand and a firm grip on old Brummel with the other.

"Anne, how nice! Tea!"

Sister was already groomed to the last curl. She danced up to Anne, and Brummel gave her a long-suffering look over one shoulder. "Sit down, Anne. I'll just finish his pompadour." Lucy turned Brummel toward her.

He accepted the buzz of the electric clipper philosophically. He was so old that his front legs were bowed, his back consequently rose like a Bedlington's, and he had almost no teeth. He was bossy, selfish and adored Lucy.

Sister leaped on Anne's lap and thrust a delicate, newly manicured paw against her shoulder and complained of the recent clipping in a high soprano.

Lucy talked while she worked, of the storm, of Brent's trip. "He phoned to me last night. I hope he doesn't run into bad weather. But those planes fly very high. Do hold still, Brummy. There . . ." She turned off the clipper and eyed her handiwork. Brummel shook himself, scattering black, shorn curls and made to jump down, but Lucy lifted him from the table. "He will try to jump," she said. "Poor old boy. Hurts his back. I'll wash my hands while Agnes brings tea."

She gathered up the newspapers and the drifts of black curls first. Agnes brought in the tea tray, put it on a low table before the fireplace, and lighted the logs already laid. "Waste of heat," she said. "All the heat we want is in the radiators.

But Miss Lucy likes it."

Lucy came back. She had removed the gloves and apron and was in trim black silk with pearls at her throat, pearls at her ears, and smelling fragrantly of cologne.

Agnes folded up the bridge table. "Drink your tea while it's hot," she said and marched out, erect as Lucy, stiff as a poker in her gray uniform.

Lucy sat down before the tea table to pour tea, ordering Sister to behave. She remembered that Anne liked milk and no sugar. She tasted her own tea, sat back and looked like a delicate and dignified and rather willful duchess and said, "Now then. You'd better tell me all about it."

Her eyes were luminous; she saw far too much. Anne put down her teacup. Lucy waited and the fire crackled and Brummel gave Sister a push as Sister advanced too closely to Lucy's knee. Lucy smiled a little. "Cassie too much for you?" she asked briskly.

FOUR

"No," Anne said firmly — too firmly, for Lucy's eyes narrowed thoughtfully.

She said after a moment, "I don't meddle, not really — but I'm going to now. Brent should sell that monstrosity of a house and get a smaller place. Let Cassie find her own home, too. There's enough money for that. She wouldn't live in the luxury she likes — but she'd have enough."

"But Brent . . ." Anne began and Lucy picked it up at once.

"Brent feels responsible for Cassie and the children. That's right; he should be. Philip was his brother and besides — well, as you know, Philip was killed during the last days of the war, in combat. Brent was in the Navy but he had a desk job. I think he's always rather felt that, in a way, he got everything and Philip had nothing. He didn't feel it was fair. So he's tried even harder than I would consider strictly his duty, to make it up to Cassie and the children. But I think he's done more than enough. The children are now of school age. Cassie's a beautiful woman, still young. She could marry again. I want Brent to have his own life. I thought when he married Melora . . ." She stopped, sipped her tea and said, "I'm going too far. Once I start to talk I say too much. But of course Brent has told

56

you about Melora." All the same, there was the flicker of a question in the quick glance she gave Anne.

"Not very much."

Lucy eyed the fire for a moment. "Has Cassie talked of her?" she said then.

"N-no. Nobody mentions her, not directly."

"But haven't you even asked Brent anything?"

"No. I felt — I don't know — I didn't think he wanted me — or any of us to talk of Melora."

Lucy said shortly, "Sounds like Brent. Shut off the thing completely. Well, it's just as well. What did he tell you about Melora?"

"He said that it was an unhappy marriage. He said Melora wanted a divorce. He said that it was all in the past."

"Men can be so stupid," Lucy said crisply. "Like Bluebeard — locking the door and telling his wife she mustn't look inside the closet. Although I must say, perhaps he was right. Mclora . . ." She hesitated. Then she rose, a slim, charming figure in her trim black silk, took Anne's cup, refilled it and brought it back. "You've been thinking about Melora, haven't you?" It wasn't a question at all. Again it struck Anne that Lucy saw far too much. "Well, don't think about her. She's nothing to Brent now. Perhaps — well, certainly he loved her when he married her. It would be easy to love Melora."

I know, Anne thought; I know.

Lucy turned her unexpectedly strong profile toward Anne and looked at the fire, as if seeing pictures. "I liked Melora — at first. But even from the first I was afraid of her."

Anne sat up. *"Afraid of her!"*

Lucy's mouth was tight, her face looked older. "Afraid of her. For two reasons, I think. One was that she had a kind of appeal, something that made you feel sorry for her. It was very disarming. You let down your guard."

"But — why not?"

Lucy flashed a glance at Anne which held a hidden, remembered anger. "That was very unwise with Melora. The other reason why I was — afraid of her was because she was completely single-minded. There was nothing she wouldn't do, if she really wanted to do it. People like that are frightening. It's as if they see nothing else in the world but a tiny, telescopic view of one thing and one thing only. And she had a remarkably well-developed sense of self-preservation. I could forgive her that. There are things I could not forgive." Lucy looked at the fire again, her profile white and stern. "I've always thought that half of Brent's reason for marrying Melora was because he felt sorry for her. Yet, really, there was no special reason to feel sorry for her except she did seem to be alone in the world. I don't know much of her background; Brent met her at somebody's cocktail party." She paused and then said rather tartly, "I told you — I liked her at first. She seemed gentle, appealing — the point was that Brent loved her or he wouldn't have married her. So I was pleased. But not for

58

long." She broke some cake in half, gave one piece to Brummel and the other to Sister. "It's bad for their teeth but life is short and you may as well enjoy it. . . . It didn't last. It didn't last at all. Melora . . ." She stopped again, watched the fire for a moment, and then became abruptly elliptical. "I don't think that Melora was ever in love with Brent. In any event, she decided that she wanted a divorce. It was done at once and quietly. I never saw Melora again. Brent gave her fifty thousand dollars."

"Fifty thousand!" Cassie had only indicated that it was a large sum.

"She wanted it like that, in a lump sum. And, I told you — Melora somehow gets what she wants."

She now wanted and had got three hundred dollars. But what had she done with fifty thousand dollars in so short a time? To Anne, brought up in habits of thrift, it seemed a fantastic expenditure.

Lucy said crisply, "So if it's anything about Melora that's worrying you — and something is — forget it." She gave Anne one of her quick, heart-warming smiles.

Anne had to ask it. "Did — Cassie like Melora?"

"Heavens, no!" Lucy was startled. Then she gave a sudden giggle, like a girl. "If you knew Melora! She was wildly untidy. Threw things everywhere. Cassie couldn't bear that either." She didn't say what else Cassie couldn't bear. She

59

went on more soberly, "Cassie had the whole house done over just before Melora and Brent were married. Then I took my own apartment. The house belongs to Brent; my brother left it to him. But of course, when Philip was married — it was a wartime marriage, they were very young, Cassie was barely seventeen — it seemed convenient for Cassie and Philip, during his leaves, to live there. Cassie — and then the children — made it their home. When Brent came back he wouldn't, of course, put them out. So they're still there." She sighed and then gave Anne a little, half-mischievous (and very Wystan) quirk of an eyebrow. "If anything's wrong it's either Cassie or Melora! Which is it?"

"Nothing is wrong . . ." Anne began and Lucy laughed shortly.

"Anne! I've got eyes!" Lucy rose with a graceful motion and brought her an enormous green plate, full of cigarettes. "I've been wanting to talk to you for a long time. You see . . ." She went back to her chair and said forthrightly, "You've changed. When Brent first brought you here you were — eager and vivid and full of life and sparkle. You're different now, you know. You seem — not frightened exactly but uncertain of yourself. Diffident. You think twice before you speak and then, sometimes, don't speak at all. The fact is, two families don't belong under the same roof. Cassie tries to be helpful to you, I know, but perhaps she's too helpful. Remember, you are yourself. Now then

— what happened today? Don't say nothing happened."

She longed to tell Lucy of Melora's visit. She said instead, "Nothing really. Except — oh, Daphne made a sort of scene this morning. She didn't want to go back to school. Then she wrote some notes and left them for me to find."

Lucy sat up very straight. Her dark eyebrows came down. *"Notes!"*

"She was cross . . ."

"What did she say?"

"Well, she — both notes said — it's so silly, Aunt Lucy."

"Said what?"

" 'I am going to kill you.' You see how absurd it was."

Lucy's face lost its look of youth; it became thinner somehow and very intent. "That doesn't sound like Daphne."

"I didn't think so either. But there was no one else who could have typed them." She explained it briefly.

"Where did you find the notes?"

"One was on the roller of the typewriter. The other — in the living room."

Old Brummel knew that Lucy was troubled. He pressed his head against her knee and Lucy's hand went down absently to ruffle his ears. She said finally, frowning, "You'll have to tell Brent. I'm sorry he's away now. But as soon as he gets home, tell him."

"But Daphne . . ."

61

"Don't worry about Daphne," Lucy said.

Agnes came in to take the tea tray and pull the wide yellow curtains so as to shut out a darkened snowy sky. Anne started up. "I must go. I didn't realize how late it is."

"Stay to dinner," Lucy said. "Stay here to-night."

"I'd love it," Anne said and meant it. "I can't. Gary Molloy wants to see me. It's something about the Cadell case."

"Oh, that!" Lucy cried with exasperation. "Well — Agnes! Mrs. Brent's coat. You did wear overshoes, didn't you, Anne?"

Anne nodded and laughed. "Thank you for everything."

"Don't thank me. . . . What do you hear from your father and mother?"

"Oh, they're well. Mother wanted more walking shoes so I sent them air express."

"How long will they be away?"

"A whole year. Two if they want to stay."

"I liked them. How did your mother manage to keep her sense of humor, living in a little college town all her life?"

Anne laughed again. She felt entirely restored, as if Lucy had brushed away cobwebs which really were merely cobwebs and as ephemeral. "You don't know a little college town."

"No," Lucy said, suddenly grave. "But I think I know one of its products. You're idealistic, Anne, not practical. And I don't want you to be hurt."

She kissed Anne lightly so it was only a quick, warm pressure and a scent of some clear and spicy perfume. She said soberly, "I do have to say this. Those notes — well, a doctor or a lawyer is vulnerable in an odd way. I mean to spite, revenge, that kind of thing. Somebody who lost a case and blames the lawyer and . . ." Lucy patted Anne's shoulder and said briskly, "Daphne must have written those notes. But just — be careful, will you? And tell Brent about them as soon as he gets home. Now make the doorman get you a taxi if he has to fight for it. Remember me to Gary." Again a mischievous, youthful smile flashed into her face. "He was once a beau of mine."

"You must have had them by the score!"

"To hear Agnes tell it, I was the belle of every ball. Don't believe it. But Gary was always a pushover for a pretty woman. Good night, my dear."

The doorman did, after some time, snare a taxi, which arrived with a passenger. It was after six though by the time Anne reached home. She shed her coat and overshoes and went back to the pantry to assemble decanter, ice and soda on a tray, remembering that Gary liked Scotch. She put out some sherry for herself and had barely done so when the doorbell rang and it was Gary, puffing and hurried, his face pink with cold.

He shook his head at the stairs and went back to the little elevator. He had a pleasant face, blunt and extremely mobile. His curly gray hair rimmed a small, bald spot. His eyes were a little faded. His voice was musical and could sway juries — it had many times. It was also a little husky with years of good living, good eating and good drinking. He said, "This is not the kind of weather for a man of my years to exercise himself. . . . Not that I did. I snatched a taxi from under the nose of a charming young girl. A lost opportunity." He chuckled and adjusted the pink rose in his buttonhole. The elevator gave its grudging bounce and stopped. He opened the door. "That Scotch is just what I want." He led the way into the library, settled down with a sigh into one of the deep, red leather-covered chairs, took the drink she poured him, turned it in his hands and said, "I think Brent has got the wrong boy."

"Oh *no!*"

"Sounds like it."

She sat down on the sofa. "But they went all over his papers, records, identification, everything. Everything seemed satisfactory."

He drank and leaned back. "I expect you know all about the Cadell case."

"Brent has told me of it."

"Of course. Brent has talked to me, too. In fact, everybody knows about it in a general way. It's one of those famous cases, something nobody ever expected to be settled." He drank again, half closed his eyes and said, "I'm sure I've got the main facts straight." He thought for a moment and then outlined it succinctly, as if

64

he were dictating notes for one of his own briefs. "This man, Jean Cadell, a Frenchman, was killed in an accident in the chemical laboratory of the Controlla Company in 1943. There was no question of his widow's right to claim an indemnity but owing to the fact that he was an independent contractor . . ." He looked at Anne. "Do you know what that means?"

"I know that there's a very large sum of money involved."

"Yes, well — you see he was not employed on a regular salary basis. He was a young and, it was thought, a brilliant chemist. So he was employed by the Controlla Company on a contract basis for a certain length of time, I've forgotten how long. Their idea I suppose was to pick his brains. But the point is the indemnity was consequently outside the usual employer's compensation laws. His widow could have sued for any sum she wanted, no ceiling to it. She didn't sue because the Controlla Company preferred to settle the thing. However, his widow was living in France, where Cadell expected to return at the end of his contract. His widow and their son. Her name was . . ." He hesitated.

Anne said, "Lisa. The boy's name is René."

"Right. Well, before the claim could be paid through a bank in France she was killed in an air raid. The boy disappeared."

Anne nodded. It had been fatally easy for a child to vanish in the wild wake of a war which had laid whole towns in waste.

Gary went on, his full, rather protuberant eyes half closed. "After the war they were able to discover the facts of his mother's death. At least they assumed them to be facts . . ."

Anne interrupted. "There was no real record of it. No grave registration. The little town was heavily bombed. Everything was a shambles. She just disappeared but the officials of the town were sure that she died in an air raid."

"Right. So the money was never paid but there was always the chance that the son, the legal heir, might turn up and claim it. It was one of those unfinished pieces of business. The legal tenure — that is, the time limit for a claim — ran out some time ago. But the Controlla Company is a substantial business" — he opened one eye and glanced at Anne with a twinkle — "well aware of the force of public opinion. And of the unpredictability of juries. Now then, I believe it was about three years ago, perhaps less, the boy — at any rate *a* boy — turned up in France and wrote to the Controlla Company, claiming to be René Cadell. They turned the thing over to Brent to settle. The Controlla Company is, of course, one of Brent's most important clients. It took a long time. The boy had to search out identification, try to find records that had been destroyed, establish his identity and claim, all that. In the end, after thorough investigation, they've decided that in all probability he is Lisa Cadell's son and are prepared to pay him the money. They could have raised the objection of

66

tenure. They waived that." He opened both eyes. "*Are* they completely satisfied?"

"I think the final decision is up to Brent. Nobody has seen the boy. They feel sure he's René Cadell but they rely on Brent, you know. So he's to question him, talk to him. If he feels satisfied, then he's to empower the bank to pay the money."

Gary nodded. "You can get more out of ten minutes' conversation with a man than years of letter-writing. Funny — but a trained lawyer gets a sense of the truth. So if Brent says pay him, they'll pay him. Well . . ." He hitched forward, reached for the decanter with unexpectedly fine and delicate hands and poured himself another drink. "I think they've got the wrong boy."

"Oh, Gary!"

"Another feller came to see me today. Says he's René Cadell. He doesn't have much in the way of papers — I mean birth certificate, marriage certificate for his parents, nothing like that. Which, oddly enough, is rather convincing. He's perfectly frank about that; says he couldn't get them, doesn't know how to get them, and in any event they would be only replacements, written up by some little town clerk or mayor, who wouldn't have been likely to know either his mother or him. He does have some letters though and" — he frowned — "he said he had one or two sentimental proofs — he said sentimental proofs, those very words — which he wouldn't show me. He could be René Cadell. He's got a good story. But it's entirely different from the other boy's story."

"What is it?"

"Well — he says that he got shipped off to England during the war. Under the name of Crayshaw — not his name."

"But how . . ."

"I'll tell you. His mother tried to get him a passage on a boat that was full of English children being sent home from France. There wasn't any passage but at the last minute a boy already booked, by the name of Crayshaw, didn't turn up. I don't know how his mother managed it — he doesn't either — but somehow she got him on the boat, saying he was the Crayshaw boy, and in the flurry and excitement nobody seems to have questioned it. He was herded off to a place in the country, full of kids who were sent out of London. Stuck to the name of Crayshaw as his mother had told him to do. Stayed there till the London bombing began. When so many English children were sent here to escape the bombing, some American woman said she'd take care of one of them, so he was shipped off again with a boatload of children. Woman's name was — March, I think he said. Anyway, apparently she wrote to his mother, Lisa Cadell, and heard from her a few times through the British agency. Then the letters stopped. After the war he stayed on with Mrs. March — he calls her his foster mother — although she didn't legally adopt him.

The point is he has the letters from his real mother and showed me one of them. I must say the whole story was convincing. Says he didn't come forward sooner because he didn't know about it. His foster mother died a few years ago but it was only recently that he went over her papers and found the letters. One of them mentions his father's death and the Controlla Company." He sighed. "There are some gaps. But just the same — well, I think he may be the right feller. So Brent's got to know about this before he pays out all that money to the feller in France. How much is it? Must be close to a quarter of a million."

"About that, I think. Thanks, Gary. Brent must know about this right away."

Gary brooded for a moment. Then he put down his glass. "Well, it's simple. I'll get hold of the air line, get them to radio a message to Brent. Now mind you, there hasn't been time to investigate this new feller's claim. May be all hogwash. All the same, it wouldn't do Brent any good if he paid over the money to the other feller and — yes, I'll get in touch with him. Leave it to me. Let's see — he left this morning . . ." He nodded. "I'll get right on the job. Give me his flight number, will you?"

She went downstairs with him. He got into his coat and wound a thick scarf around his throat. "Don't worry. I'll see to things. Seems too bad this had to happen just when Brent was about to get rid of that damned case. Some people think a lawyer has an easy life. They should know." He opened the door and braced himself for a plunge into the snow and wind.

"Thank you, Gary."

"All in the line of duty. Besides, Brent has done me some good turns — clients, that kind of thing. Dear me, such weather. Good night, my dear."

He kissed her hand politely and trotted jauntily away. She closed the door and went back upstairs.

It was, as he said, really too bad about the Cadell case — meant more work for Brent. Yet in a way it was lucky that this had developed before the case was presumably settled.

She decided to drink the sherry she had poured for herself and forgotten, listening to Gary, and then settle down with a book, something lively enough to take her mind off herself — and Melora.

But as she reached the top of the stairs Daphne's voice called down from the floor above. "Anne — Anne . . ."

She ran up the next flight. Light was streaming from the open door of Daphne's room and Daphne was in bed, sitting up, her dark hair falling around her face. "I told you I was sick!" she said. "The school nurse sent me home!"

Anne hurried to the bed.

"What's the matter? Is your throat sore?"

Daphne swallowed experimentally. "N-no. But my chest feels funny."

Anne put her hand against Daphne's face. It was hot and flushed. Oh dear, Anne thought with dismay, pneumonia? Brent gone. Cassie gone. She got a warm bed jacket. "Put this on. I'll call Dr. Cox."

Daphne eyed her sulkily but slid her arms into the woolly jacket. "Where were you?" she asked resentfully.

"At Aunt Lucy's. Then Gary Molloy came."

"Aunt Lucy's!" Daphne gave a short, un-childish laugh. "You mean you had a date with your boy friend. Just wait till Uncle Brent hears about that."

FIVE

"Oh, Daphne, don't be silly!" Anne said with exasperation. "I'll phone to the doctor."

But the doctor was out. He'd gone to a dinner party; however, he'd telephone to the house for any calls. The maid would give him Anne's message.

"Tell him she has a fever and chest pains. You're sure you've got the name?"

"Oh yes, Mrs. Wystan."

She went back to Daphne. "When did you get home?"

"It was nearly dark. The school nurse got me a cab. She tried to phone to you but nobody answered. You must have been away for a long time."

"You can ask Aunt Lucy," Anne said shortly.

Daphne gave an odd kind of snort. "Don't try to put on such an innocent act with me. I saw him. This morning."

Anne had gone to test the heat in the radiator. She turned. "What *are* you talking about?"

There was a wholly unchildish speculation in Daphne's bright blue eyes.

"Oh, maybe you did see Aunt Lucy — for a minute or two. But he was here this morning. You didn't even wait until Uncle Brent had left. I saw him."

"Saw who?"

"Your young man. This morning. In Uncle Brent's study. I suppose he was just waiting for Uncle Brent to leave."

Anne came so quickly across the room that for all her precocious poise — and precocious speculations — Daphne shrank back. "I don't know what you're talking about, Daff." She forced herself to speak quietly and reasonably as she would to a five-year-old. "Tell me, what young man?"

Daphne blinked. "Well, he *was* there," she said stubbornly. "In the study. Fussing with your typewriter." Suddenly she smiled. "Of course I don't *know* that he was your young man. He *may* have been repairing the typewriter." Her eyelids lowered over the sudden dancing mirth in them. "You've no idea how funny you looked! What a joke!"

"Not a very funny joke," Anne said crisply. But all the same, there was something that sounded true about it, as if — well, as if there *had* been a man in her study. She put her hand firmly on Daphne's. "Tell me, Daff. Don't try to make stupid jokes. *Was* there a man in the house?"

"Yes, of course. I saw him. I came upstairs to get my coat. I heard something in the study and I opened the door very quietly and — just peeked in. He didn't hear me. He didn't see me." The child looked, Anne was vaguely pleased to see, a little less complacent, even a little frightened, as if she realized that she had gone too far. "I only meant to tease you."

"You meant nothing of the kind. I found those silly notes you typed, Daff. There wasn't any man here. You typed those notes yourself. Didn't you?"

Daphne sat up, pushed back a long lock of hair and stared at Anne. *"What notes?"*

"Oh, Daff, don't lie!"

But avid curiosity was certainly in the child's eyes and voice. "Did somebody write notes to you? Who?"

"Don't pretend."

"I don't know anything about any notes! And there was a man. He was in the study. He was sitting at your typewriter."

Something strong, yet indefinable gave a kind of twitch at Anne's heart. "Are you telling me the truth?"

Daphne nodded violently. "I couldn't see his face. He didn't see me. Of course, really I thought he'd come to repair your typewriter." She stared at Anne for a second. "Why, you're scared!"

Anne moistened suddenly dry lips. "It was Cadwallader you saw."

"Cadwallader! Fat, bald — it wasn't Cadwallader." Daphne suddenly snuggled down into the bed. "I want Uncle Brent."

So do I, Anne thought. "I am going to kill you." The neatly typed words seemed to project themselves on the pink blanket cover.

It made no sense. None of it made any sense. Nobody would want to kill her. Nobody would want to frighten her, for that was all it meant. It wasn't, it couldn't be, a real threat; it was only somebody's intent to frighten her. Anne Wystan. *Why?*

Daphne said, "What did Gary Molloy want? I went to the head of the stairs and listened but I couldn't hear what he said."

Anne supposed that she really ought to say a word about listening to other people's conversations. She didn't. "It was some business. Something he wants Brent to know. . . . Daff, I didn't see any strange man in the house this morning after you left."

"He was here all the same." Daphne thought for a moment. "He could have gone out the back way — let himself out."

"I didn't send for a typewriter repairman. How was he dressed?"

"It wasn't an electrician or a plumber," Daphne said astutely. "No tools or — well, let me see, I think he wore a sort of dark suit. He was bent over, you see. Tod was shouting at me. I just thought — well, he was at your typewriter . . ."

"Actually typing?"

"N-no. I don't know. I was in a hurry."

"Daff, think. Was there anything about him that you recognized? Are you sure you don't know who it was?"

"I tell you I didn't stop to look! I just thought, what's he doing there, then thought that he was working at the typewriter and that's all. Till you came back and I — thought I'd ask you about him." She fluttered her long, black eyelashes. "I was only teasing about the boy friend." But below the deliberately assumed air of contrition, Daphne's light blue eyes were watchful. Suddenly she said, "Maybe he wrote those notes you talked about. What did they say?"

"Just — silly notes. Nothing. I'm going down to wait for the doctor."

Daphne caught her skirt as she rose. "You *are* scared!"

"That's silly, too," Anne said lightly. "I hope the doctor gets here soon. I'll go down and listen for the doorbell."

She didn't think her manner deceived Daphne but Daphne let her go without a word. In the hall the silence and emptiness of the house struck Anne with a kind of apprehension. She went down the stairs, her hand sliding along the smooth coolness of the railing. The hall was lighted. Now that it was dark outside, the lamp Melora had turned on glowed more brightly in the yellow and gray, formal drawing room. At the end of the room, the windows were black and glittering. Even from the hall it seemed to Anne that she could see snowflakes whirling past the windows.

She went into the library. Here the silence of the snow seemed less absolute. A snowplow was making its stubborn, rasping way somewhere out in the street. There were distant honks of automobiles. The book-lined room with its deep, red chairs seemed warm and protective. She went to a window and tried to peer past white, flying veils of snow. But the street lights were blurred, mere halos of moving haze. The snowplow chugged nearer. She could see snow being flung up in huge silver fans that glittered before its lights.

She wished she knew whether or not Daphne was telling the truth. Her instinct was to believe Daphne: she *hadn't* written the notes, and she *had* seen a man, a stranger, secretly in the house that morning, bending over the typewriter in the study.

An intruder didn't seem likely at a time when the house was so full of people. On the other hand, all the people in the house (except Daphne, going for her coat) had been congregated in the front hall. Cadwallader, getting away in haste for his day out before he could be snared to carry luggage, might have let in someone, a repairman or somebody claiming to be a repairman. He could have gone up the narrow back stairs without being seen by anyone.

If she believed Daphne completely, there was a logic about it, for if Daphne hadn't typed the notes, then the man Daphne said she had seen could have typed them. He could easily and quietly have placed the notes, one on the typewriter, one somewhere in the drawing room, and left by way of the back stairs again. Who?

Lucy had said a lawyer or a doctor is peculiarly

vulnerable to spite, to revenge. She could think of no one who was at all likely to wish to revenge himself upon Brent by frightening his wife — threatening murder! A more credible motive was a kind of ugly teasing, but that, too, was frightening for it suggested not a child but an evil, out-of-kilter adult.

The snowplow was almost at the corner. An automobile came along in its wake, slowly, its lights revealing a single track along the street. The plow had left jagged, heaped-up drifts, edging that single track.

Suddenly the snow itself, the wild flurries of wind, seemed obscurely ominous and threatening. She drew the brown velvet curtains across the windows.

Certainly the snow was far heavier than it was even an hour ago. However, the one car she had seen cheered her. Besides, if Dr. Cox could get out to dinner, he could come to see Daphne. The streets were still open.

She sipped the sherry and put the delicate little glass on the table with a hand that unexpectedly trembled. The sherry spilled and she mopped it up with her handkerchief, scrubbing hard at the table top with the scrap of white linen. It was not sensible to get in a panic because she was alone in a big house with a sick child, and the wind and snow seemed to shut her off from the safe, accustomed world. She could use the telephone at any time.

The doorbell rang. She ran down and opened

the door. But it wasn't Dr. Cox. Instead, a tall, slender man came into the house in a kind of burst, as if the snow and wind pushed him. He wore a dark overcoat with the collar turned up around a narrow, dark face. He reached behind him and closed the door. Anne said blankly, "But you're not Dr. Cox! I asked Dr. Cox to come to see her."

He seemed to stare at her for a moment from under the brim of his hat. Then he removed the hat, disclosing a narrow forehead and black, shining hair. He shook snow from the hat and brushed snow from the shoulders of his coat. "I'm taking his calls," he said then.

"Oh. Thank you. Your coat . . ."

He hesitated for an instant. Then he gave a kind of shrug, slid out of his overcoat, and dropped it and his hat on the table. He wore a dark suit with rather wide, light pin stripes. His coat was sharply tailored, indented at his waist-line, with wide lapels and padded shoulders. He moved with an easy flow of muscles, like a dancer. He smoothed one glossily manicured hand over his already smooth and sleek hair and simply waited, watching her.

"We'd better take the elevator." She led the way and all at once, curiously, did not like the knowledge that he was behind her, although she could not hear any sound of footsteps on the thick rug. She turned and he was much closer to her than she had thought. He stopped instantly. She pressed the button for the elevator and then knew that there was something she had missed. "You've forgotten your bag!" she said. Dr. Cox always carried a fat little bag, wherever he went.

"Oh," he said, "my — doctor's bag. Yes. I was out to dinner."

The little elevator was grunting crossly downward. It gave a thump. She opened the door and did not want to enter that small, lighted cage.

He said, "I'm Dr. Smith," and waited for her to go ahead of him.

She went into the elevator. He followed her. The door closed and she touched the third-floor button.

Dr. Smith wore, not a perfume exactly but perhaps some sort of scented oil on his gleaming black hair. She was too close to him. She couldn't move away; there was no space in the tiny cage. She listened to the rumbling ascent of the elevator. As they passed the second floor it gave a kind of sigh and click. She glanced at the man crowded into the cage with her. He was standing perfectly still, apparently looking at nothing. From the side, and in the dim light of the cage, his profile was curiously blunt, not fine and sharp as she would have expected it to be in his narrow face, and curiously youthful in its blank stillness. He must be at least in his late twenties, yet he didn't look it.

The cage thumped exhaustedly as if really too much were required of it and stopped. She led Dr. Smith into Daphne's room.

Daphne had heard the elevator. She was sitting up in bed, clutching the pink wool bed jacket around her. Her eyes widened.

Anne said, "Dr. Cox was out, Daff. He sent Dr. Smith. . . ."

Daphne eyed the young man with a bright, fixed stare. He paused for a second, then moved to the chair beside Daphne's bed. He moved like a dancer, Anne thought again — or like a young and powerful tiger!

The thought darted into her mind so forcefully that she started forward, almost as if she might need to defend Daphne. Dr. Smith said, "Open your mouth."

Daphne blinked and obeyed. He peered at her throat, adjusted the bed lamp so the light fell more directly into Daphne's face and peered again. There was no expression whatever on his face.

He didn't have a stethoscope; Anne looked for the bulge in a pocket of his sharply tailored coat — and didn't find it. He didn't even have a thermometer tucked away in his pocket. He put his hand around Daphne's wrist and counted, looking at nothing.

Anne said, "Do you want a thermometer?"

He gave her a deliberate look, seemed to think it over and then nodded.

"In Mother's bathroom," Daphne told her. "At least I think so."

Somehow she didn't want to leave Daphne alone with him. That was absurd, too.

She finally found the thermometer in a drawer

below a marble washbasin with gold dolphins for faucets. The thermometer lay amid jars and bottles and boxes, all of which sent up flowery fragrances.

When she got back to Daphne's room the doctor was just sitting there, looking at the floor. Daphne was as quiet as a rather frightened little animal.

"Thank you," Dr. Smith said and put the thermometer into Daphne's mouth. Again he seemed to count and wait, and then removed it. He rose and held it under the light, his back turned to Anne. He put it down at last and turned. "I'm going to my office to get some medication."

He walked out of the room.

It surprised Anne. Then she hurried after him. "What do you think, Doctor?"

He opened the door of the elevator, and waited for her to enter it. Again Anne tried to conquer an odd wave of reluctance, which was like a kind of atavistic fear of being closed in with anybody in such a small space. She pressed the button for the first floor. He said, "Not too bad. Nothing to worry about."

"I hope it's not pneumonia."

They clicked past the second floor before he replied.

"I don't think so."

The cage stopped. Anne went to the front door, a little too quickly for sheer politeness. Something of her odd uneasiness must have communicated itself to Dr. Smith for he fumbled with his coat and hat awkwardly. Anne opened the door. "Thank you."

He gave her a blank, yet somehow thoughtful look. "I'll be back soon," he said and went out.

She closed the door, again too quickly to be quite polite. She wished he didn't have to come back.

But he was only a young doctor, too young to have developed ease and a bedside manner.

When she reached Daphne's room again, Daphne was huddled down in bed. Her eyes were very bright in her small face. *"That wasn't a doctor!"*

"Of course he was a doctor. Dr. Cox sent him."

"How do you know?"

"Why — why, he wouldn't have come otherwise."

Daphne pulled the blankets higher so only her eyes peered out from her tousled cloud of black hair. "I think he was the man I saw at your typewriter this morning."

SIX

"Daff!"

"I think he was."

"Now, Daff . . ." Anne wished her voice were steadier. She wished her heart hadn't given a disconcerting leap to her throat. She sat down on the foot of the bed. "Now listen, I phoned for Dr. Cox. The maid said he was out but she'd give him the message. Dr. Cox isn't young — he probably always has this Dr. Smith or some other young doctor take his night calls. Especially if he doesn't think it's anything serious. Dr. Smith simply wouldn't have known you were sick, he wouldn't have come here at all if Dr. Cox hadn't sent him. Would he?"

"He had black hair," Daphne said.

"The man at the typewriter?"

Daphne nodded.

"But you said you didn't see the man at the typewriter?"

"I could see his hair. It was black."

Anne took a long breath and debated. It was perfectly possible that Daphne was enjoying a little the drama which, it was more than possible, she was inventing. In Daphne as in most fifteen-year-olds, there was a well-developed and uninhibited acting ability and zest for dramatics, especially when she herself took the center of the stage.

On the other hand, Anne hadn't been comfortable with Dr. Smith herself.

Daphne said suddenly, "He couldn't read the thermometer. I watched him. He turned it and turned it and finally looked at the wrong side of it."

"Oh, Daff!"

"He was the man at the typewriter and he's no more a doctor than you are."

Anne rose. "That's enough of that. Dr. Cox sent him and he'll be back as soon as he can get some medicine and a taxi."

Daphne sat up, wildly scattering blankets. The silk cover slid half on the floor. "Where are you going?"

Anne rescued the pink cover and put the blankets straight. "I'm going to phone to Dr. Cox's home, find out where he's having dinner, phone there and ask him if he sent Dr. Smith. Will that satisfy you?"

Daphne thought for a moment, her eyes unwavering, and said suddenly, "You're going to do that to satisfy yourself. You don't think he's a real doctor either."

"Who else would it be?" Anne said and went to the telephone in the dressing room.

Daphne's high soprano voice came across the hall. "Leave the door open. I want to hear."

But the telephone was completely silent. There was no dial tone, nothing at all. She clicked the switch and tried to dial operator and there was no buzz, nothing.

It was the storm, of course. Perhaps it affected only that extension. She went to Cassie's room, where another telephone, ivory-colored, stood on the bedside table. That was dead, too.

"There's something wrong with the phone," she called out to Daphne. "I'll try downstairs."

In a house which is built in layers like a cake there are many telephone extensions. But the library telephone was dead, and so was the extension in the kitchen, where, after she had turned on the lights, the winking, black windows seemed to watch her and the flying snow caught lights from behind the glass.

There was still no dial tone, nothing but complete, empty silence. The kitchen telephone had the irrefutable stillness of an utterly dead line.

She put it down at last. It had been working when she telephoned to Dr. Cox, and that wasn't very long ago. But then, a line could be cut off or some storm damage could occur in a second. She ought to report it.

The house seemed even more silent, and even more cut off and isolated from the safe, ordinary world that still existed somewhere beyond the wind and snow. The wide chrome steel sink shone; the great white range glittered coldly. A long worktable stood in the middle of the room, and a piece of her own letter paper lay on it.

She saw it as she turned from the telephone. She went to it as if drawn by a magnet. The typed words were clear under the bright overhead light. This time the words were different.

"It will be sooner than you expect."

Her hand jerked to snatch the paper. She crumpled it in her hand and looked all around the kitchen. Obviously no one was there. She didn't pause to examine her reason for making sure that no one was there. A door across the room led into a small back entry. There were two storerooms there, the start of the narrow back stairway which wound upward through the house, and the heavy back door which led out into the areaway and back entrance. She crossed the room, found the light button and pressed it. The doors to the storerooms were closed. She opened the back door a little, and icy air and a few stinging snowflakes hurled through the black aperture. There was a night latch on the door. She tried it swiftly. It was locked. She closed the door hard and fastened the chain bolt. No one could get into the house that way now — that is, if anyone tried to get into the house, as of course no one would.

Why would anyone leave that third note on the kitchen table? There was an immediate answer to that. She was presumably alone in the house. Sometime presumably she would come to the kitchen in order to get herself something to eat, and find the note. But why would anybody write those notes at all? It had to be somebody's idea of a joke. Not a very funny joke.

Anne left the lights burning in the big, blankly shining kitchen. She went through the pantry, where more chrome steel glistened and the glass doors over the cupboards winked in the light. A small table stood discreetly in one corner and held a radio and Cadwallader's pipe. Beside it an ancient rocking chair defied the immaculate modernity of the pantry. She left a light turned on there, too.

At the far end of the dining room the French windows, which in the summer gave upon the walled garden, also winked and glittered. She hurried down the length of the room, past the long table and the high-backed chairs, with their fine needlepoint and carved, light wood, which were ranged in orderly position like guests, watching her. There were bolts on the French windows; they were all fastened. The garden outside was now populated with white, strange shapes, dimly seen in the light that streamed from the dining room. A portrait of Philip, in uniform, looked down at her inscrutably from between crystal-hung candelabra on the black marble mantel.

There was no one, simply no one except herself and Daphne, in the house.

She snatched her coat from the closet off the hall. It would take only a moment to run to the Collins' house, next door, ask them to report the telephone and run home again.

How about leaving Daphne alone in the house which had suddenly become curiously unfamiliar and threatening? They had to have a telephone. Without the telephone they truly were cut off and isolated, herself and a sick child.

In her haste she didn't stop to put on overshoes or gloves or even a scarf over her head, but she did remember the house key and put it in her pocket. She then let herself out of the house.

The snow hurled itself upon her as if it had waited avidly, just outside the door. Her slippered feet plunged into snow that lay on the sidewalks, blown and drifted.

There was a light in the Collins' house. She was panting when she reached the step. It had been cleaned but not recently; the snow was already inches deep again. She found the doorbell and pressed it over and over again.

It was a wild night. The snow whirled around her, catching on her eyelashes, stinging her face. The street lights were merely blurred halos, seeming remarkably distant. Somewhere close again there was the sound of a snowplow and the rhythmic scrape of shovels. Mainly there was only the vicious, sharp whistle of the wind.

No one answered the bell. The Collinses were out.

She ran, sliding in the icy layers of snow on the sidewalk, back past the Wystan house; to the house beyond it. That, however, was dark.

There was not a ray of light anywhere. She remembered then, vaguely, that the Freelings had closed up the house and gone south early in the winter.

She must report the telephone. The need for it had shot up into an imperative demand. It was as if it were a life line which she must secure.

There would be drug stores on Madison

Avenue. The misty, lighted corner was not far away. There would be drug stores, lights, people and telephones. She began to run, fighting the snow and wind, toward that lighted corner.

How silly she had been not to put on over-shoes! Catch her death of cold, too, probably; nothing over her head.

She glanced over her shoulder once, tempted to give up and fight her way back home through the suddenly inimical night. Another pedestrian was trudging along behind her, bent against the wind, his figure merely a black, moving outline, half obscured.

She was so near the corner now! Silly to turn back when she was so near! She reached the brighter corner of Madison Avenue and turned.

Store windows were lighted and the sidewalk had been recently cleared. There was a small drug store, quite near now. Its windows were full of light which streamed out invitingly.

She whirled into the drug store. The warm, lighted interior came to her like a shock. She brushed snow from her eyes and hair and caught her breath and decided that somehow, some-where she had been a great fool. Everything in the world was perfectly normal and usual.

A gray-jacketed clerk looked at her with sur-prise, taking in her blown hair, her gloveless hands, her slippered feet. He came around the counter quickly. "I'm not the pharmacist," he said. "But if it's an emergency perhaps I can help."

Naturally he would think from her haste and

her appearance that there was some emergency. "No," she said, "thanks. I only want to use the telephone."

"Oh." He was curious, his eyes were bright with question, but he nodded at the telephone booth. "There it is, miss."

And then in the warm little booth she discovered that she had no money, not even a dime, only her house key and a piece of paper that rustled in her pocket. Paper? Oh yes, the third ugly little note.

She said to the clerk, "I came in such a hurry — that is, I don't have any change — I mean, anything at all."

He eyed her for a moment, still curious but very polite. "Well, I guess you can pay me the dime some other time. You live around here, don't you?"

"Right down the street. I'm Mrs. Wystan."

"That's all right. A night like this . . ."

She rushed into explanation. "You see, our telephone is out of order. I want to report it . . ."

His round pink face cleared. "Oh. Here — I'll do it." He took up the counter telephone and dialed. He asked her address and her telephone number.

She listened as he reported it. He put down the telephone. "She says they're having a lot of trouble tonight on account of the storm. She's not sure when they'll get at your telephone but it'll be as soon as they can."

"Thank you."

"Anything else, Mrs. Wystan?"

She realized then that she had been staring at the clerk, caught by a new, queer impulse. There was the telephone, a life line. If she asked him to, the friendly clerk would call the police for her and she could tell them that three notes, threatening notes, had been left for her to find.

They were typed on her own letter paper, notes which she didn't really believe that Daphne had written. Yet who, they would say (wouldn't they?), had a chance to write them?

There was nothing at all to report to the police, and she couldn't understand why it had even occurred to her to report what was — what must be simply somebody's incomprehensible idea of a joke. There was nothing real about it, and the police could see at once that there was nothing real, nothing for them to do. It would be only another of the probably multitudinous calls from frightened or hysterical women, living alone, conjuring up fanciful terrors.

The door opened with a rush of icy air. She was vaguely aware that someone entered and stood behind the tall magazine rack and cigarette counter, and of the tiniest movement of impatience on the part of the clerk as he glanced that way. "Nothing. Thank you," she said and went on. The man at the magazine counter moved around behind it as she passed.

Outside, in the wind and snow again, the street looked strangely deserted, like a city of the dead, except for all the lights that lined it. Yet she didn't want to turn away and into the darker, snow-laden cross street. She hurried; she was cold now. The snow struck through her thin stockings.

This time if another pedestrian trudged the street she did not see him or in fact look for him. She reached the Wystan house and her fingers were numb with cold and awkward with the key. She swung open the door and plunged thankfully into the lighted warm hall and closed the door hard behind her.

She leaned against it for a moment, gasping for breath, hearing the whisper and surge of the snow and wind outside. She felt as if she had escaped some enemy.

She then saw the knife.

It was rather bulky, like a large pocketknife, and open. It lay on the table, below the big mirror, close beside the green vase of red roses. She stared at it.

How long had it been there? Surely, if it had been there all that day she'd have seen it. The sharp blade caught a gleaming highlight. It was short but long enough. Long enough for what, she thought, with a clutch of terror.

Daphne said from the top of the stairs, "Where have you been? *What's wrong?*"

"Did you put that knife there?"

"What knife?" Daphne craned her thin neck over the banister. Her dark hair fell around her flushed face. She hugged a blue eiderdown around her. "Oh, that! Of course not," she said,

"Cadwallader left it there. He's getting old and careless. Mother will have to speak to him."

"But he's not here."

"Oh, not now. He must have left it there this morning early. He always clips the flowers once a day, one and a half inches off the stems to keep them fresh. I thought you knew that."

There was a touch of cool scorn in her manner, a lofty condescension. She knew all the prescribed little rules that obtained in the Wystan house; Anne didn't. But her young voice was so certain that it was reassuring. Perhaps the knife *had* been there since early morning and Anne simply hadn't seen it.

The alternative was to acknowledge an ever-advancing, invisible kind of net spreading within the house and tightening itself closer and closer.

Daphne said, "It's a funny-looking knife though, isn't it? Why, I do believe it's what they call a switchblade. How on earth did old Caddy get that? I suppose he needs a sharp knife for the flowers."

It was a switchblade, of course! But flower stems are tough.

"Go back to bed," Anne said.

Daphne edged one bare foot out over the step. Her eyes were bright with fever and extremely unchildish. "You went to meet *him*. I'll tell Uncle Brent."

Anne took off her coat. "I went to the drug store to report the telephone."

Daphne blinked. "You look terrible," she

94

cried and went up the stairs ahead of Anne, her thin, bare ankles stumbling over each other.

She was flinging herself back into bed and pulling up blankets by the time Anne reached her room. "You do look terrible." She snuggled down. "I'll tell Uncle Brent that, too. How you left me alone when I was sick and ran out in the blizzard to meet your boy friend . . ."

"Oh, Daff, *stop* it! That's so silly. Why do you talk like that?"

Daphne said smugly, "Melora had a boy friend."

Melora.

Well, naturally, Anne thought slowly. Certainly. Melora had had to have a reason for divorcing Brent and it was another man. She was vaguely surprised because it was so obvious yet had not occurred to her.

She was also suddenly and terribly curious. It would be so easy to question Daphne.

Daphne knew it. She sat up, her eyes sparkling. "Want me to tell you all about it?"

"No," Anne said. And only then, thinking that Daphne's eyes were too bright, her cheeks too pink, she remembered Dr. Smith. She had thought of the telephone, she had thought of calling the police, she had never once thought of her original intention to ask Dr. Cox if he had really sent a young man, a Dr. Smith, to see Daphne. "Did Dr. Smith get back while I was gone?"

"I didn't hear the doorbell," Daphne said absently, still smiling. But then she, too, remembered. Her eyes flared open. "Did you telephone to Dr. Cox in the drug store?"

"I forgot it," Anne said shortly. "Of course he was a doctor! Who else would know you're sick? I'm going to change my shoes."

This diverted Daphne. She leaned out to look at Anne's wet stockings and pumps.

"Goodness," the child said. "You *must* have been in a hurry to see your boy friend."

SEVEN

"Daff, listen to me. Once and for all there is no boy friend."

"But Melora . . ." Daphne began and Anne started for the door. Daphne called after her, "You think it's not proper to talk about Melora. I knew all about her boy friend — or most of it. That's the way she used to do — make some excuse to get away and meet him. That's why you went out just now. You had a date with him tonight because Uncle Brent is away. And then I came home and you weren't expecting me. You couldn't telephone from here. So you went to the drug store. That's why you didn't call Dr. Cox. All you could think about was talking to him, telling him your date was off. *Who is he?*"

Anne turned in the doorway. "You don't believe a word of that yourself! Stay in bed and don't throw the covers off. I'll be back in a minute."

She went to her own room. She slid out of her sodden pumps and stripped off her wet stockings and snatched others. Her hair was wet with snow; she toweled and brushed it. And in spite of herself she thought of Melora — and Daphne's simple reasoning that since Melora had a "boy friend" it followed that Anne, Melora's successor, had a boy friend.

How easy it would be to question Daphne —

97

who was the boy friend, did she marry him, what happened? *Does Melora regret it — and want Brent back again?*

Stop it, Anne told herself. There were things to do. She went to the telephone. It was still dead. A clock stood on the table and she looked at it with utter disbelief. It had seemed a long time since she returned from Lucy's. It was in fact only a little after eight-thirty. Neither she nor Daphne had had any dinner.

She dreaded going down to the big, empty kitchen, where she had found a third note on the table. She called to Daphne from the hall. "I'm going downstairs. I'll bring you something to eat. I'll hear Dr. Smith when he comes back."

"I don't want anything to eat," Daphne shouted back resentfully.

The kitchen was big, shining and very quiet except for the whisper of the snow against the black windows, which again made her feel that she was under some secret surveillance. She was both clumsy and too quick; dishes rattled, she dropped silver. She was in the dining room, the tray of hot food in her hands, when Dr. Cox arrived. He came in quickly, stamping snow from his feet. Over his shoulder she caught a glimpse of his car, standing in the middle of the street beyond the snow that had been heaped up at the curb by the snowplow.

"Bad night," he said and put down his overcoat. He was a thin, dry man, elderly and authoritative. He wore a small beard and Daphne called him Fuzz Face. He was in dinner jacket and a ruffled temper. "I was out to dinner and bridge. You're sure Daff's not playing possum?"

"She's got a temperature."

"She didn't put the thermometer on a hot-water bottle?"

"No!"

"She's done it before, you know. Likes attention." He trotted into the elevator and held the door for her while she manipulated the tray. He then pressed the button. "You and Brent ought to get rid of this house," he said in a disgruntled way. "How Cassie keeps servants with all these stairs, I can't imagine. She's a wonderful woman."

"Yes . . . There was a doctor here a while ago. He said his name was Dr. Smith . . ."

He interrupted sharply. "What'd you call him for?"

"I didn't. He said you were out and he was taking your calls."

"Oh!" The cage grunted and stopped. "New maid at my house. Must have got mixed up. Answering service or — that was Dr. Judson. What did he do for her?"

"Nothing. He said he'd get some medication and come back but he hasn't come. He did say his name was Dr. Smith."

He shook his head and his beard wagged decisively. "Judson," he said and trotted across to Daphne's room. "Judson takes my calls sometimes at night. I'm not getting any younger. . . .

Well, young lady," he said to Daphne. "Now let's just see if you've got anything worth missing my first rubber for."

Dr. Cox was quick, thorough and knew exactly what he was about. In fifteen minutes he was ready to leave. "You'll be all right," he told Daphne. "I've shot you full of penicillin. Here's a mild sort of sedative. Take two of them about ten. Have some dinner now. Then go to sleep. . . . All right, Anne. I'll be going. If you want me call me, but you won't. She's just got a little cold. Nothing serious. Better watch it though."

She followed him to the elevator.

"But this doctor who came — he *did* say Smith. I'm sure of it."

"Made a mistake."

"He didn't have a — a stethoscope or a bag or . . ."

"Night like this it's a wonder he got here at all," he said crossly. "Where's Cassie?"

"She went to the country for the week end."

"Where?"

"Up near Litchfield." She looked at him anxiously. "Do you mean you think I should let her know about Daphne?"

"No, no. She couldn't get home tonight anyway. Roads are impassable. Good heavens, Anne, this is turning into a real, old-time blizzard."

At the door, already bundled up in his overcoat, eager to get back to his bridge game, his face softened a little. "Now don't worry about Daff. Call me any time — I'll be here in five minutes."

"Thanks. The phone's out of order but . . ."

"They'll get that fixed up. But she'll be all right." He put out a gnarly finger and gave her chin a brusque little push. "Stop worrying. If there was anything to worry about I wouldn't leave."

"I know. Thank you, Dr. Cox."

"Good girl." He opened the door, said, "Brrr . . ." and plunged into the snow.

But she hadn't made a mistake about the name. The young doctor had distinctly said Smith, not Judson. Yet Dr. Cox must be right. The new maid had made a mistake; there was some confusion in the answering service which perhaps both Dr. Cox and Dr. Smith used; there were all sorts of explanations. Clearly Dr. Smith hadn't returned because he'd discovered the mistake. Almost certainly he had tried to telephone to her and couldn't.

Foreseeing a wakeful and troubled night she went to the pantry and made coffee on Cadwallader's small hot plate. The homely, pleasant fragrance of the bubbling coffee was heartening. She sat down to wait in Cadwallader's rocking chair and turned on his small radio. The news was full of the storm. Transportation was slowed already, halted completely in some instances. Roads were impassable. Weather forecasters saw no letup. Drivers

101

were advised to leave their automobiles at home the next day and use other means of transportation. Air travel — Anne checked the placid movement of the rocking chair and listened — air travel was halted; numerous flights canceled. There were so many inches of snow in Boston, so many in Albany, so many in New York.

She hoped that Brent's plane had got out well ahead of the storm. She thought of him, safe and warm, in a lighted, luxurious cabin, moving smoothly along high above the cold gray Atlantic, above the clouds, sleeping perhaps, reading. Perhaps thinking of her.

Perhaps thinking of Melora.

She snapped off the radio. She was filling a thermos with coffee when the doorbell rang again. It must be Dr. Smith returning to explain his mistake and to make sure that Dr. Cox had come. She hurried to open the door. However, a young man huddled in coat and hat and earmuffs stood on the step. His plump, pink face was familiar to her. He said, "I just thought I'd stop to tell you . . ."

"Oh!" She then recognized the friendly, helpful drug-store clerk. "Come in."

He did so, shivering and yanking off his hat. A gust of snow and icy air came in, too. She closed the door. He looked embarrassed but determined.

"I thought I ought to tell you. I just locked up and left the store and I was on my way home and I remembered your address and . . ."

"Tell me what?"

He turned his hat in his hands. "It was that man. That man who came in when you were in the drug store. Remember?"

"Why, I — yes."

"You see, I knew you must be alone or you wouldn't have come yourself, like that through snow. I mean, without overshoes or gloves or — and you looked sort of scared and I did think, maybe, something was wrong. And he — this man — started to talk about you. I mean, he said, wasn't it queer you were running around in the storm like that, and asked why you had come to the store. I said — but of course polite, that it wasn't his business and what did he want? He got in a hurry then to leave and said he wanted some cigarettes, but somehow I got it into my head that he had followed you into the store. So I pretended I didn't have the kind he wanted and he started to leave, but I got between him and the door and tried to talk to him about the storm and all that till I thought you had time to get a long start on him. If he was going to follow you, that is."

"Did he follow me?"

"He turned in this direction. I could see him through the window. . . . I didn't mean to scare you, Mrs. Wystan. But he sounded sort of like a crackpot. You know — some jerk with a chip on his shoulder, mad at everybody. And there've been a lot of holdups and mugging and that kind of thing, and I thought, those are big houses along that street and if she is alone — but I didn't

103

mean to scare you. It just seemed like you ought to know."

"Who was he? Had you ever seen him before?"

"N-no. Not that I remember. I guess I let my imagination run away with me, Mrs. Wystan. But with your telephone out of order and the guy — I didn't like the way he acted so I just thought I ought to stop and see you."

It had been a kind of impulse and had put him to some trouble. She said, "There's hot coffee. Would you like some? It's a cold night." Brent would have said, what he needs on a night like this is a good slug of whiskey.

He shook his head. "No, thanks. My wife's going to be worrying about whether I get a bus or not."

"You were very kind to tell me."

He opened the door. "I think I just scared you. But — I don't know — felt as if I ought to. Good night, Mrs. Wystan." She said good night and thanked him again but her words were tossed away by the wind and lost in the darkness and swirling snow which seemed to swallow him, too, instantly. She closed the door.

If the man in the drug store had followed her, she hadn't known it. So no harm was done, and in fact the incident was only a chance encounter with "some jerk with a chip on his shoulder" — who might or might not have been following her.

In fancy, of course, it was like another knot in the invisible meshes of a net that had seemed to spread itself secretly around her. So it was better to stick to facts. All the same, she wished she had looked at the man who entered the drug store.

When she got back to Daphne's room, Daphne said, "Who was that?"

Anne put the thermos on a table. "The clerk in the drug store around the corner."

"Did he bring me some medicine?"

"No."

"What did he come for then?"

"He — knew our telephone was out of order. He wondered whether it had been repaired yet or not."

Daphne leaned back. Sharp speculation was in her eyes again. "My — you do mow them down, don't you, Anne! Even the drug-store clerk."

Anne laughed and tried to stop and laughed and wiped tears from her eyes. After a suspicious, startled moment Daphne caught the contagion and began to giggle, too.

Anne didn't know why she laughed. She didn't know why she couldn't stop. All at once they did stop at the same time. Anne asked Daphne if she'd had enough to eat and Daphne said yes, that Anne ought to eat something and she was afraid the food was cold.

It was cold but it didn't matter, for she wasn't hungry. Anne took the tray to the hall and put it down and brought back blankets, which she arranged on the little sofa in Daphne's room. She turned out the light beside the bed, leaving on only a table lamp across the room. The light from the hall streamed in.

My legs ache, Anne thought, in spite of the elevator. The next time Cadwallader complains of the stairs I'll know what he's talking about. The house is safe. It is locked up, safe; nobody can get in even if anybody wants to get in.

Daphne said, "What did old Fuzz Face say about Dr. Smith?"

"He said I'd got his name wrong. It was Dr. Judson. There was some mistake — his maid or answering service. He takes Dr. Cox's calls sometimes." She shook out two of the capsules Dr. Cox had left and got a glass of water from the bathroom.

Daphne took the capsules without demur, gulped some water and said flatly, "He was *not* a doctor."

"Go to sleep now, Daff."

Daphne said suddenly, "What were you talking about — I mean when you said I wrote some notes? What were they about?"

If Daphne denied it again, positively and convincingly, all those baseless apprehensions would flood back. "We'll talk about that in the morning."

"Whatever they were they must have upset you. Go on . . ." She got on her elbow. "Tell me."

Anne lighted a cigarette. "I'm going to stay here until you go to sleep. I'll sleep in here if you want me to."

"That's what I figured when you brought in the blankets," Daphne said.

Anne leaned back against the sofa and watched the smoke from her cigarette and passionately longed for Brent. If she could hear the door open, his steps on the stairs, nothing else in the world would matter. She would cling to him; she wouldn't let anything, anything at all drive her away. Certainly not Melora. Not anybody.

After a long time she realized that Daphne was asleep. She tiptoed to the bed. With her eyes closed Daphne looked more like the portrait of her father, hanging in the dining room, less like Cassie. Anne's heart softened. There was good stuff in the child. Her little chin was as firm as Brent's; only her striking and lovely coloring, black hair and light, aquamarine eyes, was like her mother. She was breathing evenly and, to Anne's relief, without effort.

Anne went softly to her room, listening all the time for Daphne's stirring — or for any other sound in the house. It was then a little after ten. The snow was coming down as if there were no end to its reservoir. Over on Fifth Avenue a snowplow thudded along, its engine throbbing distantly. Nearer, there was the patient, scraping sound of shovels.

She tried the telephone once or twice; it was still dead. She thought of all the crews of men the storm had brought out, working away through the night and the cold. There was a small radio in the study. She turned it on low, and listened again to news of the storm, which was to continue. She wondered whether or not Gary

Molloy had managed to get in touch with Brent. If he had, then certainly Brent would turn straight around and come home. She tried to calculate the probable time of his return but it depended upon the weather, if air travel was held up or not. It seemed a long time since he had walked down the step to the car and gone — with Cassie and Tod and Daphne — and Anne had wandered up through the suddenly still and empty house to find a note.

She leaned back wearily in the chaise longue. The first thing to settle in her mind was the notes. The immediate alternatives were clear; either Daphne had written them or she hadn't. In the morning she would tackle Daphne about the notes. If she were then fully convinced that Daphne had nothing to do with the notes — then, clearly, somebody else had written them.

The motive was completely obscure. There was no use even in guessing at the motive, except again there were two alternatives: either the notes were meant merely to frighten — or they were threats of murder. The sensible answer to that was an attempt to frighten her — although that was not in fact a very sensible answer.

But clearly, too, if Daphne had not written the notes, then Anne had to do something about them. Tell Lucy? But what could Lucy do? Tell the police? She didn't really want to do that, especially in Brent's absence. Besides, there was no real evidence that anyone had tried to carry out the threat in the notes: "I'm going to kill you."

There might be, if she let fear gallop ahead full tilt, a certain contributory evidence. If Daphne were telling the truth, her story of a man in the house that morning, sitting at the typewriter, was evidence at least of an intruder. Anne looked at the typewriter and tried to envision somebody sitting before it, typing out death threats on her own letter paper, and could not.

There had been a man in the drug store. He hadn't said or done anything threatening. If he had followed her she did not know it and certainly he had made no attempt, so far as she knew, to get into the house. That too was nebulous as evidence. The drug-store clerk had *thought* he was following Anne. He had *thought* that the man's attitude was threatening to the extent that he had decided to warn Anne. But there was nothing which properly could be called proof of an intent to murder. Intent to murder, she thought with incredulity. Dr. Smith, of course, could prove to be, simply, a doctor by the name of Smith and probably would so prove to be.

Of course, the telephone wires could have been cut. It was the first time that had occurred to her and it was like the touch of icy fingers. She argued with herself for some time. But the fact which was inarguable was the storm. The girl at the telephone office had said there were so many emergency calls that she didn't know when the repairmen would come.

There was not, then, anything to tell the police

except that she had had some threatening notes, typed on her own letter paper, probably at her own typewriter. The police would be obliged to question everybody who had access to the house. She didn't want to go to the police with a story like that. Perhaps everyone was reluctant to call the police into their homes to question, investigate, upset the house and everyone concerned — for, in all likelihood, nothing. She wished someone could advise her and thought of Gary. Gary, of course. If the next morning Daphne still denied writing the notes, she would ask Gary what to do. So that was settled for the moment and the house was locked, bolted and perfectly quiet and safe.

Someone over the radio was being interviewed by somebody else about the record storms that had struck New York. Their voices were soothingly monotonous; they had got back to the blizzard of 1888. She began to feel sleepy.

Thoughts of Melora had hovered in the background though, as if waiting for just such a moment to come softly forward.

But Melora herself had gone as quietly as she had entered the house. Anne thought, again with a little shock of surprise, of the trick her imagination had played upon her, building up an image which was in fact Cassie, painting it in different colors, endowing it with a different — oh, a very different personality, and naming it Melora.

But Cassie was her friend. If Anne had resented Cassie's place in that house it was a childish, perhaps feminine but not really rooted or justifiable, resentment.

She was tired and very sleepy. Her thoughts began to shoot off into all sorts of little excursions of their own. Melora — and her "boy friend." Melora. "I was afraid of her," Lucy had said. Daphne: "That was the man in your dressing room. . . . Dr. Smith is not a doctor." Some mistake in the answering service, Dr. Cox had said. A knife beside the roses on the hall table!

She sat up, her whole body suddenly cold. Dr. Smith had dropped his coat and hat on that table. When he left he had fumbled with them awkwardly. *Could he have dropped that shiny, bulky knife on the table?*

That was nonsense. Why would he have a knife in his hand? No, she wouldn't let herself answer that. Besides, if he had had a knife in his hand — if he had come to the house intending to murder her, which was utterly unbelievable, why should he drop the knife on the table and just leave it there?

No. Cadwallader had forgotten the knife. She must remember to take the chain off the kitchen door before Cadwallader and his wife arrived in the morning.

Dance music was coming from the radio and probably had been for some time; the desk clock said twelve. She turned off the radio. The sound of snow shovels had died away. The whole city seemed mute and sleeping under its thick white blankets.

111

She tried the telephone, which was still dead, and went into her own room. She was tying the silk cord of her warmest dressing gown, preparatory to going to the sofa in Daphne's room when she heard a low, far-away kind of grumble somewhere in the house. It was the elevator!

She hadn't heard it start. She hadn't heard the heavy front door downstairs open or close either. It must be Brent! Gary's message had reached him; his plane had been delayed somewhere and he had contrived to get another plane back to New York. She knew at once though that it couldn't be Brent. There hadn't been time. So it was Cassie returning, driven home by the blizzard. Tod. Even Cadwallader or Emma, knowing that she was alone.

The little cage rumbled louder, coming up to the third floor. She went into the hall.

The small door across the elevator well was painted in gay panels of Chinese red with gold and blue and green figures. There was a little glass pane set about six feet from the floor. It was black but the hum of the elevator was nearer. The glass panel lighted up. She had a dim view of the interior of the cage. So far as she could see, it was empty.

The elevator gave a kind of bump, lurched and stopped. Then with only an increased hum it moved upward to the cold, darkened fourth floor. She watched the area of dim light vanish.

EIGHT

No one used the fourth floor. There were two or three stiff and chilly bedrooms up there. There were a few storage rooms, trunk rooms and linen closets. There was a long, narrow room where Tod's skis and tennis rackets and everybody's summer clothes, all in their neat plastic bags, were stored. There was nothing else.

She went to the door of the elevator well and listened. The door could not be opened unless the cage stood at that floor. She heard the little jolt and sigh the cage gave when it stopped at the fourth floor. Then she heard nothing.

There was no sound at all, no one opened the door, there were no footsteps in the hall above. But no one had been in the elevator. Someone could have been standing at one side or the other, close to the door, avoiding the little pane of glass.

No one could have entered the house; the doors and windows were locked and bolted. Only someone of the family, someone who had a key, could have opened the door.

Her thoughts raced, canvassing possibilities, and there was still no sound at all from the floor above. Black letters typed on white paper suddenly leaped before her eyes. "I am going to kill you." "It will be soon."

But she and Daphne were alone in the house.

The telephone was dead. She started up the stairs to the fourth floor, gripping the banister, staring up into the darkness above, listening. There must be some sensible course of action to take, but what? Halfway up the stairs a low grumble came from above. The elevator was moving again.

It had to come down; there was nowhere else for it to go. She turned, frozen, and watched. The murmur grew louder. The glass pane again showed a light, and empty interior. The elevator slowly passed down toward the second floor. It stopped again.

This was like a ghostly game of hide-and-seek.

She leaned down, over the stairwell, listening now for sounds from the library and drawing-room floor. Again there was nothing at all, no sound of the elevator door opening, no footsteps.

Suddenly an explanation, the only explanation, shot into her mind. In the storm, affecting the multitudinous wirings of the old house, a grisly sort of whimsy had overtaken the always cranky old elevator. There must be a short circuit, an unexpected crossing of wires, some erratic connection among the buttons controlling the elevator, which set it on its jaunting course up and down through the house. Cadwallader understood the ancient elevator's idiosyncrasies; nobody else. But there was a red button on that small panel marked stop. She had only to catch the elevator at some floor where it checked itself,

114

hold the door open lest the cage take another mischievous flight, and push that red button. The next morning Cadwallader, or electricians if necessary, could examine and repair it.

She had left lights everywhere below, lights in the hall, in the library, in the drawing room. The elevator door on the second floor was painted green like the walls, with a black and gold key design. The small window showed a dim light and nothing else. She had almost reached the door when the elevator gave a murmur and slid downward. The light passed tantalizingly out of sight.

All right then, the first floor. She was running, she was halfway down, before she realized that the front hall below was dark. She stopped, full flight, clutching the banister. The whole first floor now — at least what she could, or rather could not see of it — was dark, the hall, the long dining room, everything.

A tiny rectangle of dim light came into view, came farther down; the elevator stopped. The door then whispered and opened. She had one swift glimpse of a figure, dark against the dim light, sliding out of the door like a shadow. The door closed again.

There was the faintest light from the elevator window. The shadowy figure moved swiftly and furtively toward the stairs and Anne whirled around, stumbling, tripping on her long dressing gown, screaming. She knew that something leaped up the stairs toward her. There was a strong tug at the long skirt of her dressing gown. She pulled at the railing, she struggled blindly to release herself and suddenly heard Daphne screaming, too, "Mother! Tod! *Tod, hurry — burglars! Tod . . .*"

The strong downward pull was released. Anne fell in a scrambling huddle. Daphne was on the steps just above her. She was still screaming wildly, *"Tod, hurry! Bring the gun! Tod . . ."*

A blast of cold air came up the stairs. The front door closed with a heavy jar. Daphne stopped screaming. There was a long moment of silence. Daphne said coolly, "He's gone."

She was close above Anne, outlined against the thin light from above, the blue eiderdown clutched around her. She darted up the stairs and light flooded the stairway and the hall below. There was a switch, of course, at the top of the stairs. Anne had not remembered it. There hadn't been time.

She pulled herself up, holding the railing. Daphne was leaning over her, her black, soft hair swinging. "Did he hurt you?"

"No."

"Wait." Daphne crowded past her and ran down, around the newel post and flashed out of sight into the dining room. There, too, lights sprang up.

The hall was empty; no one at all was there. The elevator cage stood quiet now and stolid, behind its lighted door. Daphne came back. "Drink this," she cried, and shoved a glass into

Anne's hand. The pungent odor of brandy came from it. Daphne dashed by without so much as a second's pause, to pull open the door to the elevator. "Nobody's there now," she said and ran to the front door, opened it and tried the latch while icy air and little whiffs of snow circled around her bare ankles.

"Daff, don't! The cold!" Daphne paid no attention. She satisfied herself about the latch. She closed the door hard then and turned to Anne. "Bet he's still running. I'll fix it so he can't get in again."

She ran again to the dining room, came back tugging a dining-room chair and wedged its high back below the great brass doorknob. "There!" She dusted her hands with a kind of triumph. "He can't get back in again." She eyed Anne. "Drink that," she said sternly. "If you faint I can't possibly get you to bed."

Her thin hand grasped Anne's and forced the glass against Anne's teeth. She drank and the brandy stung her throat.

"Can you make it to the elevator?"

"Not there!" Anne cried.

Daphne frowned. Her face was tense, hard as a little rock. Her blue eyes were like sapphires. "Don't be silly. I tell you nobody's there. Come on . . ." She dragged Anne to her feet. She pushed her along the hall and into the elevator. Her young arms were strong and certain. She punched the third-floor button and huddled the blue silk eiderdown around her and waited, stern and intent, as the cage lurched and grunted in protest and then started slowly upward.

At the third floor Daphne gave a quick thrust to the door. "Come *on,*" she snapped and scurried into her bedroom and jumped into bed again.

"Finish off the brandy," she said. "Hurry up."

Anne looked with surprise at the glass she still had in her hand and obeyed, as if Daphne were the adult and Anne the child. Daphne was so strong, Anne thought dazedly. She knew just what to do and did it.

"That's right," Daphne said. "Now get over there on the sofa and wrap up. That's the thing to do for shock. Keep warm."

Again Anne obeyed. She wrapped the blankets around her. The warmth of the brandy seemed to travel through her whole body.

Daphne peered at her. "Feeling better?"

Anne lifted her head. For a long moment they looked at each other as if they were strangers, discovering each other for the first time. Anne said, "You saved my life."

Daphne's eyes widened. *"Huh?"*

"He was coming up the stairs. He got hold of my dressing gown."

Daphne sat up, staring at Anne. *"Honestly! Why?"*

"If you hadn't come, if you hadn't screamed . . ."

"We've got to call the police!"

"Yes. Yes, of course . . ." Anne started to extricate herself from blankets and Daphne said, "I forgot. The phone is still dead. Unless they've fixed it. I'll try it. . . ." Daphne started to scramble out of bed again.

"*No, no!* Stay there." Anne ran to the telephone in the study across the hall. The line was still dead.

"Well," Daphne said, "I don't know what we're going to do." She thought for a moment, her small face hard with concentration. "I'll tell you what I think. I think it's all right for now. He can't get back into the house again. Unless the back door . . ."

"I put the chain on. The windows are bolted."

"He can't get in the front door, not now," Daphne said with satisfaction. "I read about that in a book. Wedge a chair under the door-knob. . . . You can't go outside, I mean to the drug store to telephone. It's not far to Collins' house but — no." She shook her head. "That wouldn't do. He might be outside somewhere." She said with cool decision, "We'll just have to wait till they get the phone fixed. I don't think he'll come back. I think he's scared out. Probably didn't expect to wake anybody. He must have thought that you were alone here — didn't expect me to come squalling bloody murder at him." Daphne chuckled. "He's been watching the house for days, of course. Casing it. Planning robbery. It's one of those cat burglars. Well, he didn't get anything."

"Daff — how did you think of it?"

"Think of what?"

"Screaming like that for Tod and again for your mother. As if they were in the house."

"Oh." She looked blank. "I don't know. I guess it just struck me it would scare him off, if he thought there were other people in the house. It *was* rather quick of me, wasn't it?" Daphne looked a little surprised. "I guess I didn't really stop to think. I heard the elevator, you see. I heard you run out. I thought it was Uncle Brent, but then I knew it couldn't be. I thought of Tod and then I heard the cage jumping around from floor to floor so I went to see. I knew right away it was a cat burglar."

"Yes," Anne said after a moment. Three typed messages threatening her life, left where she would find them, within the solid walls of the house. "I am going to kill you." "It will be soon."

Daphne knew nothing of the notes. Anne was sure now of that. A burglar wouldn't have set the elevator in motion. He would have known at once that the sound of its ancient machinery would wake anybody in the house. A burglar wouldn't have taken the cage up and down tantalizingly, from one floor to the other, forcing Anne to follow it. A burglar wouldn't have leaped up the stairs out of the darkness toward her. A real burglar wouldn't have been frightened away by Daphne's scream.

She wasn't sure of that. She wanted to tell Daphne all about it and fling herself upon the unexpected practicality and strength the child had so swiftly displayed.

Daphne gave a pleased little flounce. "Just wait till Tod hears this! He'll be furious because he missed the excitement." She eyed Anne shrewdly. "I gave you a walloping slug of brandy. It's going to hit you any minute." And then she became all child. "You will sleep on the sofa in here tonight, won't you? There's no key. Mother took it away one time when I locked myself in, but the key to her room fits that lock."

Murder or attempted murder was a word for headlines, remote, nothing that could happen in the house or to anyone she knew. Especially it couldn't happen to Anne. Cassie's key did fit the lock to Daphne's door. Daphne tossed a pillow from her bed, expertly, so Anne caught it.

Presently Daphne gave a little giggle which sounded very far away. "You'll sleep it off," she said comfortingly.

But later she roused and peered across at Anne. "Did you say he grabbed your dressing gown?"

"Yes . . ."

After what seemed a long, long time she heard Daphne's high voice again, drifting out of a maze of shadows. "That's a queer thing for a burglar to do. It's queer he'd take the elevator up and down like that, too. He must have known somebody would hear it."

She couldn't possibly sleep, Anne thought hazily, but did, for when next she roused she knew that it was morning and the snow had stopped. There was an unearthly silence everywhere, but she could hear Daphne's light, regular breathing, which *was* light and regular, not hoarse and gasping.

She slid quietly from the sofa, wincing at aching and tired muscles. The bright cap of the thermos on the table caught her eyes. She took it, glanced again at Daphne, who was only a little mound under the blankets, unlocked the door quietly and crossed the hall — which was just as usual except it was still lighted. Nothing stirred within the house and over all lay a deathly hush.

She drank some hot coffee and looked out the window. The street below was heaped with snow. The single track the snowplow had made the night before was almost covered over again. The day was gray. There were then no more flying veils of snow, obscuring the world, yet the sky lay very heavy and close above.

She must get down to the back door and take the chain off before Cadwallader and Emma arrived. The hot coffee and a hot shower were reviving. She dressed quickly and went down the stairs. At the turn between drawing room and library she caught a glimpse of the ash tray Melora had used, drawn out of its usual place, holding a burned cigarette and charred black fragments of paper. In the library, the decanter and glass Gary Molloy had used and her own sherry glass still stood on the table. But on the stairway leading down to the hall there was no evidence whatever of that feral figure which had leaped up from the darkness toward her. Attempted murder?

She removed the chair from under the door-knob and carried it back to the dining room. The night before she had not drawn the curtains over the French windows. Daylight streaked drearily into the room. The stone benches and the bird-bath in the garden were heaped and utterly disguised with snow.

She went into the kitchen and tried the telephone, which was still dead. She took the chain off the back door and drank more coffee.

In the clear gray light of morning, it struck her forcibly that there was a kind of ugly prankishness, too, in taking the elevator up and down while she pursued it. It had the flavor of a cruel joke, a Grand Guignol sense of humor, which seemed to link itself to the typed notes. Yet the figure which slid furtively and so swiftly from the elevator, and leaped upward from the darkness of the hall, was real.

She was pouring orange juice when Cadwallader arrived red-faced, puffing and alone. Emma, he said, had a cold, so knowing that Mrs. Wystan would be alone and there was no company coming, he had made Emma stay at home in their own apartment. When he heard that Daphne was at home and sick he lifted his sparse eyebrows frostily but said he could probably manage the meals if Mrs. Wystan would see to the trays. He also opined that Daisy, the maid, wouldn't come at all; buses were late and scarce.

"The radio says the city is paralyzed," he quoted with smug gloom.

"Cadwallader, did you — that is, yesterday morning before you and Emma went out — did a man come to repair my typewriter?"

He shrugged. "No, Mrs. Wystan. Not a soul." He put a coffeepot on the stove. "Someone may have come after we left. I believe Mr. Wystan and Mrs. Wystan and the children hadn't gone yet. We didn't wait. It was after ten when we left and Mrs. Wystan never expects us to stay in when it's our full day out." He clearly referred now to Cassie, when he said Mrs. Wystan.

"How about Daisy? When did she leave?"

"That girl!" He adjusted the blue points of the gas flame. "She's out like a rabbit as soon as she can make the beds. Got a new boy friend. Can't think of anything else. She was gone long before we left."

"You're sure you locked the back door?"

He gave her an annoyed glance. "Certainly, Mrs. Wystan."

So far her questions had not roused so much as a flicker of interest in his pale eyes. She said, "There's a knife on the hall table. I expect you left it there when you cut the roses yesterday."

"Roses?" he said vaguely, leaning over to dive into the refrigerator. "I didn't cut the flowers yesterday. I knew there'd be fresh ones today. Mrs. Wystan gave orders for fresh flowers to be delivered Mondays and Fridays. I daresay you'll

124

not want much breakfast — since Emma isn't here."

"Just give us what you have," she said rather meanly, knowing that Cadwallader never stinted himself when it came to food, and sure enough, presently the odors of coffee and bacon drifted up the stairs to the library where she stood again at the telephone. It now was in working order. The dial tone was strong and clear and sounded just then like music.

What exactly would she report to the police? She had a hearty respect for the thoroughness of a police inquiry. If she reported the notes they would question everybody available, including Daphne, who had the opportunity and in a way the motive for writing them — but who hadn't written them.

She dialed and when a voice answered, her decision about the notes made itself. She reported an intruder, possibly a burglar. She reported her name and address. She said, when asked, that she didn't know who the intruder was, she didn't see his face, he had been frightened away. It had happened about a quarter after twelve, the previous night. No, he had not robbed the house, there hadn't been time. The voice assured her pleasantly, but rather hurriedly, as if a dozen other telephones were ringing near by, that someone would come to see her as soon as possible. It added that owing to the storm there were a number of emergency calls and if her report did not constitute an emergency, it might be some time before the police got around to see her. She said that it was not an emergency, not now, thanked the voice and put down the telephone.

She then, after some thought, telephoned to Dr. Cox. Daphne, she said, seemed about the same, certainly no worse. "Dr. Cox, is there any way you can check on the man who called himself Dr. Smith?"

He, too, sounded hurried, "My dear, I told you that was Dr. Judson."

"He said Dr. Smith. And — you see we had a — a burglar last night . . ."

"Burglar!"

"At least someone got into the house and — I thought of Dr. Smith; that is, he *didn't* seem like a doctor!"

"What! Are you implying that *he* — why, that's nonsense! There was only some mistake!"

"Will you check on it, Dr. Cox?"

"Good heavens, Anne! Do you realize how many Dr. Smiths there are?"

"You could ask Dr. Judson if he came."

"You said his name was Smith!" Dr. Cox snapped inconsistently.

"That's what he said. Dr. Cox, I've reported the burglar to the police."

"Police!"

"When I see them I'll have to tell them about the — well, about Dr. Smith. I thought perhaps you could get at the truth and then I wouldn't need to tell the police. That is, if it really was a Dr. Smith."

126

He was spluttering, angry, no longer indulgent. "*You can't do that!* Send the police around to question a perfectly reputable doctor who *happened,* somehow — heaven knows how, to get one of my calls!"

Yesterday, she thought, oddly surprised, she would have yielded to the authoritative voice of the Wystan family doctor and old-time friend. Today she said firmly, "I'll have to, Dr. Cox."

There was a pause. Then he said, "All right, all right! I'll see about it. But really — who else but a doctor would know that Daphne was sick?"

He hung up with a bang.

If the "burglar" *were* the man calling himself Dr. Smith, she could describe him to the police. If by any chance he were the man in the drug store who had asked questions, then the drugstore clerk could describe him.

It might be neither.

But "I'm going to kill you" the notes had said. "Soon . . ."

NINE

The elevator rumbled and Cadwallader came puffing in, gave her a laden breakfast tray in an injured manner and told her that a man from the telephone company had been there. "He's just gone," he said. "He told me to tell you that the telephone wire had been cut on the outside and he thought you ought to know it. . . . Mrs. Wystan! You're tipping over the orange juice!"

She righted it, her hand still unsteady. She had thought herself so sensible, winning that argument with herself, plumping for the likely reason. It would be easy for someone to dart into that narrow areaway, shielded by the neighboring walls and by the snow, and cut the wire. She would tell that to the police when they came. That was evidence.

Daphne was awake but very thoughtful. "Have you phoned the police?"

"Yes. They'll send somebody to see us."

"Oh." Daphne thought for a moment, her little chin very square. "Well, I want to talk to them, too. It *was* that man that called himself Dr. Smith, you know. I've got it all figured out. He'd planned a robbery; he'd cased the house. That's what they call it. I mean he'd found out when Caddy and Emma were to be out, and that you were going to be alone. Then when he came you must have said something about expecting

128

the doctor. Didn't you?"

"I — yes, I did. That is, I think I said 'You're not Dr. Cox — I asked Dr. Cox to see her' — something like that."

"You see? So he jumped at it, pretended to be a doctor so as to get in the house and to take a look around . . ."

"If he was going to rob the house he had a chance to then."

"No," Daphne said with cool logic. "He decided to get an idea of the layout of the house and whether or not anybody else was here. Probably I was a surprise. He expected you to be alone. . . . That's how I know it was that man. I thought and thought and couldn't see how anybody could get in. That's the answer. He turned the night latch when he went out. Nothing simpler."

"I went out to the drug store after he was here. I used my key to open the door again."

"You turned the key in the lock but I'll bet you don't know whether or not the door was really locked."

"I used the key. But I was hurried and it was snowing so hard — no, I couldn't possibly be sure whether the door was locked or not."

"You wouldn't have noticed. The key would turn whether the night latch was off or on."

"Dr. Cox came later, too. And the drug-store clerk. I don't remember testing the night latch. I closed the door hard, though. . . . Sometimes it jars itself open."

"*It does what?*"

"Opens itself. I mean — just a little, I suppose if the latch doesn't quite catch."

Daphne gave her a blank look. "No, it doesn't."

"But . . ." But Melora had found it so, and come into the house. Anne said, "It might if it wasn't closed hard enough. But last night I made sure it was closed."

"But not locked," Daphne said. "Why did you ask me if I had written some notes? You wouldn't tell me anything about them. What notes?"

But Daphne had not written them. Anne said, "There were some notes, one was on my typewriter. They may have been a sort of joke."

"What did they say?" There was only frank curiosity in Daphne's eyes.

"Just silly notes. Somebody trying to frighten me. I threw them away. It's not important."

"Then why don't you tell me about them?" Daphne thought for a moment and said, "Kidnap notes! That's what they were. No — that's not right. The kidnap notes are sent after somebody's kidnapped. Anne, what were they?"

Strangely she wanted to tell Daphne. But why frighten her? "I told you, nothing really. Here . . ." She shook the thermometer and stopped Daphne's questions by putting it in her mouth.

"How high is it?" Daphne asked when she removed it.

"About a hundred. Finish your breakfast."

130

She ran a tub for Daphne. She got out a fresh nightgown and while Daphne was in the tub she put fresh linen on the bed and aired the room. She then went to the telephone and called Lucy.

"Good morning, dear." Lucy's voice sounded different somehow, tired and a little strained.

"Aunt Lucy — you know those silly notes I told you about."

"What's wrong?"

"Daphne didn't write them. I'm sure she didn't. She's at home with a cold. Dr. Cox came last night. She's better this morning but . . ."

"Go on."

"Well — a man got into the house last night."

"Anne!"

"It's all right. He just ran the elevator up and down and — Daphne heard and scared him away. Everything is all right. I reported it to the police. But, Aunt Lucy, you said that a doctor or a lawyer was vulnerable. I wondered if Brent had ever told you about anybody who might have a grudge against him and — well, take it out this way. I mean, trying to frighten me. You see — there was another note last night on the kitchen table. It said, 'It will be sooner than you expect.' The telephone wire was cut, too."

There was a long pause. Then Lucy said, "I think I'd better come," and rang off abruptly.

Anne had barely put down the telephone when it rang. It was Max, snowed in at Danbury. "Shall I leave the car here and take the train home, or shall I stay with the car till

131

they get the parkways cleared?"

She told him to stay with the car. He thanked her and hung up very quickly as if he were afraid she'd change her mind. It was perhaps an hour later and Lucy had still not arrived, when the telephone rang again. She answered and a distant voice said, "Is this Anne?"

It was Melora.

"Yes."

Melora said rapidly, so her soft words slurred together, "I've got to see you, right away. Meet me at the Forty-ninth Street Longchamps. I'll be near the Forty-ninth Street door. Bring me some money."

Money again! "I'm sorry. I can't do that."

"I've got to have money," Melora said simply.

"But you had three hundred yesterday . . ."

"Don't write a check. That won't do. There must be more in the safe. . . . I'll be waiting there for you."

The telephone clicked.

The strange thing about it was not that Melora wanted more money, not that she had fixed a meeting place which obviously she had already planned. It was the perfectly matter-of-fact way in which Anne went to the safe and took out the remaining two hundred dollars.

"I've got to go on an errand," she told Daphne, and thought: to see my husband's divorced wife because Melora has only to ask for something to get it.

"What about the police? Tell old Caddy to

send them up here."

"I expect I'll be back before they get here. And don't call him Caddy. Your mother doesn't like it," she added automatically.

Daphne grinned. "Too much like her name. . . . The police. Just wait till Tod hears this."

Anne had not told Cadwallader of the intruder of the previous night. She did so briefly, as she got her coat.

His eyes popped and his face turned mauve. "Good heavens! What did he get?"

She was zipping up galoshes and turned to stare at him blankly. "I never thought of looking. I don't think he got anything. There wasn't time."

"There's Mrs. Wystan's jewels — no, she probably took most of them with her. How about the safe?"

"It was still locked this morning."

"*They cut the telephone wire! They've been casing the house!* They knew you'd be alone!" He and Daphne had clearly an unsuspected bond. His eyes were glittering avidly. "It's a gang! I'll check the valuables in the house at once."

"The police will be here sometime today. I'll be back in — oh, an hour at the most."

"Certainly, certainly," he said absently, thinking of the flat silver, for he was already waddling back to the dining room. But at the door he turned and gave Anne an austerely reproving look. "You thought I left a knife on that table,

Mrs. Wystan. I didn't. There's no knife there at all and none missing from the kitchen. I just thought I'd tell you that you were mistaken."

He was perfectly right. The green vase stood on the table. The roses in it were turning faintly purple, like Cadwallader, around the edges. There was now no glittering, razor-edged knife.

She said slowly, "What kind of knife do you use for the flowers? I mean — is it like a switchblade?"

Cadwallader's eyes bulged. "Certainly not! I use just any knife so long as it's good and sharp." He lifted all three of his chins in righteous vindication and marched away.

But the knife *had* been there. Anne had seen it. Daphne had seen it and said it was like a switchblade. Perhaps Cadwallader had coolly put it away and denied it. She wanted to accept that and couldn't. Had there been a knife in the hand of that feral, swift figure, leaping out of the darkness toward her? The cold seemed to creep in around the door.

She had to go to meet Melora. She let herself out into a scarcely recognizable street, heaped with snow. The gray sky seemed low enough now to touch the housetops. There were great, chunky drifts which had been kicked up by the snowplow, along the curbs.

She crossed Fifth Avenue in the hope of finding a southbound taxi. That day there were no nursemaids with perambulators, nobody feeding the squirrels. Beyond the wall the trees and shrubs in the park looked like a colony of humped-up, prehistoric monsters with no faces, all covered in white. Such luckless cars as had been caught by the snow were mounds of white, too, like gigantic turtles. It was rough and breathless walking. There was little traffic. Twice she saw an occupied taxi which chugged past her. After a long time a bus came rumbling along and she got in.

The trip to Forty-ninth Street was long, too, slow and difficult. She began to feel uneasy about time before the bus stopped at Rockefeller Plaza. She glanced at the Plaza, which looked strange and wintry with snow-laden shrubbery instead of flowers, and started over toward Madison. The store windows were all lighted, but the streets looked strange and deserted, heaped up with snow. There were great gray trucks scooping away at the drifts. Even busy Madison Avenue looked as if it had been struck by some mysterious blight overnight. There were pedestrians but they were few in comparison to its usual flood tide of hurrying people. The stores had a bleak and empty look.

The huge red and black Longchamps sign was bright and inviting. She whirled around the revolving door. The restaurant was not empty — perhaps it was never empty — but it was not full. Melora was seated in a corner. Anne threaded her way between tables and Melora said, "It took you a long time."

"I know." She sat down and a waiter appeared. The table before Melora had a napkin and some silver and nothing else. "Coffee?" Anne said.

Melora nodded. "And a sweet roll," she told the waiter. He left. Anne unfastened her coat collar. Melora said, "Did you bring the money?"

"Two hundred dollars. It's all there is in the house." She opened her handbag and Melora took the money from her hand as swiftly and adroitly as a pickpocket. One instant the bills were in Anne's hand; the next instant they had vanished inside Melora's handbag.

"I knew there was more in the safe," she said coolly.

"That's all I'm going to give you. Please don't ask for any more."

"This will do," Melora said.

She wore again the black sweater she had worn the first time Anne saw her and did not know it was Melora. Anne said, "I did see you! At the Museum, in the restaurant."

"I don't know what you're talking about." Melora examined the catch on her handbag.

"Yes. You sat near me."

Melora's hazy brown eyes seemed to look straight at Anne. "I was never in the Museum in my life."

"But — I saw you! I told you! A man came in and sat down with you. You must remember!"

This time Melora didn't even trouble to deny it. The waiter put down coffee and two enormous sweet rolls. Melora snatched one of them hungrily and said, "Are you going to send for Brent?"

"Send for — you mean because of that note you found and read?"

Melora nodded. "Take my advice. Send for him."

"But — that note was only to — to frighten me . . ."

"Who?" Melora asked elliptically, biting into the sweet roll with sharp little teeth.

"I don't know. But . . ."

Melora said coolly, "I'd take it seriously if I were you. Send for Brent. Or get out of that house. You'll have to sooner or later, you know. Cassie hates you."

"That isn't true!"

"Isn't it?"

Melora drank some coffee, said, "Brandy wouldn't hurt this — well, there isn't time," finished her sweet roll and eyed the other one. "Do you want that?"

"No."

"Thanks." Melora took the remaining sweet roll. Her little white teeth dug into it hungrily.

Anne said sharply, "Melora — haven't you had anything to eat today?"

"None of your business," Melora mumbled.

"But — if it's money — you had three hundred yesterday . . ."

Melora laughed softly and eyed the sweet roll. "I'm hungry," she said simply. "I didn't eat much breakfast. But you needn't look like that.

I'm not starving. . . . Listen, Cassie hated me and she hates you because she wants to marry Brent."

"I don't believe you!"

Melora shrugged. "Use your eyes. . . . Are you going to send for Brent?"

"Because of those notes? No, of course not!"

Melora's hazy, myopic gaze seemed to fix for a moment upon nothing. Then she thrust the remaining half of the sweet roll into her pocket, drank the last drop of coffee in her cup and instantly rose.

"Melora — wait . . ."

Melora was tying the green scarf over her head. She said coolly, "Take a plane. Take a train. Hide somewhere in the city. Do anything — but get out of that house."

"But you — those notes . . ."

"People do murder other people. As easily as you would kill a fly."

Anne seized Melora's coat sleeve. "Don't go! What do you mean? You've got to explain . . ." Melora's coat sleeve gave a kind of twitch and slid away from Anne's hand. Melora moved as lightly as a little animal. Already she was two tables away. Anne sprang up to follow her. The waiter shoved a tray upon the table.

By the time Anne had found enough money in her coin purse, Melora's green scarf had circled through the revolving door and disappeared into the street.

Anne followed her. She had to find her, catch

138

up with her, make her explain what she meant —
or what she knew. The green scarf was already a
block away, heading for Fifth Avenue, when
Anne got into the street. It bobbed out of sight
behind two men. There weren't many pedestrians but there were enough to make Anne's
pursuit difficult. It was also beginning to snow
again, great, thick, white flakes. The sidewalks
instantly became slippery. The green scarf
turned on Fifth and headed north.

Anne was caught by the traffic light and a
stream of trucks and taxis and cars, jerking
through the snow, getting stuck, jerking on. By
the time the light changed and a truck heaved
itself out of the way, the green scarf was far
ahead.

She lost it completely at the subway entrance.

TEN

Anne was, then, almost a block behind. She bumped into pedestrians and umbrellas, hurrying, trying to watch the green scarf which bobbed into sight and out again — and saw it turn and go down and out of sight. By the time Anne reached the cross street the traffic light changed again. By the time she could cross the street it was too late.

She stopped at the subway steps and looked down but there was no green scarf anywhere, no hurrying figure, nobody at all. It looked like the entrance to a deserted cave. There was no chance of finding Melora. She was almost certainly by then in a train, hurtling beneath the snow-laden city. Going where? Anne wondered.

"People do murder other people," Melora had said. "Cassie hates you."

Cassie wouldn't have typed those ugly little notes. She wasn't afraid of Cassie.

Melora had said, send for Brent — or get out of that house, in so many words.

It was too late to ask Melora questions, even if Melora had chosen to answer them.

She looked for an empty taxi or a bus, didn't see one and started walking north. The snow was heavier now, the flakes finer and colder, driven by the wind, full in her face.

It struck Anne suddenly that this time she

hadn't felt sorry for Melora, she hadn't been aware of the slightest current of the disarming appeal which, on their first meeting, had caught her so strongly. She had instead felt a little repelled by something a little too evasive and yet a little too purposeful about her. What was the purpose?

The patent answer was, first to get more money. But she *had* warned Anne of danger, because she had read one of the notes, and because she knew — or seemed to guess — the source of that danger. "Cassie hates you. She wants to marry Brent."

That was only a sly little touch of spite on Melora's part. All the same Anne wished that Melora had not said exactly that.

But the immediate question was what did Melora know, did she really know anything which gave validity to her warning?

It was odd that Melora had lied about so trivial and unimportant a thing as taking coffee in the restaurant of the Museum.

Anne struggled through the snow and wind to a hotel entrance, waited her turn and eventually secured a cab which arrived with a passenger. The house was lighted when she reached it. Cadwallader heard the door open and came to meet her. His pale eyes bulged with curiosity as if he wanted to say, where *have* you been? He said, "The police have come and gone! They questioned me, too, but, of course, I couldn't tell them anything except that the telephone wire

141

had been cut. They're all upstairs. Miss Lucy and Mrs. Wystan and . . ."

"*Who?*"

"Mrs. Wystan is home. She got here just as the police were leaving. It seems she didn't care for the blizzard and came home."

They were all in Daphne's room, not only Lucy and Daphne and Cassie, but surprisingly, Tod, too, draped over the sofa, his long legs dangling over the arm. And they were clearly in the middle of a more or less heated family conference.

Daphne saw her first. "Oh, Anne, you've missed it all. They couldn't wait for you any longer. But I told them everything."

Tod said, "Daff, *did* you write those notes?"

Lucy sighed. She was sitting beside Daphne, very straight and handsome in her brown tweed suit and white silk blouse, and very intent. She flashed a look of apology at Anne. "I had to tell the police about the notes, Anne. So they questioned Daff."

Daphne said, "I didn't write them, I tell you! Anne, why didn't you tell me they were threats? Murder! *That's* why you were so scared last night. I told them all about the man at the typewriter and the fake Dr. Smith and everything."

Cassie was standing before the window. Her green wool dress outlined her lovely, slender figure. Her black hair was as smooth and shining as satin. She said in the softest, lightest voice, "I've heard of people writing unpleasant letters

142

to themselves! I believe they simply wish to attract attention, sympathy, something of the kind."

There was a sudden, complete silence in the room. Lucy turned very deliberately to look at Cassie and for a blank second or two Anne did not believe her own ears. Cassie didn't mean that. She couldn't mean it!

"Cassie," she began, and Lucy said sternly, "That's a wicked thing to say!"

Cassie lifted her black eyebrows with an effect of surprise. "What have I — oh, why Anne! I didn't mean — *you* wouldn't have done anything so silly. Why, you'd know that Brent would see through it in a second. Now do tell us the *facts* about this burglar."

Daphne sat up, her face pink, hugging her knees. She glared at her mother like an angry and reckless kitten. "There was somebody! I saw him myself. And I scared him away."

"So now," Cassie said, smiling, "you're a heroine, dear. And we'll be in the papers." She turned to Anne again. "The police said they'd be in touch with you later. They thought it odd, I'm afraid, that you sent for them but didn't wait to see them."

Tod unfolded, magically assembling legs and arms. "They said they'll want you to identify him, Anne, if you can. Daff told them about the drug-store clerk, too, and the man in the drug store . . ."

"And I described Dr. Smith!" Daphne said,

very pleased with herself. "Anne, *did* you think I'd written those horrible notes?"

"I thought you might have, at first. Then I knew you didn't."

"Oh, that's all right," Daphne said calmly, replying to Anne's unspoken apology. "I was mad enough to write them. But I didn't."

Cassie put her hand on Lucy's arm. "Aunt Lucy, you'll stay to lunch."

Lucy was frowning, her face seemed older, a little drawn and bleak. "No, thanks," she said and rose. "Cadwallader would have a fit — all of us to lunch and Emma not here." She eyed Daphne doubtfully, bit her lip and finally said, "I believe you, Daff. Don't work up a temperature."

Cassie glanced at Anne and then back to Lucy. "*I'll* see that she's taken care of."

Anne felt herself flushing. The implication was that Anne had permitted Daphne to run around in the cold, chasing burglars, inviting pneumonia. And, of course, it was true. Cassie went out of the room, smiling and pleasant and very beautiful. Lucy frowned after her and then turned to Tod. "You told your mother you came home because classes were dismissed. I've brought up two boys. Now tell me the truth. Why did they send you home? What did you do?"

Tod shoved his hands in his pockets and avoided her eyes. "I told you. It's the blizzard."

"All right," Lucy said shortly, "Brent will get it

144

out of you." She put her hand on Anne's shoulder. Her gray eyes were very clear and dark. "Good-bye, my dear. I really had to tell them about the notes. But I'm afraid they believe that Daphne wrote them."

"Of course they think so," Daphne said and gave a hoarse chuckle. "Won't they feel silly when they find out I didn't!"

Lucy patted Anne's shoulder and went out. Anne said, "I'm sorry I thought you'd written them, Daff."

Daphne eyed Anne candidly. "No harm's done." She wriggled her feet under the blankets, shoved her hair back and said, "I guess I wasn't very nice to you."

"Love feast," Tod said in disgust and walked out of the room.

"The trouble is," Daphne said, "I don't think the police really believed *any* of it. Except that the telephone wire had been cut. Old Caddy told them that. But there's nothing missing, so whoever it was didn't steal anything. I told them all about the elevator and the man that jumped up the stairway and then ran away when I screamed, and I don't think they believed a word of it. But that was after Aunt Lucy told them about those . . ." She frowned, exactly like Lucy. "Those queer notes you found. They decided that I typed them, I know they did. And then you weren't here so they said they couldn't wait any longer but they'd make a report of it and then talk to you later." She sat up, hugging her knees, her eyes eager. "One of them said he might ask you to come and take a look at pictures of his beauties. He meant gunmen, didn't he?"

"Well — petty thieves — thugs." There was a flicker of disappointment on Daphne's face. "Yes — I expect gunmen. When did your mother get here?"

"Oh, she missed most of it." Daphne lay back on the pillows again. "She got too cold up there at the Moores'. They've got one of those huge, old-fashioned houses, on a hill. She said she ought to have turned right around and had Max bring her home as soon as she saw it was going to be a heavy snow. But anyway, she nearly froze to death — arctic breezes, she said, right through the house. So she got up before breakfast and got somebody to take her to the station and got a train back to New York. Then she had to wait, she said, an hour and a half in Grand Central Station, trying to get a taxi. She got here just as the police left."

"When did Tod come?"

"About half an hour ago. He was surprised, too. Where *were* you all that time?"

"Errand," Anne replied evasively. "I couldn't get a taxi. . . . So you told them about Dr. Smith?"

Daphne nodded. "They're going to talk to Dr. Cox." Her lips tucked up mischievously. "Won't old Fuzz Face be mad?"

Cassie from the doorway said, "Daphne, darling, don't call him that. Cadwallader wants to serve lunch, Anne."

They sat at the table in the great, formal dining room, Tod and Cassie and Anne, and it seemed to Anne that a very long time had passed since they had sat together. Yet that was only Wednesday night, and this was Friday noon. Tod was unusually quiet. Cassie seemed entirely at ease as if she had put the notes, the intruder into the house, even the visit of the police into their proper, unimportant niches. All the same, she seemed different to Anne. It was as if she were seeing Cassie in a new light, and in that new light it seemed to Anne that Cassie did have an air of complete authority, the woman in possession.

Cassie said unexpectedly, "Darling, you're staring. What's wrong?"

"Nothing," Anne replied. She wouldn't let herself be influenced by Melora. Melora, really, was not important in her life, or Brent's, or Cassie's.

Melora became very important about four o'clock that afternoon.

It was a quiet afternoon, muffled again by the heavy snow outside. The police did not return to talk to Anne; they were busy. It was a day of problems, traffic accidents, fires from over-heated stoves, all the varied emergencies which a blizzard can bring in its wake. Tod disappeared immediately after lunch. Daphne went to sleep.

Cassie got Emma on the telephone in the library and had apparently a frustrated conversation with her, for Cassie said at last in a defeated way that she hoped Emma would be able to come to work soon. She then telephoned to Daisy.

She was more successful with Daisy, who had been employed only that fall, after Anne's marriage to Brent. Cadwallader and Emma had been in the house for years, and bullied Cassie as much as Cassie bullied them, but Daisy was new to her job. Anne had a fellow feeling for Daisy, both of them strangers in that house which Melora — no, no, it was Cassie who organized the household with such perfection of smooth running detail, never Melora.

Daisy apparently yielded, for Cassie snapped down the telephone and said, "Anything for an excuse! If I can get home from Litchfield, she can get here from the Bronx." She looked at Anne. "How do you think this — burglar — last night got into the house?"

There was a delicate, smiling skepticism in her inquiry.

"There *was* somebody here, Cassie."

"My dear, I don't doubt for a minute that *something* happened that upset you. I do think that perhaps you and Daphne — well, got a little frightened and hysterical. You see, there really is no way anybody can get into the house without a key. All that nonsense Daff talked about your Dr. Smith turning the night latch *is* nonsense. I'm sure the police must think so, too. In fact, I imagine they think the whole thing was built up, not intentionally, of course, but — perhaps I should say it built itself up between you and Daphne. I understand it. I'm sure they do. You and Daff alone in the house, the telephone cut off and all that . . ."

"But the wire was cut."

Cassie shrugged. "That could happen a dozen ways. The point is nobody had a key to the house." Her brilliant eyes narrowed between those long black eyelashes. "What's the matter?"

Melora might have had a key! She had said the door was ajar, but it now struck Anne as a little too glib an explanation. If Melora had a key, she could have written the ugly little notes — sheerly to make trouble. But Daphne had seen a man at the typewriter.

"What *is* the matter, Anne? Why don't you answer me?" Something very bright and hard leaped like a flame into Cassie's eyes. She said slowly, watching Anne, "An odd thing has just occurred to me. Melora, of course, had a key once. She might have returned it to Brent. But certainly she didn't give it to me." She bit her lip for a thoughtful instant, her bright, sharp eyes probing, and said as if she plucked it out of the air, "You've seen Melora."

"Yes, I have. She was here yesterday."

"*You* . . ." Cassie drew in a sharp breath. "She wants Brent back! I knew it. I knew it when I saw them together."

"She wanted money. I gave it to her."

Cassie debated for an instant. "How much?"

"Five hundred."

"Five — where did you get it?"

"Out of the safe."

"Why did you give it to her?"

"She said she needed it."

"Melora always wants money."

"I thought Brent would want me to give it to her."

"I wouldn't have given her a cent! Unless . . ." Anne could see a swift speculation flicker in Cassie's eyes. She leaned forward and said gently, "Did she promise you to stay away from Brent? I mean — if you gave her some money?"

"No! She wanted money so I gave it to her, that's all. Five hundred wouldn't have stopped her, Cassie. Not if she had any reason to believe that Brent — wants her back."

Cassie shook her head. "You don't know Melora. She'd take anything, promise anything and then do whatever she wanted to do. I'm sorry. But I did warn you, dear. I told you Brent had been seeing her."

Cassie was all kindness, all confiding friendliness. But Anne said suddenly, "Why did you tell me that, Cassie?"

"Why because — because I thought you ought to know it. I saw them together. Having cocktails in a little place — oh, never mind, I saw them. And you see, dear, Melora has — I don't know — a sort of attraction. I can't see it myself, I never could. When Brent married you, of course, I tried to do everything to help you. So I — warned you." Cassie's eyes flicked away from Anne's. She went to the table, took a cigarette and lighted it. "Darling, I wouldn't have hurt you for anything. I didn't intend to do that."

"You didn't hurt me. I'm Brent's wife."

Cassie smiled. "You're very sure of yourself, dear. I wouldn't be so sure." She put out the cigarette she had just lighted and started for the door, grace in every curve of her lovely figure. It was never quite possible to believe that Cassie with her beauty, her slender youthfulness, could be the mother of two teen-age children.

"Wait, Cassie. What exactly do you mean?"

Cassie's eyebrows lifted. "Darling, how very stern you are! I meant — why, that's all I meant! A woman should never be too sure of herself with a man."

"I am sure that Brent loves me," Anne said steadily — but was she so sure? She lifted her head and met Cassie's eyes. "I'm his wife."

Cassie laughed softly, "Darling, you said that. Nobody denies it. But Melora was once his wife, too. . . . I only felt that you should get your eyes open. I'm sure there's nothing for you to worry about. Brent is very — kind." She walked out of the room and up the stairs, humming softly.

A book lay on the table beside Anne. She was surprised by the intensity of her longing to take the book and fling it at Cassie. Luckily Cassie was already out of sight.

After a while Anne followed Cassie upstairs

151

and went to the refuge of the little study, curled herself in the chaise longue, and watched the snow drifting steadily past the windows.

Once it occurred to her to telephone to Gary Molloy and ask if he had got a message through to Brent and a reply. But if Gary had news he'd have told her.

By four o'clock it was almost dark and still snowing. Anne turned on the radio beside the chaise longue. She was thinking only of the possibility of Brent's return and the weather reports and whether or not the storm would permit plane travel.

The announcer's voice spoke clearly and impersonally from the little box. The city was stormbound, trains running late, traffic almost at a standstill. The weather forecast was for continued snow and cold. And now for the news. A woman had been murdered in the subway. He gave the street and station and Anne sat up as if a hand had jerked her upright and tense.

"About noon today," the voice continued brightly. "She was in her twenties, blond, wearing a fur coat. Her handbag was taken and thus far the murdered woman has not been identified. She was stabbed twice. No knife was found. The motive they believe was robbery. At that time the passage leading to the subway platform was almost deserted. Attendants have been questioned but so far as it is now known her murderer escaped without being seen. An odd note developed with the discovery of a small gold clock, believed to be an antique of considerable value, and half a sweet roll in the pocket of her coat, which is mink. These two unusual items, the police hope, will lead to her identification. . . ."

Anne's hand moved as if it had a life of its own and snapped off the radio.

ELEVEN

It was Melora.

The sweet roll in the pocket of her mink coat was not only an odd note, it was an utterly convincing one. Blond, in her twenties, a sweet roll in the pocket of a mink coat, in the subway at the very street and station where Anne had seen the green scarf disappear.

An antique gold clock. It seemed to Anne that she thought of the clock at once, in only a few seconds. In fact, it must have been several stunned moments before she remembered the small table, velvet-lined and glass-topped like a box, which stood in the drawing room close beside the chair where Melora had sat.

She ran downstairs. Cassie and Tod were already there, bending over the table, and the glass top was open. There was still the varied little assortment of more or less valuable objects which collect in a house which has been lived in by several generations: some jade and rose quartz snuff bottles, a few miniatures, some charming old Battersea boxes. The tiny gold clock, scarcely larger than an old-fashioned watch, was gone.

Cassie turned with a swift movement that set the white silk lounge coat she wore rustling sharply. "It's the Louis Sixteenth! The most valuable thing here and she knew it. Anne, how could you have let her take it!"

"But it may not be Melora," Tod said. His face was white and the skin looked as if it were stretched over his sharp bones.

"Blond, in her twenties and the clock — the instant I heard of the clock I knew. She came into the house yesterday. . . ." Cassie stopped, thought and cried, "She meant to open the safe! That's why she came. She knew it was Thursday. She came in and — then Anne came home so she didn't have a chance to open the safe. She asked for money and you gave it to her, Anne. And while you were gone she took the Louis Sixteenth clock."

Tod muttered, "It may not be a Louis Sixteenth. That's not certain."

"Of course it is. He made it himself. That's why it's valuable. . . ."

"Can't prove it," Tod said contumaciously.

"That doesn't matter. Melora thought it was valuable." Cassie turned to Anne again. "Anne! Listen — we heard it on the radio! A woman was murdered in the subway and she had a gold clock and I came to look — and there — see, it's gone!"

She pointed at the blank space where there was now only a faintly marked oval on the black velvet.

Anne said, "It was Melora. She ate one of the sweet rolls and part of another and — put the rest of it in her pocket and went to the subway and I followed her that far — and then I came home."

155

Tod's eyes were like black pits in his white face.

"*You* saw her? *You* met her. . . . *Why?*"

Cassie flashed, "Oh, Tod, don't be stupid! She came here yesterday when we were all gone. She asked Anne for money and Anne gave it to her!" She whirled around to Anne. "What's this about a sweet roll and the subway?"

"She phoned. This morning. She wanted more money. I met her at Longchamps. We talked a few minutes. . . ."

"That's where you were when the police were here! What did she say? Why did you follow her?"

"She had found one of those notes yesterday. It must have been somewhere in this room. She didn't say anything about it then. But this morning she — she seemed to warn me."

"Warn you?" Tod cried. "You mean she thought — she *believed* the note?"

"Oh, Tod, be quiet," Cassie cried. "What did Melora *say?*"

Anne thought, she told me you hated me and hated her. Aloud she said, "She urged that I should get Brent to come home, said I should leave — go away somewhere — that there were people who would murder as easily as I would kill a fly. Then she left and I wanted to know what she meant — what she knew of those notes — why she said" — Anne swallowed hard — "the things she did. So I followed her as far as the subway."

156

There was a long silence while Tod stared at her and Cassie stared at her and the snow drifted slowly past the window at the end of the room.

Finally Tod said, "Did you see anyone else — following her, I mean?"

"She went down into the subway. By the time I got there she had disappeared. There wasn't anybody there. Nobody at all. I came home."

Cassie stirred suddenly. She put out a hand and closed the glass top of the table with a snap. "It was Melora," she said. "I warned you, Anne. She was trying to make trouble between you and Brent. It's all perfectly clear. She still had a key. She knows the routine of the house. *She* wrote those notes, to frighten you. She told you to leave the house — so she could come back. In the meantime she needed money. She intended to sell the clock. She had the five hundred you gave her in her handbag and a thug robbed her. She resisted — she would, so he . . ." Cassie shrugged.

Anne's lips were dry. She turned toward the library and Cassie caught her arm.

"Where are you going?"

"Why — we should call the police. Tell them who she is . . ."

"You'll do no such thing. Melora has always meant trouble to us. Do you want to rake it all up again?"

"She can't just — lie there. Nobody to see to things . . ."

"Anne," Tod said, his face glistening white,

157

"that's why I came home."

Cassie cried, "Tod! What do you mean?"

He met his mother's eyes with a kind of miserable defiance. "She sent for me."

"Melora!"

"Last night. She phoned. She said she had to have some money. She asked if I had any. I said I had my Christmas present and pocket money for the month but it wasn't much. She said to come to town and meet her at the bus terminal as soon after one-thirty as I could. I explained I didn't know how the trains were running and I might be late, but she said it didn't matter. . . ." Tod's voice roughed as if he choked back a sob. "It didn't matter," he repeated, holding sternly to his self-control. "So I came home and then there were the police and all that and lunch was late and — so I was late. I was too late. She wasn't there because . . ." His mouth quivered. He turned away abruptly and went to stand at the window, his back turned to them and his hands shoved in his pockets.

"Tod," Cassie said, letting out her breath in a gasp. *"Why* did you do it? Why didn't you *tell* me? *Why* . . ." She flung out her hands in a hopeless gesture. "I don't understand it! You and Daff are the same! You'd do anything — just anything for Melora. All she had to do was ask it. Even now — why, it's been nearly three years. You were children!" Her eyes were drained of color except for black, hard pupils. "Have you kept in touch with her all this time?"

"N-no," Tod said. "That is — sometimes she wrote to me — just post cards, nothing much but . . ."

"But the minute she phones to you, you leave school and rush off to get some money for her!"

Tod turned around. He was angry, too, but very white. "Suppose I did! What's wrong with that?"

"But you knew — at least you must have guessed . . ." Cassie took a long breath and said softly, "It's as if she put a — a spell on you and Daff. Both of you were perfectly silly about her. You still are. I don't understand it. I told you to forget all about her. I told you what she . . ."

Tod said in a suddenly adult voice, "Stop that, Mother. She's dead."

"That doesn't change anything." Cassie's silk robe rustled as she moved around to Anne. "Now then — somebody will identify her but not you. Think of Brent."

"Brent would tell the police who she is," Anne said.

"But that's not your decision to make. Besides . . ." Cassie's eyes widened thoughtfully. She stared at Anne for a second. Then she put her arm around Anne. Her voice became warm and affectionate. "Darling, you must listen to me. You see, you *were* one of the last persons to see her. And you say you followed her as far as the subway."

"But I did. She was alone. . . ."

159

Tod said, again in that suddenly adult and cold voice, "She means the police will question you and me, too. We'll be suspects. Isn't that right, Mother?"

"*Suspects* . . ." Anne cried and Cassie said softly, "I'm afraid so, dear. You met Melora — you say because Melora wanted money — and gave it to her, and of course I believe you. But do you think they'll believe that? I'm afraid they are far more likely to believe that you and Melora quarreled. Perhaps that you were afraid she would come between you and Brent, or that you — were — well, jealous of her."

"That's not true!"

"Mother!" Tod said. "Anne didn't kill her! I didn't . . ." He put a thin, urgent hand on Anne's arm. "But we've got to think about Uncle Brent, just the same."

"Anne dear," Cassie said in a reasonable, gentle way, "identify her if you feel you must. But do think of Brent — newspapers, police — everything!"

It was a convincing argument. Anne had only to lift the telephone and dial a number and a deluge would descend upon them. Floodlights would be turned upon every facet of their lives but particularly upon Brent's life and would strip it of reticence, expose every fact and every possible surmise of his marriage to Melora.

Tod said, "Mother is right. I hate to think of Melora — like that . . ." His voice trembled. "But all the same — Mother is right."

"Of course I'm right. It's tragic and terrible but it has nothing to do with us. Now Tod — don't tell Daff. She was absurdly fond of Melora and she's stubborn and . . ."

Tod cried, "Those notes! Daff didn't write them. . . ."

"Melora wrote them," Cassie said.

"No, no. Listen! They were *meant* for Melora! Whoever wrote them thought Melora was still living here! He didn't know about the divorce, he didn't know that Uncle Brent was married to Aunt Anne. He meant them for Melora! And the man last night meant to kill Melora then. He discovered it wasn't Melora — I mean it was Anne on the stairs — that's why he left."

There was a long, packed silence. So all of them heard the front door open and close. All of them heard Brent's voice.

"Anne!"

"It's Uncle Brent!"

Brent came up the stairs, meeting them in the hall. He held Anne and kissed her and she clung to him and Tod cried, "Uncle Brent — listen — Uncle Brent . . ."

Cassie told him. Tod told him. When he questioned her, Anne told him.

The long library windows were black and glittering and reflected Brent, pacing up and down the room, toward the windows so Anne could see his face, white and tense, hard as a rock like Daphne's the night before, mirrored in the black

161

glass, and then, as he turned, his tall figure, his shoulders — tired-looking and stooped a little, his hands thrust in his pockets as he paced back again. A glass of whiskey and soda stood on the table before the sofa.

She could see herself, too, sitting hunched on the big footstool, watching him. There was no way to tell how much or how deeply Melora's murder affected him. There was no way to tell, either, what he was going to do.

He had listened and asked questions and listened. Cassie had sent Tod to bring the whiskey and soda. Anne wished that she had thought of it. He had explained his return. The plane had run into bad weather and was obliged to wait for some hours at Gander, the flight having been diverted owing to the storm. While there he had Gary's message and had contrived to get a flight back to Boston. From there he had come back to New York by train. He had agreed, absently, with Cassie when she said it was better not to let Daphne know of Melora's death that night. "She'll know soon enough," she said. "We can't keep it from her. But — she was foolishly fond of Melora."

"Daff will raise hell," Tod said gloomily. "I'll take her radio."

But when Cassie asked if he intended to go to the police Brent said that he wanted to talk to Anne alone. Tod and Cassie had gone — reluctantly, but had gone.

He turned at the door to the hall and paced

162

back again, head bent, toward the glittering windows.

Was he going to say — Anne, I was still in love with Melora, bear with me?

She couldn't ask. Love has its own barriers and its own reticences. She could only wait. Yet in fact she couldn't wait and watch that troubled pacing. She said, "Brent — I'm sorry. If I had followed her down into the subway it might not have happened."

His head jerked up. "Thank God you didn't!" He came to her, sat down in the deep red chair near the footstool and took her hands. "Anne, you couldn't have helped it."

"But I'm so — so *sorry*, Brent. It's horrible. . . ."

"You tried to help her. It was right to give her money. There was nothing else you could have done for her."

But she couldn't say, "Brent, tell me. I'll understand. I love you. But tell me — did you still love Melora?"

He looked very tired. He stretched out his long legs and took up the glass and sipped from it, his face abstracted, deep in thought. Finally he said, "Is there anything, anything at all that you haven't told me? Some — small detail, something Melora said or did — anything?"

There was, of course, and it was not a detail. She had automatically, as if somebody else had made the decision, locked deep in her knowledge the accusation of Cassie, which Melora had

163

tossed out so matter-of-factly. "Cassie hates you — she wants to marry Brent." She couldn't tell anybody that. She wouldn't tell anybody. It had nothing to do with Melora's murder. She hesitated between an outright lie and some sort of evasion which would be in effect the same thing, and Brent said, "Go over it again, Anne. All of it. From the time you found the first note."

Again he listened, his eyes narrowed and thoughtful. Again she omitted Melora's words about Cassie — but she was sure she omitted nothing else. This time, however, she remembered the knife on the hall table. "But oh, Brent — there was a knife on the table. . . ."

He listened and sent for Cadwallader, who knew of Melora's murder, who always knew everything that happened in the house, who was shocked and ashy pale, but who insisted he knew nothing of a knife, like a big pocketknife, on the table beside the roses.

"Have you ever seen a switchblade?" Brent asked.

"Well — I'm not sure," Cadwallader said and thought for a moment. "But there are some short paring and carving knives in the kitchen. Mrs. Wystan may have been mistaken. But I did not leave a knife by the roses and I didn't — I'm sure I didn't see a knife there this morning. However," he said in a harassed way, "it's been an upsetting sort of day."

After he had gone, Brent sighed. "Probably Cadwallader did pick it up and forgot it. He's

164

getting old and fidgety. On the other hand — the man in the elevator last night might have taken it. Melora was . . ." He stopped and Anne, too, could not quite face the dreadful mental picture of Melora, crumpled down in her shabby mink coat in the subway, terribly alone — stabbed, the announcer had said.

Brent said, "You said you destroyed the notes."

"Yes. No! I think the third one — the one on the kitchen table . . ."

"Do you still have that?"

"I don't know what I did with it. . . ."

"What were you wearing?"

"My red dress . . ."

"I like that dress," Brent said unexpectedly. "Look in the pocket."

"No, it doesn't have a pocket. Oh yes! My coat — I went to the Collinses right after that to get them to report the telephone and . . ."

"Get the note, Anne."

The coat was in the closet downstairs. She ran down through a neat, quiet house, with everything in perfect order — and a tiny clock gone from the glass-topped table. There were fresh flowers in vases. An enormous clump of pale pink quince blossoms with straggling brown branches reflected itself in the mirror above the hall table. The note was in her pocket, crumpled down with her key.

Back in the dining room she had a glimpse of Daisy, returned to work, in her black uniform and decorous white apron, putting silver on the table. Everything in the house was proceeding in its orderly routine quite as if Melora had never lived there, never visited there the previous day, never touched upon its life.

TWELVE

Brent took the note and read it. "Not very nice," he said in a voice that had no relation to the icy hardness that came into his eyes. He put it in his wallet. "I'll see about this."

"Daphne didn't write it. I'm sure she didn't."

"I'll talk to Daff. It's more than likely that some petty thief, some thug, killed Melora. Snatched at her handbag and she resisted and — that's what probably happened. But these notes — the man last night — that knife . . ." He put his arm around her, drawing her very close to him. "I shouldn't have left you alone. Oh, Anne . . ." He put his face down against her own for a moment. Then he got up and paced the room again, but now, talking. "The point is this. Either Melora was murdered by a thug, or it was a deliberate, planned murder. If it was a planned murder, there could be some relation between it — and those notes, the man last night in the elevator — Dr. Smith, the man in the drug store — Melora's demand for money. I think it *likely* that a thug killed Melora. If that is so, then all the business of threatening notes and a man entering the house belongs to some other — call it scheme, some other plan. I don't know what."

Anne said slowly, "But at first it seemed like a

joke. An unpleasant sort of joke. I can't think of anybody who would think that that kind of thing was a joke. But all the same . . ."

"That's a natural reaction. It's something that's entirely foreign to your experience, something outside — normal behavior." He eyed her for a moment, thinking. "I think Melora still had a key to the house. I think she came here yesterday, knowing it was Caddy's day out, hoping to get into the safe, get some money and leave without being seen. You came home before she had a chance to open the safe. She took the little clock, of course. She'd have thought it was valuable and she might be able to sell it. The coincidence of the notes, the man last night, Melora's need for money does seem to hook it all together. All of it happened at once, as if somebody planned it like that. Yet somehow — Melora's murder doesn't seem to fit in."

And murder, too, lay outside the protective, safe fences of civilization. Brent said, "Melora obviously wanted money. Suppose some scheme, which included all these things, was put into operation with the intent of getting money. From me, I suppose, although I don't know just how it was expected to succeed. Threats to you would have been the lever but — I don't think Melora herself would have gone about it so indirectly. But suppose somebody she knew . . ."

There was another fact she had unintentionally omitted. She hadn't told him of her first view of Melora! "Oh, Brent, I forgot! I saw Melora. I

168

mean before she came here yesterday. She was with a man. . . ."

"When was this?"

"Weeks ago. Early in December, I think. She was in the restaurant at the Museum. I sat near her. A man came and sat with her."

"Was it this Dr. Smith?"

"I don't know. I didn't notice him particularly. He was young, I think. I can't remember anything about him really. But I remembered her, even the black sweater and a locket she wore. I told her. But Melora denied it. She said she'd never been in the Museum in her life."

"Probably the man was Delayne."

"Delayne?"

"Reginald Delayne."

The boy friend Daphne had talked of? Anne said slowly, "That doesn't sound like a real name."

Brent gave a short, dry laugh. "He's real cnough. You see — Melora was in love with him."

"That's why . . ." Anne began and Brent nodded. "I never saw him. I never knew where or how she met him. But she — it was like a sickness really. I don't think she could help it. She had to have him," he said and sat down on the arm of the chair. "Anne, when we were married I told you that Melora and all that was in the past, and I meant it to be in the past. But a few weeks ago I saw Melora."

She had known that, too, Anne thought;

169

Cassie told her. She dug her hands hard into the footstool. Brent said, "She phoned to me at the office. She said she had to see me. I guessed she wanted money. I knew — that is, I guessed, that Delayne had got away with her settlement. I told her at the time to hang onto it — I thought then that she wanted a lump sum because Delayne wanted it. Well, I met her. She asked for money. I gave her a couple of hundred. She wanted more. I told her that I wouldn't give her any more money for Delayne. She said she needed it only for herself. Then she admitted that Delayne had got most of her money. She didn't seem to know or probably didn't want to tell me what he'd done with it. However, she said she'd have nothing more to do with him if I'd give her enough money to stake her until she could get herself on her feet again. I told her that if she ever really needed help, of course I'd try to help her. She took the money I had with me and was gone. I never heard from her again. Anne — I didn't tell you about it."

"No, of course. No — then is Melora married to Delayne?"

"I don't know. I don't think so. She didn't say so definitely and I didn't ask. I didn't care. They seem to have been leading a wandering sort of life, I did gather that. If she told Delayne that I had advised her to get away from him, as in a way I had, he might have got some idea of revenge into his head. He *could* have got hold of Melora's house key, if she still had it. He *could* have got into the house by the kitchen door (it's the same lock) without being seen by the servants, after they left. He could have gone up the back stairs and typed those notes. He could have been the man Daphne saw. It was taking a chance but Melora could have phoned to the office and discovered that I was going to Paris, and Delayne could have thought the house would be empty except for you. That's the way it looks. He could have been the man in the drug store — following you as the clerk said. He could have been this Dr. Smith. None of us ever saw Delayne. I've no idea what he looks like. Whether he really meant to murder you — is something different. I would be inclined to think that it was simply and sheerly a kind of program of revenge — he meant to frighten you and revenge himself upon me. Revenge — or some sort of scheme to get money. Taking that elevator up and down through the house, that would frighten you, too. But he did make an overt attack. If hc did havc a knife — if Daff hadn't scared him . . ."

She said, staring at the rug, "Melora said there were people who could kill as easily as I would kill a fly. She told me to leave this house. . . ."

Brent's voice was rough. "She knew — or guessed — something of his plan. It is Delayne. We have no real proof of that. It does sound as if Melora didn't go along with him, as if she really tried to get you to leave, get away from him — but of course she couldn't tell you the truth. She wouldn't have got Delayne into trouble, you see.

171

Her flat denial that she was the woman you saw in the Museum suggests that it was Delayne with her and that she was trying to protect him — perhaps so you would not connect the man in the restaurant with her with — say — Dr. Smith. If Delayne is back of all this — I think Melora knew it. Since she warned you so urgently, she must have been afraid that Delayne might — get out of hand and instead of merely frightening you, revenging himself upon me in that way, he might actually murder you. Did you feel she was sincere about that?"

She met his eyes fully. It was easier somehow now for he was speaking of Melora in a direct, yet impersonal way. "Yes. She wouldn't tell me why. She said to send for you — or get out of this house — take a plane, take a train — but go." There was an odd little light in his eyes. He said gently, "And you wouldn't."

"Why no!"

"Did she talk of any person, any name at all? I mean did she seem to suggest any one person, any specific source of danger to you?"

Only Cassie, Anne thought. Only Cassie. But Cassie wouldn't have written those notes; and it was a man in the elevator. Upstairs a radio was going, a man's voice was speaking steadily and indistinctly at that distance. In the street below an automobile honked impatiently. Anne said, "No."

There was another long silence. She wouldn't look at Brent, yet she knew he was watching her.

Finally he said, "She could have quarreled with Delayne. But somehow I don't think he murdered her. She was his source of money. Obviously he sent Melora to ask me for money — and to ask you for money. Even Tod. For that reason alone I don't think he'd have murdered her. But the first thing to do is go to the police."

"What are you going to tell them?"

"Who she is," he said, his voice suddenly rough again. "Who she was — and enough about Delayne so they'll question him. As to the rest of it . . ." He paused for a long moment and then said, "I'm a lawyer. I've undertaken to interpret the law as truly as I can, and abide by the law. On the other hand I've undertaken, too, to shield and protect my wife." He came to her and put his hand on her cheek, turning her face up toward him. "So I intend to do that, too."

Cassie said from the doorway, "Oh, I'm sorry." Her clear light eyes were observing. Brent's hand dropped. Cassie said, "I thought you ought to know. It's on the radio. They've identified her! Brent, she married him! Did you know that? They say she was identified as Mrs. Reginald Delayne."

"Who identified her?"

"The announcer didn't say. He just told about the murder again and her name and — the point is, you needn't identify her at all, Brent. You needn't get us into the thing at all. Brent . . ." She put her lovely face against his arm. "Don't go to the police. Don't tell them anything. You

173

don't have to. It's so horrible for you. And for all of us."

"I know, Cassie. I'm sorry about it all."

She said softly, "Oh, I don't blame you for bringing Melora here, for marrying her. I understood that. You felt sorry for her, you felt . . ." She stopped and looked at Anne. It was a pleasant, almost smiling look and it shut Anne out as if she were an intruder, as if what Cassie had to say lay between her and Brent alone.

The telephone rang. It was so sharp and imperative a sound that perhaps all three felt it significant, a summons. Brent took two strides to the table and picked up the telephone.

Cassie's white hands pressed down upon the table. A great aquamarine hung on a single fine chain at her white throat and glittered in the light, exactly the color of her eyes. Brent said, "Oh, Aunt Lucy. Yes, I got back this afternoon. . . . I know. . . . Yes, we heard it over the radio." He listened for what seemed a long time. Anne strained her ears to distinguish words but there was only the quick staccato of Lucy's voice. Cassie, nearer, seemed to understand something of what Lucy said for her eyes brightened hopefully, as she watched Brent. Then Brent said, "Listen, Aunt Lucy. I was on the train. Nobody would suspect me. There's no reason for it. . . ."

Lucy's voice seemed to quicken. Brent said at last, "Yes, I understand. But it'll be all right. I'll call you later."

He put down the telephone. Cassie cried tautly, "*You* didn't kill her! They can't suspect *you*. What did Aunt Lucy mean?"

"She had just heard about it, over the radio. The instant she knew I was at home she — oh, you know Aunt Lucy. She said that the police always suspect a husband or wife or — even a former husband." His matter-of-fact way of speaking was purposeful, Anne knew. It was intended to define Lucy's anxiety as fanciful. Yet Lucy was not fanciful. She had clear, hard common sense.

"That doesn't sound like Aunt Lucy," Cassie said.

"In a way, she's right. People don't as a rule murder perfect strangers."

"But it was a thug, a pickpocket — he took her handbag — there was nobody on that part of the platform, the radio said so. He got away. Nobody saw him. It's nothing to you, Melora's nothing to you. Think of what she did to you, how she . . ."

Brent said to Anne, cutting through Cassie's voice, "Don't look like that, Anne." He bent and kissed her lips. "I'll be back before you know it."

He went out of the room. The house was so still that they could hear his steps on the stairs, his voice as apparently he spoke to Daisy or Cadwallader in the hall below. The front door opened and closed.

Cassie then turned to Anne. She was still wearing the white silk lounge coat; the red lining

175

flashed as she moved. She leaned across the table, closer to Anne, and the aquamarine at her throat swung back and forth. "He's doing this because of you," she said in a deliberate, very quiet voice. "He'll drag us all — and himself — through the mud because you're such a fool. *Why* did you talk to Melora? *Why* did you go to meet her this morning? He should never have married you. You don't belong here. We don't need you. We don't want you."

It was like a slap in the face. It would have been easier to believe if Cassie had not been so controlled, so quiet and reasonable.

So Melora was right.

Cassie leaned nearer. "This is for your own good, dear. You must see that you're really not the wife for Brent. . . ."

Cassie broke off. Daisy stood in the doorway. Her eyes were wide and excited between pale lashes. Her carroty hair flared out wildly. With no pause, no break whatever in her even, reasonable voice, Cassie said, "What is it, Daisy?"

Daisy had a small silver tray in one hand. "It's a note."

"Give it to me," Cassie said.

"But it's for . . ." Daisy checked herself with a swift glance at Anne, and Cassie snatched the note.

Anne said, *"It's another one. . . ."*

This time it was in an envelope. Cassie slid out a single sheet of paper. She read it at a glance and looked at Daisy. "Did you read this?"

"Oh no! No, Mrs. Wystan!"

"Why did you bring it here?" Cassie glanced at the envelope. "There's no name on the envelope."

"Well — but — I thought . . ." Daisy twisted her white apron and said, "Caddy told me about the notes so I — I brought it to — to the other Mrs. Wystan."

"You can go, Daisy."

"Yes'm." Daisy gulped and fled.

"Give it to me," Anne said.

In a swift movement Cassie took the cigarette lighter on the table, crumpled up the note and envelope and crossed the room to the fireplace. There was the tiny click of the lighter.

"Cassie — don't . . ."

"Be quiet." She held the paper over the lighter.

"Cassie . . ." Anne ran to her. She reached for the note which was already touched with flame and Cassic's othcr arm came out, with a swift hard thrust which sent Anne stumbling back against the sofa.

"But you can't do that, Cassie! I've got to see it! Brent — the police . . ."

The last corner of the small paper was already burning. In a second it was brown and crumbling. The envelope still made a bright little flame.

THIRTEEN

"Cassie, why did you do that? What did it say?"

"I'd better light the fire," Cassie said and did so, kneeling, her white silk skirt spread outward around her, on the floor. Flames shot upward, the kindling crackled. Cassie rose and dusted her hands together. "That's that," she said coolly.

"Why did you burn that?"

"Because it was best. Believe me, Anne."

"What did it say?"

"Nothing."

"Cassie, you've got to answer me."

"All right." Cassie thought for a moment, her eyes so clear and purposeful that it seemed strange that Anne could not see through them and follow the course of her thoughts. Finally she said, "Dear, I'm older than you. Be guided by me. There was no note."

"You mean I'm not to tell anybody. Cassie, that's silly. . . ."

"There was no note."

"But it's important, Cassie. They have to try to trace those notes. . . ."

"I suppose you'll tell Brent."

"Of course I'll tell Brent."

"All right," Cassie said. "I'll tell him you're lying."

"You *can't* . . ." Anne turned from Cassie's

178

composed smile, which said she could. She went quickly to the small button set into the casing of the door and pressed it.

Cassie came in a swirl of white silk after her. "What are you going to do?"

"I'm going to ask Daisy where she got it."

"No . . ." Cassie's white hand gripped Anne's wrist hard. Anne kept her hand on the bell and suddenly the two women were locked together in a swift, hard struggle as if they were fighting each other for life, over a dangerous abyss.

Perhaps Cassie sensed that abyss as Anne did, for in the same second they drew apart and looked at each other. Cassie was breathing quickly. Anne's heart was thudding. And all at once another woman seemed to enter the room and stood there, watching them, with hazy brown eyes, saying matter-of-factly, "Cassie hates you."

But Anne couldn't hate Cassie and she couldn't fear her. Hatred like that, fear, went back to an older time. It had to do with the struggle to survive. Hatred could not exist in that house between two women. Or between three women, Anne thought — for Melora seemed to laugh softly, watching them.

And then, in the flicker of an eyelash, Cassie was in control of herself, beautiful, calm, half smiling. "Darling," she said, "we needn't fight over it. Really, dear, you were so violent! If you want to question Daisy, go ahead."

She strolled over to the book shelves. She took

out a book without looking at the title. She opened it and turned a page or two with steady, lovely white hands.

Daisy came, running up the stairs and into the room, where she stopped and said breathlessly, as Cassie had taught her to say, "Yes, madam?"

The fire was burning brightly now and the brown fragments of the note were mixing indissolubly with the burning logs.

Anne said, "Daisy, did you read the note you brought just now?"

Daisy's eyes flickered uneasily away from her, traveled around the room, avoided Cassie. "Read it! Oh, *no*, Mrs. Wystan."

"Listen, Daisy, it's quite all right if you just happened to look at it. There was no name on the envelope so it would be very natural — right — to open it and see what was in it. Don't be afraid to tell me if you read it."

Daisy fastened her gaze stubbornly upon a point just above Anne's head. "But I didn't, Mrs. Wystan. I wouldn't do that."

"Yes, I know. Not an ordinary letter. But this wasn't addressed — it wasn't an ordinary letter." And that was terribly true, Anne thought.

But Daisy shook her head virtuously and stubbornly. "I don't read other people's letters."

Cassie said gently, "Of course she doesn't do that, Anne," and turned over a page with a crisp rustle.

"Well, then," Anne said, "who brought it? Where did you get it?"

Daisy consented to meet her eyes. "Well . . ." She moistened her lips. "Well, it was very queer."

"What do you mean?"

"Nobody delivered it. I mean, not a postman or a messenger or — but somehow it got into the house. I mean — well, there it was, Mrs. Wystan. . . ." Cassie's silk coat rustled and Daisy apparently remembered her training and said nervously, "I mean, madam, there it was — in the hall. Mr. Wystan had gone. He said not to wait dinner, he might not be home in time for dinner, and I went back to the kitchen to tell Caddy — I mean Mr. Cadwallader . . ."

Cassie's cold silence was unnerving to Daisy. She twisted her apron and glanced at Cassie. Anne said, "Yes, go on."

"To tell him that Mr. Wystan wouldn't be home to dinner. You see, Caddy — Mr. Cadwallader — is already in such a state about the cooking. He seemed to think I ought to do the cooking and I wasn't hired to cook . . ."

"Get to the point," Cassie said.

"Yes'm. Well, I told him and came to ask you if it was time for cocktails and there was the letter on the floor."

Cassie lifted her head. Anne said, "On the floor?"

"Yes'm." Daisy had twisted her apron into a roll. "As if it had been shoved under the door. But nobody rang. I'm sure nobody rang. . . ."

"Thank you," Anne said. "That's all."

181

"Daisy," Cassie said sharply, and Daisy whirled to give her a sullen, badgered look. "You may bring the tray for cocktails now. Put on a fresh apron first."

Daisy stood perfectly still. She did then an unexpected thing. She untied her apron with slow deliberation, advanced to Cassie and dropped the apron at Cassie's feet.

Cassie caught her breath. "Daisy! Pick that up!"

"I won't!" Daisy said. "I'm tired of you giving me orders. I don't have to take them. And if you want to know what was in that letter, I'll tell you. I'll tell everybody. It said . . ."

"Daisy, don't lie. . . ." Cassie said.

"It said, 'Cassie killed her and she'll kill you!' That's what it said." She looked at Anne. "It was meant for you, Mrs. Wystan. It was meant for you. . . ."

"Daisy!" Cassie said with an air of calm reproval, "you knew that I burned that paper."

"No, I didn't. . . ."

"You were in the hall. You heard. You're lying because you think I can't prove it's a lie." She turned to Anne. "It's between me and Daisy. Whose word will you — and Brent — believe?"

"But it's true!" Daisy was white with fury. "Cassie killed her and she'll kill you and . . ."

"Daisy," Cassie said evenly. "Get back to your work."

"Wait," Anne said. "Was it typed or . . ."

182

"Written!" Daisy cried. "With a pencil."

"Was it — signed?"

"Oh no!"

"Well, then . . ." Anne thought swiftly. "Who wrote it? I mean did you recognize the handwriting? Think, Daisy — think hard. Have you ever seen the handwriting before?"

"Oh no . . ." Daisy began and stopped and stared at Anne as if transfixed. Two bright spots of color came up into her cheeks. *"No . . ."* she said but as if arguing to herself. "Oh — *no . . ."*

"Who wrote it, Daisy?"

Cassie did not move. Daisy didn't move. As suddenly as they had come the two bright spots ebbed out of her cheeks. She said in a mumbling, unsteady voice, "Oh no! No . . ." and made for the door.

Cassie said, "Daisy! Come back here and pick up this apron. . . ."

There was only the hard, rapid thump of her heels on the stairs.

"She knows who wrote that," Anne said.

Cassie didn't speak.

"Cassie — *was* it that?"

Cassie turned at last. "The girl was lying. She was angry. She's always resented taking orders. This is simply her petty little idea of revenge."

"But if that is really what was written in that note you burned — don't you see, it's some — some enemy, somebody who is trying to make trouble — for you and me and all of us. You didn't kill Melora. You didn't try to . . ."

Cassie was again in perfect control. She gave a tolerant little laugh. "Darling, I didn't try to kill you last night! I wasn't even here. I have an alibi, dear, if you want to phone the Moores'."

"Oh, Cassie, don't! *You* didn't — *You* wouldn't . . . Besides — why, it was a man in the house last night! I saw him! Those other notes were typed — on my own letter paper. This one was different. But *somebody* wrote it. Somebody somehow got it into the house so it would be found and . . ."

"And the police might think I murdered Melora," Cassie said softly. "And so they might think that I mean to murder you. So I burned the note. Is that what you believe?"

"I think we ought to tell Brent and tell the police and . . ."

"Darling, Daisy was lying. But I'll tell you exactly what was written in that note. It was like the other notes — the typed notes. It said simply — 'I am going to kill you.' That's all."

"I am going to kill you."

Cassie continued. "So I burned it. Daphne wrote those notes. I know my own child. I'm sorry she did this. But I don't want her to get into trouble — real trouble. Of course, I couldn't give it to the police! They'd discover it was Daphne. It's — well, I'm afraid it *was* in her handwriting. I had to burn it."

It sounded true. Cassie saw the acknowledgment in Anne's face and pressed her advantage. "You'd have done that, too, Anne — burn it and

184

protect Daphne. We know that those notes were only a child's trick. A very wicked trick. I couldn't really believe that Daphne had written them until I saw this one. It's a serious thing. I'll have to make Daphne see how serious it is and — I don't know what, but see that she's punished. But the point now is, Melora was murdered. The police will question all of us. They may now take a very — well, they may think it's not just a child's prank. Don't you see? I can't let them suspect my own child of having anything to do with murder."

"She didn't kill Melora . . ." Anne said with horror.

"What a dreadful thing even to suggest!"

"But I didn't . . ."

"Anne! Oh, we mustn't quarrel like this! I simply could not let that written note fall into the hands of the police."

"Brent wouldn't have given it to them. He'd have faced Daphne with it."

Cassie went to the table, took a cigarette and turned it over in her fingers, absently. Then she looked up with an air of frankness and friendliness. "Perhaps I acted impulsively. Yes, I ought to have let Brent see it. But I didn't. And no harm is done. . . . Anne, I must apologize to you. I'm sorry I said that — that we don't want you here. I was upset and . . ." She smiled at Anne a little ruefully, a little whimsically as if inviting Anne to share her feelings of regret for some minor impoliteness. "That was very wrong of me. I didn't mean a word of it. I'm nervous and upset. Shall we forget it all and be friends again?"

She believed Cassie. Yes, she had to believe her. She couldn't look into Cassie's clear — now surely affectionate — eyes and had to believe her.

Cassie again sensed her yielding. "That's better, darling. Now we've made peace. . . . We'll tell Brent about the note I burned as soon as he gets back. I'll go and get dressed."

She patted Anne's arm lightly and smiled, her eyes affectionate and candid — surely candid — and went out.

The rustle of her white silk skirt died away. The fire sighed and crackled. And all at once Melora — dead Melora, murdered Melora, Melora who would never speak or move again — seemed to chuckle softly and derisively somewhere near.

Anne went upstairs, too. Cassie's door was closed. She wouldn't question Daisy herself. Brent would do that. Brent would question Daphne as well.

Daisy had recognized the handwriting. That was clear. She liked Daphne; everybody in the house liked Daphne. Daisy had heard enough of what had happened during the past two days to realize that now that it was murder and attempted murder, Daphne could find herself in very serious trouble if the police or anyone knew for a fact that Daphne had written the notes. So Daisy had protected Daphne. It was a reasonable, sensible ex-

186

planation, as reasonable and sensible as Cassie's explanation had been. Cassie had said it was Daphne's handwriting. Daisy had not admitted it. Indeed, it was only when Anne insisted that Daisy slowly, frozen and transfixed, seemed to reëxamine in her mind the handwriting in the note — and discover that she knew it.

So Anne was back at the same question: If Daphne had not written any of the notes, who had?

There was another question, a corollary: If by any chance Daisy *had* told the truth, then who had accused Cassie of murder? And the intent to murder: "Cassie killed her and she'll kill you"?

There were no more news bulletins about the murder over the radio. Anne left it going, listening for the news while she showered and changed to a short, dark blue taffeta dress, and brushed her hair and put on red lipstick as if it were any day, every day.

She had a perfume bottle in her hand when it struck her sharply again as strange that the house and everybody in it went on as if Melora had never lived there, had never visited there — had not died, terribly, suddenly, in the cold, bare cave of the subway. The perfume sent up a delicate fragrance of lilacs. She tipped the bottle against her fingers, touched her throat and her arms, replaced the glass stopper and put the bottle very softly on the table as if a sudden noise might arouse someone or something.

Brent had still not returned when she went

downstairs. The snow and wind had stopped. It was so quiet that on the stairs she heard the murmur of voices and the light clink of glass and ice from the library.

Cassie and Tod were there. Cassie looked very elegant in a long, black and lacy tea gown. She had a cocktail in her hand. "Oh, there you are, Anne. I was about to send Tod for you."

The white crumpled apron had disappeared. Cassie saw Anne's glance and said lightly, "Daisy has gone. Good riddance, I'm sure. Don't you agree, Anne dear?"

"Do you mean she's — left? Just like that?"

Cassie nodded. "It doesn't matter. I have her address and phone number."

For once Tod's ears did not prick at the hint of something he did not understand. He said gloomily that old Caddy was in a state. "Says Daisy simply walked through the kitchen, took her coat, and left without saying a word. He says she's got a new boy friend and she's been talking of marriage. Maybe she's eloped. . . . I think we'd better get to dinner soon. Caddy's beside himself. I wish Uncle Brent would get back."

"We'll go down to dinner," Cassie said and swept ahead of them with elegant composure.

Brent had still not returned by the time they finished dinner, which was an odd and uncomfortable meal marked mainly by a silence which had settled in the house; a thick, almost tangible silence so they could hear Cadwallader muttering crossly to himself in the pantry. The telephone did not ring, the doorbell did not ring. Yet the house itself seemed to be listening and waiting for some sound — perhaps the soft crunch of snow beneath a stealthy tread somewhere outside, or the faint skittering of a cheap envelope, slid furtively below a door.

There was nothing.

Dinner was marked too, more overtly, by an extreme and deferent politeness, which seemed to project itself between Cassie and Anne. That was natural of course, Anne thought, in a remote way. It was their mutual defense, their bridge for the precipice which had so suddenly and dangerously opened itself between them. It was bridged now with "Anne dears" and "Anne darlings" and "don't you agree with me, Anne," in Cassie's light, cool voice.

Gary Molloy arrived after dinner. Anne was in Daphne's room taking her temperature, which still hovered around a hundred, when Tod called her.

Daphne was sulky and suspicious. "I know Uncle Brent came home. I heard his voice. Then all of you talked and talked and I couldn't hear a word. Did you tell him about last night? Did he go to the police?"

"Yes. Don't talk."

But she mumbled around the thermometer. "Tod took my radio. Why? What's happening that you don't want me to know about?"

"Hold the thermometer steady."

"Anne," Tod called from the stairway. "Gary

189

Molloy's here, he's been talking to Mother. He wants to see you."

Tod had been helping Cadwallader. He was in shirt sleeves, and a huge striped apron was wrapped nearly twice around him. He relieved her of Daphne's dinner tray, caught Anne's glance at the apron and said, "He's giving me three bucks. If Emma can't come tomorrow he'll give me six. . . . They're in there."

He jerked his black head toward the library and plunged down the stairs, the dishes on the tray clattering perilously.

Gary seemed subtly different. Perhaps all of them were different. Gary sat as usual in one of the red chairs, nursing a highball in his fine, small hands, but his face had sagged. There were bluish gray shadows in it. "Lucy sent me," he told Anne. "You ought not to have let Brent go to the police. Although nobody can stop Brent. However, since he *has* gone — I've been telling Cassie — it's just as well to get some facts clear. I understand you saw Melora this morning."

Cassie leaned forward. The light sparkled in her great aquamarine. "I told Gary about your meeting her, Anne darling."

"Why did you follow her, Anne?" Gary asked.

"Because she seemed to know something, she had read a — one of the notes. . . ."

Cassie interrupted. "I told him about that, too."

"The point is," Gary said, "if Brent tells them that . . . Well, you *were* probably one of the last

190

people to see and talk to Melora." He leaned forward, poured himself another drink and said, apparently addressing the decanter, "None of you seem to have an alibi for the presumable time of her death. You, Anne, were actually following her and then getting a taxi, coming home. Cassie was in Grand Central Station about that time — for an hour and a half, didn't you say, Cassie? — trying to get a taxi. The train from Litchfield arrived at . . ." He glanced at Cassie and Cassie waited a second and said lightly, "About eleven. Perhaps eleven-thirty. *I* didn't kill Melora! How would I possibly have known that she was going to be in the subway at exactly that time , Gary? Even if I *could* have . . ." She gave a faint, small shudder and said, "Absurd."

"So long as the police think so." Gary watched Cassie. He and Cassie were always very polite to each other but it was a guarded politeness. And with Cassie, Gary's air of gallantry disappeared. There was now a cold dislike in his eyes.

Cassie thrust back neatly and instantly. "But of course, if the police *should* ask for such things as alibis, merely because Melora was once married to Brent — what about Aunt Lucy?"

Anne stared with utter frozen astonishment at Cassie. Cassie's face was all concern, yet the faintest, smallest smile seemed to touch the very corners of her mouth. She said, "That's really why you came, isn't it? You knew that Lucy would rather have killed Melora than let her enter Brent's life again. Lucy hated her. . . . Did

191

Lucy see her lately? Yesterday? This morning?"

Gary's plump chin set. "You hated Melora yourself, Cassie. You would never have permitted her to set foot in this house again."

"But it's Anne who took Melora's place! Anne who met her and talked to her." Cassie rose with a whisper of silk, crossed to Anne and took her hand in a cool clasp. "But Anne didn't murder her. Why, that's a dreadful accusation! Simply because Melora and Brent had been seeing each other again, and Anne admits she followed Melora — as far as the subway," Cassie said in a delicate and thoughtful way. "That's very unfair of you, Gary."

"You made the accusation; I didn't!" Gary's voice was uneven. And Brent said from the doorway, "Hello, Gary. Aunt Lucy send you?"

None of them had heard his arrival. His eyes sought Anne. He gave a reassuring little nod, said, "I'm starving. I told Caddy to bring me something to eat," went to the table and poured himself a drink.

Cassie cried, "Brent! How did it go? What are they doing? Who identified her . . . ?"

But Brent turned abruptly toward the door, the decanter arrested in his hand. They all heard Cadwallader puffing and thudding from the elevator. Tod came galloping after him, the apron dangling from his hand. Both of them shouted in a wild antiphony, which Tod began. "It's on the radio — another murder . . . ."

Cadwallader gasped. "It's Daisy. I'll swear it!

192

It's that Daisy! They said a woman . . . Wearing that new coat she got last week, a gabardine coat, just as much like the coat Mrs. Wystan wears as she could find."

"And a dark blue beret," Tod said, "like Anne's."

"Found in the snow. On her way to the subway . . ."

"Just at the entrance!"

"With a knife," Cadwallader said.

FOURTEEN

Cadwallader was the star witness and took the center of the stage with considerable aplomb. He also had a theory. Daisy had been upset about something. He didn't know what, but she sailed straight through the kitchen, and went into the big closet off the kitchen, changed — he supposed from her uniform to a dress — put on the coat she had recently bought . . . "She did admire Mrs. Wystan's coat and that little cap she wears," and the first thing he knew there she was at the kitchen door, wearing coat and beret. "She just walked out. And I think she went to meet this new boy friend of hers, and I think he killed her."

"Oh, my God," Gary Molloy said. His air of gallant youth dropped away. He looked shriveled and old.

"What new boy friend? What are you talking about?" Brent asked.

"She's talked of nothing else," Cadwallader said. "But I don't think she ever spoke his name. Or, come to think of it, where he worked or anything. She just talked about him as if she was going to get married, and went around her work in a dream and — I think he decided things had gone too far. I think she decided to quit her job and maybe she phoned to him from a drug store or somewhere and told him she'd left her job and now they were going to be married and made

194

him meet her and . . ." Cadwallader made an unexpected and horrible swishing sound through
his false teeth and a swift cutting motion with his
arm.

Poor Daisy, Anne thought, making her gesture
of defiance and then walking out into the treacherous night to meet murder.

Cassie cried, "That note! I wonder — Anne,
she recognized the handwriting! Suppose her
boy friend wrote it and she accused him of it
and . . ."

"*What note?*" Brent demanded.

Cassie told it. She told it exactly as it happened. "But Daisy was lying. She never liked me
and she was angry so she said that the words
were 'Cassie killed her and she'll kill you!' That
wasn't true. The note I burned was just like the
others Anne found."

There was a long silence. Gary, sunk in his
chair, eyed Cassie stonily. Tod stood like a
frozen beanpole, staring. Brent said at last, "And
the note really said, 'I am going to kill you.' "

Cassie nodded. "Just like the others Anne told
us about. Except this was written with pencil."

"But you think Daisy had recognized the
handwriting."

"Of course. Not at first, but when Anne questioned her she seemed to think about it, and
then, just all at once, she looked scared. I think
that she had snatched up the envelope, taken out
the paper and read it, and she was so excited she
just ran upstairs as fast as she could and gave it to

us. But then Anne insisted about the hand-writing and — well, I was sure that Daisy thought about it and suddenly realized that she knew the handwriting. Or she had a good idea who had written it. At the time I thought she knew it was Daphne and Daisy wouldn't say so. She liked Daff."

There was, then, something not quite accurate in Cassie's story. Anne said, "But — Cassie — *you* said it was Daphne's handwriting."

"I thought it was," Cassie said. "It was just a scrawl, you know. But I was so sure that Daphne had written the other notes that I . . . Oh, perhaps I leaped to conclusions. I'm sorry I burned it, Brent. But I was so sure it was Daff."

"I don't think Daff wrote the notes," Anne said. "I don't think she had anything to do with them."

Brent looked at her and looked at Cassie. Gary poured himself another drink and sank back in the chair.

Brent said, "It doesn't sound like Daff. I'll talk to her. But this boy friend of Daisy's . . ." He thought for a moment and shook his head. "I can't see why he would write anything like that. I can't see what he'd hope to gain. I can't see how he could possibly be connected with . . ."

"Melora!" Tod finished as Brent hesitated. "Uncle Brent — *was* it Melora?"

Brent nodded. "I didn't have to identify her," he said slowly. "Her landlady had already done that, and traffic was so bad tonight there was no point in taking me down to the morgue just to identify her again. But they showed me her coat and the clock."

I'm glad he didn't have to look at her, Anne thought.

Cassie said, "Of course it *was* our clock?"

"Oh yes.

Gary stirred. "What did you tell the police?"

"I said I had heard of her murder. She was my former wife."

"They questioned you?"

"Of course. There wasn't much I could tell them. I didn't know where she lived but the landlady had told them that. They asked me about Delayne. I told them what I could. He hasn't turned up. They're trying to find him. I said I considered it urgent in view of the threats to Anne and the man in the house last night. But of course I have no proof that that was Delayne. I want you all — and we'll tell Daff, too — to understand this." Brent gave a commanding look around the room which took in every person there as directly as if he spoke to that person alone. "I did *not* tell them that Melora had seen Anne in the restaurant this morning. I expect you all to keep quiet about that. I did tell them that Melora had been here yesterday, asked for money and, presumably, had taken the clock then. I gave them an account of the notes and the man who was in the house last night. I referred them to the policemen who were here today. If they should question Anne directly about

Melora — well, we'll cross that bridge when we come to it. Up to now — that's all they know."

Gary surged up out of his chair. "That was right. Brent, that was right."

Cassie said, "Gary, dear — *did* Aunt Lucy see Melora? I mean, recently?"

"I didn't say that! And if you think that Lucy followed this maid to the subway and — and knifed her . . . Good God, Cassie!"

Brent said, "There's no question of that. Cassie, where did this maid come from? Had she any relatives?"

"I don't remember. I'll look in the house-keeping book," Cassie replied with prompt efficiency and went out of the room.

Gary got out a handkerchief and wiped his face.

Tod said suddenly, "But I think those notes were meant for Melora. . . ."

"Then why was there another one tonight?" Brent said. "Caddy . . ."

"Yes, sir." Cadwallader was different all at once, very prompt and terse with a sudden air of cool mastery in his manner, which vaguely reminded Anne of someone, somewhere, a type perhaps, no one in particular. Tod gave her the clue when he muttered, "The great detective . . ."

Brent said, "This boy friend. Do you think he could have got Daisy to help him in any sort of . . ."

"Criminal activity?" Cadwallader said, pursed

198

his lips, thought, and shook his head rather regretfully.

"No, I really don't think so, Mr. Wystan. Daisy was talkative. She'd probably told him everything she knew about the house. But — yes, I think she was an honest girl. Talkative, yes. Rattlebrained. Not too bright, if I may say so, poor thing. Knifed . . . Well, as I was saying, she was not the criminal type. While her boy friend may have influenced her to a certain degree, she'd have stopped at anything criminal. In fact" — his eyes bulged a little — "in fact, sir, if, say, it *was* his handwriting on the note and she suddenly tumbled — that is, became aware of it, I suggest that she might have phoned to him at once, accused him of it — or at least questioned him about it. So in that event, he might have met her and — to keep her quiet . . ."

"Did she know anything of — my former wife?"

In a less stately person it would have been an uneasy wriggle; with Cadwallader it was merely a kind of quiver. "I rather fancy she did, sir. In fact," he admitted with a burst of candor, "she did. I told her. And I dare say I told her about the notes and the intruder last night but since the police knew of it, I did not consider it a matter for discretion."

Gary sighed. "Brent, we may be all wrong about this. It may not be your maid at all. Could be anybody . . ."

Cadwallader said firmly, "It was Daisy."

Gary gave him an exasperated look. "I don't see how you can be so sure. . . . Look here, Brent, I don't see how any of these things — I mean the notes and the burglar last night, or Daisy's being killed, if it *is* Daisy — could possibly have anything to do with Melora's murder."

"I don't either," Brent said, "except they happened at the same time."

"And you say the police are trying to find this — Delayne feller?"

"Oh yes. The minute the landlady identified her they started asking questions about the husband. She couldn't tell them anything, apparently — or if she did, they didn't tell me. It seems Melora lived alone. She may have left him. I — tacitly — advised her to leave him."

Nobody said a word. Even Gary felt, or at least showed no surprise. Brent went on. "That was, I think, about a month ago. So of course Delayne might have an idea of revenge."

Cassie said, "Where did Melora live?"

"She had a room, with a kitchenette. The landlady got the idea she was packing to leave so she kept an eye on her. Melora, it seems, got away from her this morning, simply walked out when the landlady was in the back of the house. She had lived there only a few weeks. Her landlady heard the announcement on the radio. She went to the police and identified her. The police have already searched Melora's room. They found nothing of any special interest — or if they did, they didn't tell me about it."

"Uncle Brent." Tod thrust his face forward, his eyes bright as a squirrel's. "Didn't the police think the notes were meant for Melora? Didn't they say anything like that?"

Brent said slowly, "I don't know what they think. The man in charge of the investigation into the murder wasn't there. I waited. Then I got hold of one of the policemen who were here this morning. I told him that I had one of the notes and he took it. He seemed to think that Daphne had written them but he said they'd investigate further. By that time I was sent in to see the man in homicide." He shrugged. "He simply made notes, thanked me. That was that."

Tod said, "*Could* Daisy have known — well, had any evidence about Melora's murder? So whoever killed Melora had to kill Daisy?"

Cadwallader replied. "I can assure you, Mr. Wystan, she didn't. She'd never have kept it to herself."

Cassie came back into the room with the red housekeeping book in her hand. "I've looked. I made a note of her references and her Social Security number and the date she came to work here. She said she lived alone — here's her address and phone number — but I don't know about relatives. Did she tell you anything, Cadwallader?"

He thought, one eye squinted in a very astute manner, which availed him nothing. "I can't say she did, madam. I may remember something, however. A clue . . ."

"Emma might know," Tod said.

Gary put down his glass with a shaky hand. "What are you going to do, Brent? If you're thinking of going to the police about this — this maid, you know what will happen."

Brent didn't reply. Instead he turned to Anne, his eyes very dark and intent. "What shall I do, Anne?"

She understood him. "I think we have to."

Cassie cried, "You can't! Brent, you can't drag us all into this. You don't even know that this girl is Daisy!"

Brent went to the telephone and paused, his hand upon it. Anne had a flashing view, which was queer, of headlines in black and white, as clear as if she held a newspaper in her hands.

Gary sighed and pushed himself up out of the armchair. "You're making a mistake, Brent. I'd better tell you. Lucy had a violent quarrel with Melora last night."

Brent's head turned slowly toward Gary. "Lucy!"

Cassie said, "I knew it! That's why Gary came here. He'd protect Lucy if he saw her kill Melora with his own eyes!"

"Lucy didn't kill her! That's absurd. But she did see her. That is, Melora came to see her. Lucy said that she just arrived out of the blue last night about ten. She told Lucy that she had been seeing you, Brent. She said that she regretted her divorce and — so did you."

Brent dropped the telephone and stared at Gary. "Melora told Lucy that? But Lucy couldn't have believed it!"

Gary's eyes went to Cassie, to Anne, to the floor. He said remotely, merely stating a fact, "Melora is a very attractive woman."

"So you thought, Gary," Cassie said. "You always liked her."

"You always disliked her, Cassie," Gary said. "You never gave the child an even break."

"Child!" Cassie cried scornfully.

Brent said, "Go on, Gary. What did Lucy say to Melora? What did Lucy do?"

"Well, Lucy told me that right away she felt that Melora wanted some money. So she gave her some."

A little grin tugged at the corners of Brent's mouth. "Lucy is very direct."

"Too damn direct," Gary said. "She gave Melora what cash she had in the house. She said she had to get rid of her. But before she showed her the door, she told Melora what she thought of her. In fact, Lucy said to me, 'I hated her. I wouldn't have let her come back into Brent's life. I'd have killed her first!' Lucy said those very words. Of course she didn't mean it. But you wouldn't want the police to know that Lucy felt like that about Melora."

Cassie cried sharply, "But there wasn't a word of truth in what Melora told Lucy about regretting her divorce and Brent regretting it, too!"

"I did see Melora," Brent said. "But that

wasn't the reason. I'd better talk to Aunt Lucy. I think we can keep her out of it."

"You've got to eat," Anne said. "You've had no dinner." She turned to Cadwallader but he was already hurrying out. "I'll get something for him, Mrs. Wystan," he said and disappeared.

Gary took the telephone. "I'll call Lucy. . . ."

"No," Brent said. "Get the police first. I'm going to have a twenty-four-hour guard in the house."

"For Anne?" Tod cried incredulously. He stared at Anne. "Because of those notes? But that would be murder!"

Gary flashed a look at Tod. "For God's sake, boy, it *is* murder."

"Get the police, Gary," Brent said. "I'll talk."

"Now listen, Brent." Gary took a deep breath and drew himself up as if addressing a jury. He became suave and kind and very reasonable. "In the first place, we don't know that this girl they found tonight was your maid. How was she dressed? In a coat like one that Anne wears. Was there anything special about that coat, Anne? What does it look like?"

"It's a gabardine coat. Tailored. Light brown."

"It wasn't especially made for you, now, was it?" Anne shook her head. "Wouldn't you say there were many of those coats made? Hundreds, perhaps? She had a beret on her head. Well, that isn't the only one in the city of New York. She had red hair — that's certainly not exclusive . . ."

Tod came out with a burst like a firecracker. "Suppose whoever killed her thought she was Anne!"

Brent sat down on the sofa and looked at Tod. Gary stammered and stopped and passed one hand over his bald head. Tod said, "Well, it's possible, isn't it? Those notes to Anne threatening to kill her. Daisy always tried to ape Anne's clothes. She got that coat and beret because Anne wears a tailored coat and beret. She got a dress too that was like Anne's. I saw it. A kind of red dress." He paused momentarily and said candidly, "She didn't look like Aunt Anne in it. But it was red and Anne's got a red dress . . ."

Cassie seemed to get her breath. She swirled down upon Tod. "Stop that! I never heard of anything so silly. Nobody would think she was Anne. Gary is right. We have no real reason to think this girl was Daisy. And if she was, let the police find out about it. It's their job. It's nothing to us. . . ."

"We have to know," Brent said. "And I have to tell them about the note you burned, Cassie. We've got to find out what's behind this."

Daphne came running down the stairs, thudding in her bare feet, sobbing as she came.

"Oh, Lord," Tod cried. "She's heard about Melora."

Brent said, "Give me the telephone, Gary."

FIFTEEN

Daphne evaded Tod and darted into the room. She was again wrapped in the blue eiderdown and clutched it up around her and sobbed. "Melora — the radio said Melora was killed. . . ."

Cassie and Gary paid no attention to her. They were both listening as Brent asked for somebody, some name, and waited. Tod showed unexpected firmness with Daphne. "We didn't want you to know about it. Not tonight anyway. There's nothing anybody can do about it and you're going back to bed."

Brent said into the telephone, "Oh, Lieutenant? This is Brent Wystan. I talked to you earlier this evening. . . ."

Tod got an urgent hand under Daphne's elbow. "Come on . . ."

Daphne resisted, her eyes on Brent, her sobs suddenly stilled. "What's he doing?"

"Talking to the police."

Brent said, "Yes, I'd like to see you. I'm not sure whether it's evidence or not but my wife has received another threatening note . . ."

"Oh . . ." Daphne squealed.

". . . and this girl — it was on the radio — who was killed tonight near the subway entrance — have you identified her?"

Daphne whirled around to Anne. "What girl?"

"Sh —" Tod said. "He's talking. . . ."

206

"I'm not sure," Brent said. "Her description . . ."

"*Who . . . ?*" Daphne cried.

"Daisy," Tod said in a sharp whisper. "Now shut up."

". . . worked as a maid in my house," Brent said. "I'm not sure. . . . I see. . . . No, no, that's quite all right. I understand. . . . Yes. Right away."

He put down the telephone. Gary said, "Well, what?"

"He told me where to meet him."

Cadwallader came puffing in with a tray, the dishes clinking lightly.

"But aren't the police coming here?" Cassie asked sharply. "I thought they'd come here and — and question all of us about everything."

Gary gave her a cold look. "They will," he said heavily, "but just now they want Brent to identify this girl, this Daisy. If she *is* Daisy. I'll go with you, Brent."

Daphne ran to him. "Uncle Brent, what happened? Who killed her? They said it was Melora — you said Daisy . . ."

"Come here, Daff," Brent said and as Daphne approached, he drew her close to him and looked down into her wide eyes. "It was Melora, Daff. Nobody could have done anything to stop it. It was all over very quickly. I know you liked her. I wish you hadn't had to know about it at all. But now there is something you can do to help me and Anne and all of us. Will you?"

"Yes," Daphne whispered, her eyes intent.

"The police think that you may have written those notes just for a trick."

"I didn't. . . ."

"Wait. There was another one tonight. Daisy thought it . . ."

"Daisy . . ."

He put his hand under her square little chin. "Now I want you to tell me. Did you write the notes?"

"No," Daphne said. There was a little quaver in her voice but she wasn't angry or defiant.

"Do you know who did write them?"

"No."

He held her gaze for a moment. Then he said, "All right. I believe you." He smoothed back her tumbled hair. "Tod, see that she gets back in bed."

Daphne went like a lamb, but a disconsolate lamb, very young, trailing her blue eiderdown. Tod went with her. How adult they could be, Anne thought with a catch in her throat, and how very, very young.

Brent said, "I do believe her."

"Then," Cassie said, "who did write the notes?"

Nobody answered that. Cadwallader sighed. "Your dinner, Mr. Wystan."

He did eat something while Gary telephoned to Lucy. They listened as intently while he told Lucy of Daisy and the burned note, and reported Brent's visit to the police, as if they had not

208

heard any of it before, as if the very repetition of it might disclose some revealing fact. It didn't and Gary at last put down the telephone. "She says it's right for you to go straight to the police," Gary said. "She says to tell them whatever you think best. But if I were you I'd keep Lucy out of it."

"I knew she'd say that." Brent pushed aside the tray and rose. "All right. Caddy, stay here tonight, will you?"

"Oh yes, Mr. Wystan!"

"Bolt the doors and windows. Don't let anybody, no matter who it is, into the house. You know where my revolver is. Get it, will you? But be careful about loading it."

"Oh yes, sir!"

Anne followed Brent and Gary down the stairs. Brent put on his coat. "Anne, I don't want to leave now. But I've got to talk to the police again. I'm going to have a police guard here."

Anne wanted to say, "Don't go."

After they had gone out into the darkness and cold she tried the night latch and made sure that the door was locked. She stood there for a long time beside the table, with the great brown branches and pink quince blossoms in the vase making a pattern in the mirror through which her own face looked white and strange. She thought again of Melora.

It seemed clear, from the landlady's story to the police that Melora had been living alone. So therefore even though she was Mrs. Reginald

Delayne she must have left Delayne.

She had told Anne to leave that house — take a plane, take a train — leave. Was that because Melora wanted Anne to leave Brent and thus prepare the way for Melora's return?

Yet Brent had said with blank astonishment that Lucy couldn't have believed Melora's claim that he wanted her back. But Melora was dead. Anne wouldn't have wanted Melora to die, like that.

The house was too quiet. Cold seeped in from around the door. Something outside seemed to watch and know that the house and everybody in it were vulnerable, so it could wait and strike at leisure.

She wouldn't think about Melora's little figure plodding along through the snow. She went back to the kitchen. She'd make sure that Cadwallader had put the chain on the kitchen door.

Cadwallader was in the pantry talking to Emma over the telephone. He said, "Well, it may not be Daisy but we believe it is . . ." and saw Anne. "The madam is here," he said hastily into the telephone. "I'll call you later."

"Did Emma know anything about Daisy?" she asked the butler.

"Not a thing that she could remember. She was very shocked but she said she knew that girl would come to no good end. Not after she met this man she's been going around with."

"Did Emma know anything about him?"

He shook his head gloomily. "She's never seen him. Daisy talked about him, but nothing definite, not his name or where he worked, nothing."

"How about Daisy's relatives?"

"Emma didn't know. She had an idea that Daisy came from some little town upstate. Never cared much for her jobs. Emma said she was just looking for a man and wanted to get married. Ah, well . . ." he said with an air of vast philosophy. "That's the way it is with girls. Natural." He sighed and said unexpectedly, "Poor Daisy. Doesn't seem right, you know."

"It's horrible."

He looked at her quickly. "You'd better sit down, madam. Here, I'll give you some coffee."

She didn't want the coffee but she sat down in his rocking chair — which, as a matter of fact, was sacred to his use but he seemed to feel the circumstances required it — and took the steaming hot coffee he brought her.

He leaned against the chrome-topped counter, his hands spread out upon it. "It's horrible, too, about Mrs. Wys— the first Mrs. Wys—" He wrestled for a second with the three Mrs. Wystans and said, "About her."

Melora.

"Yes," Anne said.

He said in a shaken, odd voice, "I liked her."

"You better sit down, too."

"Well, it — certainly, madam." He dragged forth a high kitchen stool and hunched on it, fat,

211

pompous, kind — and suddenly rather old and haggard. "I liked her," he said, staring at the floor. "That is — oh, she wasn't what we expected. Not at all what we expected Mr. Wystan's wife to be. I knew that at once. And then, of course — very soon, too, things began to go wrong. She didn't belong here and that was a fact."

It was what Cassie had said to Anne; you don't belong here. She sipped the hot coffee and Cadwallader sighed heavily. "She knew it herself. I could see that. She began to go out — more and more. Nobody knew where exactly but . . ." He got down from the stool, said, "If you'll excuse me, madam," and poured coffee for himself.

"Many's the time she's come out here and told me to give her some cloves. Quick. Many's the time." He drank some coffee and arched his eyebrows high as the hot liquid struck his throat. "I guessed — it's queer but I'm rather observant that way — a sort of gift I think" — he interpolated modestly — "but I guessed when she met him."

"When she met *him?*"

"Delayne. Yes, I knew — the very night she came in here and took a quick cocktail off the tray I was setting. There was something about her — sort of as if all at once she had a — a secret. A fine secret. I said to Emma, I said, 'It's happened.' She said, 'What's happened?' I said, 'You'll see.' And I was right."

She couldn't have stopped him. She didn't want to stop him. It seemed important to listen.

"She made more and more excuses to get away. She'd leave — well, really at all hours. He used to telephone. I got so I knew his voice. She asked me to — to say it was some woman friend — a Mrs. Bridges. There really was a Mrs. Bridges. We never knew her." His eyebrows arched rather haughtily. "But she was about the only woman friend who ever phoned to her. There were men — and then toward the last it was always the same man. I knew his voice. Delayne, I suppose. But she told me to say Mrs. Bridges had called her. It wasn't right, of course. I didn't know what to do but — when *she* asked you to do anything, somehow you did it. Emma soon saw the way the wind was blowing. 'The madam's in love,' she said. 'She's got to have the man. We'll soon have a divorce here,' she said. 'Mark my words.' She was right, of course. And I can't say that I didn't think it was for the best. She didn't belong here," he said again. "And there was Tod, you know. And Miss Daff. She wasn't what you'd call a good influence for them. But they were mad about her. They'd do anything she wanted them to do. That was bad, too. Even after the divorce she used to write to the children — a postal card or a birthday card. Postmarks from all over — Tia Duana, Las Vegas, Cuba. One this winter was mailed in New York. I saw to it that they went directly to the children — their mother wouldn't have liked it.

That was wrong of me, too, but — the children liked her. The divorce was all for the best. Yet I wouldn't have wanted her to die."

"No," Anne said.

But he was philosophical, too. He heaved another sigh and said, "She had everything a woman could have wanted here. But she didn't like it. It wasn't the — the kind of air she lived in, if you know what I mean. A fish out of water. And once she met that man, Delayne — it was like a spell on her. No — that's wrong. It was as if she found what she did want and what she had to have. Nobody could have changed her, nobody could have stopped her." He gave her a sudden, surprised look. "I oughtn't to be talking to you like this, madam."

"It's all right."

But suppose, really, Brent wanted Melora. The way Melora had to have Delayne. He loved Anne, yes; she was his wife. But suppose with Melora it was different.

Cadwallader hesitated, fumbled for words and said diffidently, "I'm sorry, madam." He set down his cup. "Mr. Wystan may be away for some time. I've got the windows and the door bolted. French windows, too."

"That's right."

He followed her anxiously to the door. "If there's anything you need, just ring."

"Thank you."

"And mark my words, madam," he said suddenly, "money's at the bottom of it! I don't know just how, but money. Money's the reason for most murders."

"You'd better have coffee and some sand-wiches ready for Mr. Wystan. He didn't eat much dinner."

He drew himself up reprovingly. "Why, cer-tainly, I intended to. I'll stay up until he returns. Nobody's going to get in the house while I'm here." He slid into his impersonation of the great detective. "But it's money," he said with an air of sharp perspicuity. "And that man, Delayne."

Again as she went upstairs the house seemed to have reverted to its silence and emptiness of the previous night. Cassie was not in the library. There was no sound from anywhere. She hoped that Daphne had gone to sleep.

She straightened the library absently, smoothing cushions, emptying ash trays. The fire Cassie had lighted had died down long ago. She put on more logs, which caught quickly in the still-warm hearth and crackled as flames shot upward. She huddled there for a long time, watching the fire and seeing too much: Melora, in her shabby coat, shoving the sweet roll into her pocket. She wondered exactly when Melora had taken the clock. There had been nothing in her hand when she left the house; she had pushed the roll of bills down below the tight collar of her shabby black dress. But the clock was small, about the size of an old-fashioned watch. She might have concealed it easily some-where about her.

Anne could see Daisy, too: Daisy, with the angry red spots growing in her cheeks and then so suddenly draining away; Daisy, flinging down the crumpled, white apron and walking out of the house, into the snow, to her death.

And there was Lucy, facing Melora, denying Melora's claims — certainly she must have denied them but afraid of Melora, too — paying her off; Lucy, who that morning had looked so white and drawn and anxious because she had seen Melora.

And in the end there were Daisy and Melora, together making a link between the Wystan house and murder.

She got up, went to the windows and parted the curtains to look down to the street, where the night before, a man, a lonely, dark figure struggling against the wind and snow, had walked behind her toward Madison, toward the lighted little drug store.

They must ask the drug-store clerk for a clearer description of the man who had entered the store and kept carefully behind the magazine rack.

She watched for a long time but no taxi came struggling through the drifted street. Perhaps Brent would return in a police car, its big center light shining redly. The snow had stopped again.

Tod came down the stairs, quietly for Tod, and peered in at her. "It'll take a long time. Even policemen have to sleep. Do you know it's past midnight? Daff's asleep. I gave her one of

Mother's sleeping pills and she's out like a light." He went on around the turn of the stairs and down.

By the time, he came back the fire had burned down to red and ashy embers and there were no more logs. "All serene," Tod said. "Cadwallader is sitting in his rocking chair, listening to the radio, and what do you think! He's got Uncle Brent's gun in his lap. You ought to see him, rocking away with that gun on his lap, just as if he's singing it to sleep. I'm going to sit down there in the hall near the front door, keep an eye on things." He looked at her seriously. "You ought to go to bed. You look like Death warmed over. . . ." He caught his breath and put a thin hand over his mouth. "I didn't mean — I'm sorry . . ." He seemed to brood upon life in general and said, "It's the damnedest thing. The things we say and don't, you know, mean them. When Aunt Lucy told Gary she'd have killed Melora rather than let her come back here, she didn't mean that."

He looked very young and his eyes were too dark and brooding in his thin, young face.

"Tod, don't think about Melora."

"No. Well, it happened. But I — I liked her."

"I know."

"I knew I shouldn't like her. I was just a kid when it all happened. Melora and — and Delayne and the divorce and all that. I was only thirteen or so. Just a kid," he said, looking down from the infinitely superior height of going on

217

sixteen. "But I couldn't help knowing what was going on. Besides, Melora used to talk to me some. Once she took me with her to a . . ." He stopped himself with a wary glance at Anne and went to the window. "Stopped snowing," he said with an elaborate air of nonchalance.

"Where did Melora take you?"

He coughed, wriggled and replied jerkily, "To a bar. Over on Third Avenue. Don't tell Mother."

Anne waited a moment. Then she said, "No, I'll not tell Cassie."

He turned around. "You see — I think she was expecting to meet Delayne, I guess. Because all at once she sort of sat up and her — her eyes began to shine and . . ."

"Did you see Delayne?"

"Well, no. She sent me home then. I never saw Delayne. None of us did. So he might be this Dr. Smith. Except I can't see why he — I mean, if he *was* Delayne — why he came into the house like that. Or why he came back later, if he did, and ran the elevator up and down and then made a grab for you and . . . It doesn't make sense. I mean, why would he try to kill *you?* What's he got to gain? What's he got against you? And why would he kill Melora?" He got up and took her hand. "Come on," he said with his sudden shift to maturity, "you go on to bed. I'll wait up for Uncle Brent."

She put her hand on his shoulder. "Tod, I'm sorry about Melora."

"Well," he said thoughtfully, "I guess Mother was right. She always said Melora wasn't a good influence. Maybe she wasn't. I mean — she'd let me give her my allowance and then she'd put it on a horse and sometimes I'd win and — she said, why tell the truth and get yourself into trouble when it's so easy just to forget it! She — but I liked her," he said. "Good night, Anne."

He bent unexpectedly and kissed her cheek shyly. "You're a better aunt. I can sort of — I don't know — count on you," he said with an unprecedented tenderness, for Tod, and then, embarrassed, hurried out of the room, all angles and awkwardness like a young colt.

She went upstairs. Cassie's door was closed. Daphne's door was closed. She might have been alone in the great house — except Tod sat at the front door and in the pantry Cadwallader rocked and listened to the radio and cradled a gun in his lap. She turned down Brent's bed. She curled up again on the chaise longue in the tiny study and listened. She heard only the distant thudding of snowplows.

It was a faraway, monotonous sound which was almost hypnotic — that and the silence in the house. A long time had passed. She must have slept without knowing it when she roused, feeling that there had been another sound, nearer, within the house. She struggled for full consciousness. There *had* been some sound, a kind of faraway jar. The front door, of course! Brent had returned.

219

She had slipped down on the chaise longue. Her cheek was pressed against the pillows. She sat up and pushed back her tumbled hair, fought back the lethargy of sleep and went out into the hall, down the stairs, around the turn between library and drawing room and on down the steps to the front hall but Brent wasn't there.

Nobody was there. But Tod had said, "I'm going to sit near the door, keep my eye on things." Probably Tod and Brent had both gone back to the kitchen. She rounded the newel post and started for the kitchen and stopped.

Tod had gone to sleep. He lay at the end of the hall, sprawled flat on the floor with a cushion from the library sofa, which he had thoughtfully placed under his head.

She had clearly been mistaken about the sound she thought — or dreamed — that she had heard. Some street sound had roused her. She ought to wake Tod and send him to bed. Oddly a dining-room chair lay turned over on the bare parquet floor just behind him. There was something odd, too, in his sprawled position, something odd in his complete immobility, something odd — she ran to him.

There was an ugly bruise on his temple. She found the pulse in his bony wrist. It was beating, slowly but strongly. She ran then for the pantry and Cadwallader with his gun. He, too, was asleep, sagging in the rocking chair. The gun had slipped to the floor.

"Caddy — wake up . . ."

He started up wildly and stared at her.

"Tod's been hurt. Somebody hit him . . ."

He started for the hall, remembered the gun, charged back and scooped it up and plunged out the door. Anne snatched a kitchen towel and held it under the cold-water faucet. By the time she got back to Tod, Cadwallader was bending over him, the gun in one hand and his other hand on Tod's face. "Somebody's in the house — somebody — what'll we do?"

Anne applied the cold towel to Tod's face. "Phone the police. Hurry!" But Cadwallader was already running heavily back to the pantry and the nearest telephone. "I'll search the house," he called back and the pantry door swung.

Tod's eyelids fluttered. He took a long struggling breath and another. And then Daphne, upstairs, screamed.

Tod heard it, opened his eyes and looked dazedly at Anne. "Daphne!" The elevator door was beside Anne. She said in a queer, high voice that didn't belong to her, "Stay there, Tod. Stay there," whirled into the elevator and pressed the third-floor button. It gave its usual grumble and started upward.

Cadwallader would get the police. But it would take even the nearest police car some time to push its way through the snow-drifted streets. Daphne, Daphne, she thought, and frantically willed the old elevator to hurry. It was so slow, so deliberate, yet quicker than the stairs. Surely

Cassie would have heard that scream.

She had reached the second floor and could see the lights from the hall. Then she saw a man, on the stairway. She couldn't see his face, only his legs and a hand which held a bulky knife, a switchblade knife, which was open. He seemed to be standing still, arrested, looking up, toward the third floor.

The elevator ground upward and the lighted picture vanished.

SIXTEEN

She had to get out of the elevator, it was like a terrible little cage, and there was no escape. The cage had to go on either to the third floor or, if she touched the button, reverse itself and go back down. It seemed an aeon of time before it leisurely came to a halt at the third floor and she could see the hall through its tiny lighted window. Cassie and Daphne were there at the top of the stairs, looking down.

"Anne!" Daphne cried. "Somebody's in the house. He came up the back stairs. I heard him, he went into your room and then he came out and I — screamed. He's in the house. . . ."

"He's on the stairs," Anne said in a queer whisper and pushed past them.

He was not on the stairs. Cassie tried to hold them back. She whispered sharply something about the police, they must get the police, but Daphne jerked away and ran to the stair railing and peered down and Anne looked, too, and nobody was there. He had vanished like a shadow. There was no sound at all.

Daphne clutched Anne's arm. "What'll we do?"

"Phone the police, of course!" Cassie said.

"I told Cadwallader to do that. . . ." Anne began, and a gunshot rocked the house, reverberated up the stairs, seemed to shock against her ears.

The man on the stairs had had a switchblade knife, not a gun.

"It's Cadwallader. He's got Brent's gun," Anne said, whispering again.

There was another gunshot, heavy and echoing, which seemed to destroy the sedate inviolability of the house forever.

"I'm going down," Anne said. Daphne clutched her hand and came close behind her. Cassie seemed to remonstrate. She whispered, saying what could they do, but she followed them.

They had reached the curve of the stairs — the hall between library and drawing room was lighted and empty — when there were sounds from below. The front door closed with a heavy bang and Tod shouted, *Uncle Brent — Uncle Brent . . ."*

No one came from the library. No one came from the drawing room. Brent came running up the stairs to meet them and saw Anne and reached up for her. "Anne — Anne . . ."

"No, it's all right. I'm all right. But he was here. He had a knife. I saw him . . ."

The next hour was a chaos, yet it was an organized chaos for Brent had brought a young policeman with him, tall and stalwart in his blue uniform. They had barely begun to search the house ("He went out the kitchen door," Cadwallader kept saying. "I saw the door move and the chain is off — he went out the kitchen door") when a prowl car arrived. Suddenly the house seemed full of quick-moving, blessedly adequate figures in blue uniforms although there were in fact only three of them.

But the man on the stairs had vanished. By the time they finished an efficient and systematic search there was not a square inch of the house that had not been explored.

Somebody made coffee. Somebody turned on the sconce lights in the long dining room. It looked like an odd sort of dinner party, with the lights reflecting themselves upon the polished surface of the long, stately table, the chairs pushed anyhow around it. One of the policemen, notebook in hand, leaned on his elbow at the great sideboard, with the huge, old-fashioned silver coffee service gleaming behind him.

Somebody, too, had persuaded Daphne to get into a heavy flannel dressing gown and slippers. Anne had done that herself, she realized suddenly. She had tried to make Daphne go back to bed and Daphne had refused and Cassic had finally said, "Oh, let her stay."

She wondered if that elegant and decorous room had ever witnessed just that kind of assemblage and for that purpose and knew that it hadn't. Tod said, "I was sleepy. I put the cushion under my head but I was sure I'd wake up if anybody came in the front door. And I wasn't sure that Caddy would stay awake, so I propped a dining-room chair across the door, you know, tilted against the door casing so if anybody did get into the house — from the back,

I mean — he'd run into it and knock it over." He rubbed the purple splotch on his temple. "I guess it wasn't such a good idea but . . ."

One of the young policemen grinned faintly. "It worked. Did you see him?"

"No," said Tod with disgust. "I just heard a kind of clatter and thought the chair went over, and then, wham. Just a kind of bang on my head and I went out."

Cadwallader came in with a coffeepot in one hand and his gun still clutched firmly in the other.

One of the policemen eyed Cadwallader. "You said you took some shots at him?"

"Well." Cadwallader looked a little embarrassed. "It's this way. I called the police from the pantry phone. It took a few minutes to get the — the desk sergeant, he said he was. Then I came back in here and Tod was up and sort of staggering but he said somebody upstairs had screamed, and Mrs. Wystan had gone up in the elevator. So we started for the stairs but then I thought of the back door and I ran back down again through the pantry. Just as I got there the back door was moving. I could see it through the kitchen and I fired a couple of shots and — I guess they just hit the back door. Then I heard Mr. Wystan and Tod in the front hall. And — I'll get cups," he said and hurried for the pantry.

The policeman with the notebook whipped out a pencil. "Now then," he said, "for my report . . ."

Anne listened while they pieced it together, drank the coffee and seemed to appreciate the sandwiches Cadwallader brought them.

Cadwallader admitted to having fallen asleep in the rocking chair in the pantry but he insisted that nobody could have entered the house by the back door, for the chain was then on the door. The alternative was that someone had entered by the front door, although that was locked, too ("There are ways of slipping night latches," one of the policemen said in a matter-of-fact way), tiptoed past Tod but knocked over the chair and then . . . "Sapped Tod," Cadwallader said wisely, caught himself and said with great dignity, "I believe that is the term for it."

There was some discussion about his later movements. Cadwallader said defensively that even though he had gone to sleep, he was sure no one could have passed him and gone up the back stairs. However, he admitted that his radio was going "right in my ear. I thought it would keep me awake." If the intruder had gone up the front stairs he might have heard Anne, roused by the clatter of the chair and starting down from the third floor. Hearing her footsteps, he must have ducked out of sight, through the door which led from the second-floor hall to the narrow back stairway — and by way of the back stairway up to the third floor where Daphne heard him. For Daphne insisted that she had heard somebody come from the back stairway. The door into the third-floor hall had, Daphne said positively, a peculiar kind of squeak and she heard it.

"You were asleep when I left you," Tod said. "I gave you a pill."

"I wasn't asleep at all," Daphne retorted. "I just pretended to take that pill. I knew Uncle Brent had gone to the police and I was waiting for him to come home."

At the word police the man with the notebook jerked up his head and looked at Brent. Brent said, in a kind of aside, "I saw Lieutenant Donovan. We'd better report this directly to him. . . ."

"Oh. Why — sure," the policeman said but looked curious.

Daphne said, "So I *did* hear the door squeak and I *did* hear somebody sort of tiptoeing along the hall and I thought he went into Anne's room. Then there was all that talk about the notes."

The two policemen who had come in the prowl car said, startled, *"Notes!"*

The young policeman who had returned with Brent said, "The lieutenant knows all about it. That's why I'm here. Threatening notes."

Daphne's high voice rode over the deeper voices of the men. "So I screamed. I didn't know what else to do. It was like last night and . . ."

The policeman with the notebook said, *"Last night! See here . . ."*

Brent said quickly, "Somebody was in the house last night, too. Lieutenant Donovan knows all about it."

"Okay, okay," the policeman said. "All I'm in-

228

terested in right now is my report. I'll see the lieutenant later." He turned to Anne. "You say you heard something downstairs, Mrs. Wystan? I don't understand how you could have heard that chair knocked over, away up on the third floor, when this man with the gun, Cadwallader, didn't hear it and he was right there in the pantry."

Tod grinned. "You would if you knew Caddy. He gets that radio going full blast, goes to sleep and he wouldn't hear the crack of doom."

Rather fortunately at that moment Cadwallader was in the kitchen, concerned with more sandwiches. "I was half awake," Anne said. "I didn't know what it was. I just knew I had heard something. . . ." She watched the pencil making a full record of her account. The policeman's hand looked very young, very brown and awkward with the pencil, as if it would be more at ease, say, with the wheel of a car, or with the gun which was strapped on him. He looked up when she finished.

"You're sure, now, Mrs. Wystan, that you saw this man on the stairs?"

"Yes."

"And he had a switchblade knife?"

"Yes. I saw that. Then the elevator went on up."

"Could you identify him?"

"No." Legs in dark trousers, a hand holding a knife. Nothing else.

Brent said, "Anne, do you think it was this — Dr. Smith?"

Again all three policemen seemed to listen tensely, with the same quality of cool, sharp inquiry in their faces. This, too, was something new. The policeman who had come home with Brent looked as alertly curious as the other two, but said in an aside, "Lieutenant Donovan ordered me here. They've had some trouble — I'm to report directly to him."

The man with the notebook shrugged. "Okay."

Anne replied to Brent, "I don't know. I just saw — a man with a knife there on the stairs, as if he were listening."

The policeman with the notebook eyed Brent and took another sandwich. "He got out the back way, Mr. Wystan. No other way he could go, and the chain was off the door. There's nobody in the house now. I think I'd better talk to Lieutenant Donovan right away." He looked at the watch strapped on his wrist. "He's not going to like this. It's been a hell — heck of a day. Snow and accidents and — well, Mr. Wystan, we'll get right on the car radio, do everything we can."

The young policeman who had come with Brent followed the other two into the hall. There was a low-voiced conference at the front door. Then it opened and closed hard and the young policeman came back and said that they could all go to bed, nothing anybody could do just then that wasn't already done or about to be done, and he'd suggest they just leave things to him.

Cadwallader surrendered his gun to Brent with reluctance and an enormous yawn. Daphne went upstairs with Cassie. Brent lingered to speak to the young policeman, and Anne went with Tod to wash his bruise, salve and bandage it.

"*Was* it Daisy?" Tod asked, sitting on the rim of the tub.

"I don't know. Brent didn't say."

He brooded for a moment. "Anne, don't mind if I ask but *is* there anybody, I mean somebody you knew before you married Uncle Brent — who might have a grudge against you?"

"No! Hold still — it will sting for only a minute."

He held still heroically. "I just asked. I just *can't* see why anybody would — write those notes and kill Melora and then Daisy and then come here." But he eyed his bandaged head in the mirror with a certain complacence. "Look as if I'd been in the wars, don't I?"

Brent was in the study, sunk wearily into the chaise longue. Cassie sat at the foot of it, beautiful and composed in her white silk lounge coat, her dark hair tied back with a red ribbon. It made a curiously domestic little scene, which stopped Anne in the doorway with a sense of being a stranger, an outsider. Brent saw her though and put out his hand. "Come here, Anne. I've been telling Cassie. It *was* Daisy."

Cassie rose. "I'll do anything you say, Brent, of course."

231

"See that the children know."

"You can do more with them than I can," Cassie said. "But I'll tell them. You ought to get some sleep, Brent." She put her hand on his shoulder. "Good night, dear."

"Good night, Cassie."

Cassie paused for a second to adjust the lamp shade and went away.

Brent said, "I had to tell the police almost everything, Anne. It *was* Daisy. They don't know who did it. They have no line on him. It was dark and snowing. Nobody seems to have seen the thing. Somebody going along the street saw her and reported it. Maybe an hour after it happened."

Daisy, Anne thought again, flinging down her crumpled apron and walking out of the house to murder.

She sat down at the foot of the chaise longue where Cassie had sat. Brent said, "I don't know how it is hooked up with Melora's murder but there must be something — something perhaps Daisy knew. Possibly the handwriting on that last note. That's what the police think. This Lieutenant Donovan is a very capable man — quiet, easy, intelligent. I hope he didn't see that I was not telling the whole story but I wouldn't be sure of it. That's what I was warning Cassie about. We'll have to make Daff and Tod understand what they can tell the police tomorrow, and what they can't tell. I still didn't tell them that you had met Melora at Longchamps yesterday, and I didn't tell them that she had seen Aunt Lucy last night. Of course I told them all about the note Daisy found and Cassie burned. They asked if Cassie had any, say, enemy — spiteful, who would accuse her of murder. I told them no. But I'm not sure that they believe Cassie's version of the note."

Anne's heart began to pound. "Do you believe her, Brent?"

"Don't you?" Brent's eyes sharpened. "Do you think Daisy was telling the truth? That would mean that somebody tried to turn suspicion of murder to Cassie. Who would do that?"

Melora had accused Cassie, not of murder, but she had said, "Cassie hated me and she hates you." Once perhaps Melora could have written or said anything of Cassie, spitefully, but not an accusation of Melora's murder.

"I don't know," Anne said. "What happened then?"

"Oh, that was toward the last. I asked for a police guard here in the house, right around the clock. The lieutenant seemed willing, in fact more than willing to give it to me. Melora and the notes and now Daisy."

"Did they make you — look at Daisy?"

"Yes," he said shortly. "They took us — Gary and me — to the morgue. And then since we were there, they asked me to identify Melora just to confirm the landlady's statement."

"Oh, Brent . . ."

He rubbed his eyes wearily. "Gary was still

with me. They pulled out — oh, well, never mind. Gary said he would, took a quick look, said it was Melora and got us out of the place. It was hard for Gary. He'd always liked Melora. The police want to question you, Anne. I don't know when. Right now they're trying to get some kind of line on Melora, where she lived and how, who were her friends, all that, before she took this room and left Delayne — if she did leave him. And Daisy — all about her. But they'll want to question you and Cassie and the children. Probably tomorrow."

After a moment she said, "What about Delayne?"

"Oh, they're after him. Trying to find him. They had searched Melora's room. The lieutenant said there wasn't much in it in the way of clothes or in fact anything. No letters. It was all very neat, almost empty. He suggested that Melora had taken it for only a short time and meant to leave. He thought possibly that was why she wanted money, to get away. And of course she had told Tod to meet her at the bus terminal, so it looks as if she'd intended to leave from there. She might have been afraid."

"Of Delayne?"

"The lieutenant suggested that. I don't think Melora would ever leave Delayne."

He reached forward suddenly and drew her close into his arms. "Anne, that man tonight — if it was Delayne — whoever it was . . ." He stopped and simply held her, close and warm.

After a while he said something, half mumbled, she couldn't hear it, and then very slowly his arms began to relax. She lifted her head. He was almost asleep. His face, so close to her own, was drawn and tired. She rose, moving very quietly, got a blanket from his bedroom and put it lightly over him. He looked young, asleep like that. The tired lines were smoothing out. He moved his dark head to a more comfortable position on the pillows, and put out his hand toward her. It was a searching, confiding gesture. She leaned over to put her own hand in his and as she did so he said clearly, "Melora . . ."

She stood still. His hand dropped, empty.

Finally she turned off the lights and went into her own room. The city, the house, everything was quiet.

In his sleep, troubled and tired, Brent reached for Melora's hand. Nobody could know Melora and love her and forget her.

After a long time the clock downstairs struck three times as if it marked the three syllables, Me-lor-a, in measured cadence and would mark the name forever.

Down in the hall the policeman listened to the clock strike, too, debated and lighted a cigarette. His name was Walsh. He didn't like the house and the silence that enfolded it. Elegant all right, must have cost a lot in its day. Funny old place really, all those stairs and that little box of an elevator. He didn't like the snow either. It reminded him too much of snowy, cold nights in

Korea when any hump of snow might turn out to be a man, draped in white, with a gun in his hand. Or a knife. He'd been just a kid, a green kid. But he'd never forget it. Well, his job was to stay awake and keep his gun handy. Better take a look around the house every so often.

In the kitchen he found some cake in the refrigerator and was tempted to sit for a while in the rocking chair in the pantry. Funny place for a rocking chair. Reminded him of his grandmother's rocking chair. Seemed out of place in that shining, clean pantry. He munched the cake, resisted the temptation of the rocking chair, made a round of doors and windows and settled down in a straight chair in the hall again.

About six he went to the kitchen again and made coffee. It was still dark. The slow, cold winter dawn had barely outlined the heaped-up snow in the garden. The house was still quiet and no one stirring anywhere when another policeman arrived, rang the doorbell and relieved him.

"What's it all about?" the newcomer asked.

Walsh shrugged. "Look out for a guy with a knife."

SEVENTEEN

The day continued gray and cold but there was no more snow and the dazed city began slowly to dig itself out of the accumulated drifts, which were no longer a dazzling white but were speckled with soot and had hard, frozen crusts. There were tons and tons of snow, in the gutters, on the roofs, in the alleys, along the streets except for the tracks which slowly began to widen as traffic became more and more venturesome. Great garbage trucks were diverted from their usual courses to scoop up and haul away snow. Gray snowplows and small orange tractors thudded their way along the streets. There was, though, still a kind of paralyzed slowness of all traffic. The bustling, swift activities of the city seemed lethargic, dulled by the cold and the difficulties of movement.

There were, however, at least two segments of the city which were of necessity even more active than usual, and these were the Fire Department and the Police Department. After a day and two nights of emergency, the Fire Department trucks still shrieked their way through the barely cleared streets and the Police Department still worked overtime.

A third and vital segment of the city worked overtime, too, reporting not only the stories of the storm but the stories of two women, murdered the previous day. The newspapers were

237

delivered rather late but had headlined accounts of Melora's death (Mrs. Reginald Delayne, formerly the wife of Brent Wystan, a well-known attorney of this city) and of Daisy Mills, a maid in the Wystan residence. It was a headlined account but a scanty account. The police probably had kept it down to the bare facts. However, the inference that there was some connection between the murder of Brent Wystan's former wife and a maid presently working in his home was too obvious to be ignored and could not be put down to coincidence. There was no mention of threatening notes, or a man (with a knife) who had twice entered the Wystan house.

Tod brought Anne the papers. She read them with a curious feeling that none of the story had anything to do with her. It was like looking at a scene which ought to be familiar and well known but had removed itself to an almost indecipherable distance. Brent, Tod said, was seeing reporters.

There were as a matter of fact only two reporters and one cameraman; the city and the newspapers were jammed with news that day, nevertheless murder was murder. Brent, sensibly, answered what questions he could answer. The cameraman was in a hurry. A fire had broken out in a loft downtown. He photographed only the outside of the house and left. The photograph appeared eventually, a little smudged with snow, with the caption: HISTORIC BROWNSTONE BACKGROUND FOR MURDER.

238

The house was not historic. It was merely old. It was not a brownstone but it belonged to the brownstone era. It was without question, by the time the photograph appeared, the background for murder.

The police arrived shortly after the reporters left. Tod came for Anne. "They're here. They're in the library and the door is shut and — I think Uncle Brent wanted to talk to you himself but they wouldn't let him." He looked pale but excited. "I think they've got onto something. The way Uncle Brent looked . . . Now take it easy."

He waited while she brushed her hair and put on lipstick but he needn't have told her to take it easy. She felt dulled and lethargic, going through automatic motions. She was Brent's wife, she was Mrs. Wystan — but somehow in the night — Melora — murdered, never to enter that house again — had nevertheless displaced her. It was as if Anne herself had no real claim, no real position in that house, and consequently was walled off from a deep concern for what happened there.

Tod went with her down the stairs and pushed back the old-fashioned sliding door to the library, which never, in Anne's short knowledge of the house, had been used.

Brent and two men were waiting for her. Brent took her hand and one of the policemen said, "Is this Mrs. Wystan?" rather quickly, forestalling any word on Brent's lips. He introduced them, then. The tall man, rather loose-jointed and shambly with a long, kind face and shrewd eyes, was Lieutenant Donovan. The other name Anne did not hear. Lieutenant Donovan said, "Leave this to me, please, Wystan," and addressed her directly. "You'd better sit down, Mrs. Wystan." She did so. Lieutenant Donovan said, "Now, Mrs. Wystan, will you tell us all about your meeting with the former Mrs. Wystan — that is, Mrs. Delayne, yesterday morning at Longchamps?"

So they knew that. "I think they got onto something," Tod had said. But it was unreal, all of it was unreal. She looked at Brent and Brent said, "They know about that. I don't know how. Just — tell them the truth, Anne."

Lieutenant Donovan eyed him with a half-smile. "I'd have thanked you if you'd seen fit to tell me about it yourself, Mr. Wystan."

Brent said coolly but watching Anne, "You know why I didn't. My wife didn't murder her. It was my decision to keep that meeting in the restaurant a secret, not my wife's decision. This is the first time you have questioned her, remember."

Lieutenant Donovan nodded, almost approvingly. "So your wife will have no previous statement to retract. You're a lawyer, Mr. Wystan. Now then, Mrs. Wystan, suppose you just begin at the beginning and tell us the whole thing, everything you can remember. This is not a formal statement. I'll not ask you now to sign anything. I only want all the information you can give me."

His manner was kind, quiet and disarming. He sat down and the gray light from the north windows fell directly upon his face, revealing weary lines. But that was wrong, Anne thought queerly; it was the suspect they put directly before the light so they could see any change of expression, note any attempt at evasion.

Lieutenant Donovan eased his collar and said, "Let me get it chronologically. Begin when you found the first note."

She went over the entire story again. She had told it now so many times that it fell into prescribed lines. Nobody stopped her. Once Brent lighted a cigarette for her. When she came at last to the meeting with Melora in the restaurant, she automatically, as she had done before, omitted Melora's reference to Cassie.

When she finished, Lieutenant Donovan questioned her minutely. Was she sure that it was Melora she had seen in the Museum restaurant? . . . Yes, though Melora denied it. . . . Would she be able to identify the man who had come to Melora's table? . . . No. It might have been this — Dr. Smith. She didn't know. . . . About the notes now — the third note, the one Mr. Wystan gave them, had been written on Mrs. Wystan's own typewriter — who did Mrs. Wystan think wrote them?

She didn't know that either. . . . Well, then, the handwritten note the maid had found — did she think the maid had recognized the handwriting . . . ? Oh, she did. But the maid had given no indication, no hint, as to the writer . . . ? Oh, she hadn't. Now what about the knife in the hand of the man on the stairway? Was it like the knife she had seen on the hall table . . . ? It was. . . . Was she sure of that? She was sure.

Eventually Lieutenant Donovan extracted from his coat pocket a thick, folded document which he read in silence, apparently checking various items with a pencil. He then handed it to Anne. "This is the full report the police who came in answer to your call yesterday gave me. Will you look at it, please. . . . Take your time."

She read it slowly. It was Daphne's account of the previous night.

"Is it substantially correct?" Lieutenant Donovan asked.

She gave it back to him. "Yes."

But he questioned her, all the same, about each detail. It went on and the clock struck twelve and Brent was sitting now, crumbling cigarettes in his fingers, wanting to take over, holding himself in, growing angry and holding that in, too. She knew that.

"Is that all?" Lieutenant Donovan asked at last. "Are you sure, Mrs. Wystan? Think now, is there anything at all that you've left out?"

She'd said nothing of Melora's accusation of Cassie and she wouldn't say anything of that. She looked straight back at Lieutenant Donovan and said firmly that there was nothing she'd left out.

Lieutenant Donovan rose, went to the window and looked down. The other detective, who hadn't said a word, who only sat and smoked and listened, stretched out his legs thoughtfully and looked at his shoes.

The room was full of cigarette smoke. The ash trays were full. Brent said, "Is that all, Lieutenant? My wife is tired. . . ."

It wasn't all. Lieutenant Donovan turned from the window and came back. "Now let's go over that business of following Mrs. Delayne to the subway. You're sure you didn't go down the subway stairs."

"I'm sure," Anne said and Brent stirred suddenly as if he couldn't hold himself in any longer. "You'd have to find somebody who saw her in the subway, Lieutenant," he said.

"There's the lawyer again," Lieutenant Donovan said pleasantly and shook his head with an air of reproach.

Brent rose with an effect of bottled-up energy now released, like a spring let loose. "See here, Lieutenant, how did you know that my wife had met her? Who told you?"

Lieutenant Donovan considered him for a moment. The other detective wriggled wearily and lighted another cigarette. Finally Lieutenant Donovan shook his head. "We found out," he said, and turned to Anne and said calmly, "Thank you, Mrs. Wystan. Just one more question. Did you, say, quarrel with Mrs. Delayne?"

"No!"

"But you knew your husband had been seeing her?"

Brent said, "I saw her once. I told you that."

"You also said that you had advised her to leave Delayne."

"Not in so many words."

"I think you told me last night that if she had left Delayne, you would have — I believe you said, helped her, given her enough money to take care of her until she got herself — settled. Wasn't that it?"

"That was it."

"You're perfectly sure that there was no suggestion of, say, a reconciliation between you and your former wife."

"Perfectly sure," Brent said and Anne tried not to look at him and couldn't keep herself from one quick glance. There was no change in his expression at all and Lieutenant Donovan noted the question in her eyes. He said, his own eyes meeting Anne's with shrewd perception, "Sure about that, Mr. Wystan?"

"I'm sure!" Brent snapped.

"But you, Mrs. Wystan — you did know that your husband had seen his former wife."

"Yes."

Brent said, "I told her. There was nothing to conceal — no reason for it."

"When did you tell her?" Lieutenant Donovan asked.

"Yesterday — after I got home." Brent's eyes flashed angrily. "*After* the murder, Lieutenant."

But Cassie had told her *before* Melora was killed. Would the police consider it a motive? Brent had seen the trap; Anne didn't until then. Brent said, "Is that all, Lieutenant?"

"Why yes," Lieutenant Donovan said pleasantly. "Of course, we'll have to get a formal statement from Mrs. Wystan. You understand that?"

"Certainly. She's perfectly willing to give it. But understand this, Lieutenant. My wife didn't kill her! Good God, she's been threatened herself! There've been two attempts to murder her!"

"I haven't accused your wife of murder. Now have I?"

"You've been very cautious, Lieutenant. I'll say that."

The lieutenant sighed. "I'm doing my best. It's a queer setup — some angles . . ." He broke off and said with an effect of frankness, "You've got police protection. You can have a police guard here in the house as long as you want it. Now I'd like to see Mrs. — the other Mrs. Wystan. You can stay, if you want to, Wystan. No objection at all to a lawyer being present."

Anne felt as if she were in a dream, an ugly, frightening kind of dream but a dream. Brent opened the door for her. He put his arm around her. His eyes were anxious. Tod was sitting on the edge of a chair in the drawing room, hunched forward listening, his ears sticking out. "Take Anne upstairs," Brent said. "Then call Cassie."

She didn't need help, Anne thought, but as Tod sprang to take her arm, she found she did need it. Her knees were wobbly, her whole body queerly uncertain.

She waited then in the study, again listening, although there was almost nothing to hear.

They questioned Cassie and time went on. They questioned Tod. They came up to Daphne's room and shut the door and stayed there for a long time, too. Cassie came into the study while the police and Brent were with Daphne. She was different, dressed in a gray suit and a white silk blouse. With no jewels and no make-up she looked somehow domestic and kind and very motherly, very elder-sisterly. "Did they talk to you about alibis?"

"They asked me about seeing Melora yesterday in the restaurant. Following her to the subway. How and when I got home. . . . They wouldn't say how they knew I'd met her."

Cassie's eyes were very clear and blue. "I suppose the police who came yesterday told them that you weren't here. They asked me where I was — and of course I was either in Grand Central or on my way home at about the time Melora was killed. Grand Central isn't far from the subway entrance where they found her. But — they did see I was telling the truth about that burned note. Daisy was lying."

"Was she, Cassie?" Anne said suddenly.

Cassie's eyes widened. "But I *told* you. The note said, 'I am going to kill you.' That's all."

Cadwallader came to the door and peered in and Cassie said, "Yes, what is it?"

"Lunch is served, madam."

"You'll have to wait. The police are still here."

"Ah," Cadwallader said. A gleam came into his eyes. "I daresay they'll wish to talk to me. I'll be in the kitchen, madam."

And they did talk to Cadwallader, rather lengthily, before at last they went away. Anne heard nothing of that. She and Cassie went into Daphne's room as soon as the police and Brent left it. Daphne was excited. "They asked me all about everything again," she cried. "That man I saw at the typewriter and Dr. Smith and everything. I told them I didn't write those horrible notes and I'm sure they believed me. And they said I was a very smart girl to scare the burglar away that night when he was in the elevator. Except it wasn't a burglar — it was the murderer and he was going to murder Anne! I told them that. I'm going to get up and dress. I feel fine." She flung off the covers, put her feet out and said thoughtfully, "They let Uncle Brent stay all the time. That's because he's a lawyer, I guess. They always let a lawyer stay with a witness — or a suspect."

"You're not a suspect, Daff," Anne said.

Daphne reached for stockings and looked up at Anne with clear blue eyes. Her Wystan chin stuck out. "You know what I think? I think we're all suspects."

EIGHTEEN

It was starting to snow again, in a desultory way, when at last the police left. "What did they say?" Cassie asked Brent. "What are they going to do?"

"I don't know. I think right now they were going to talk to the drug-store clerk. They asked me if it was the drug store nearest the corner. Is that right, Anne?"

She nodded.

Daphne cried, "Uncle Brent, *are* we suspects? All of us? Are you going to be our lawyer and defend us?"

The worried lines in Brent's face relaxed a little. "I don't think you're going to need a lawyer, Daff. It'll take time. They're snowed under. They've got to find out everything they can about Melora — where she lived, who were her friends, all that. Same thing with Daisy. All we can do is wait." He added rather grimly, "And keep a police guard here."

But after lunch, alone with Anne for a moment, he said, "I'd like to know who tipped them off about your seeing Melora yesterday morning. It couldn't have been Daphne or Tod or Cassie. If Cadwallader knew it, he wouldn't have told them. Of course, the police who were here in the house yesterday noon would have reported that you were not here. But how did they know what restaurant? How did they know you followed her to the subway?"

"Brent, *am* I a suspect?"

"Of course not," he said too quickly. "This is all simply in the line of inquiry. Maybe I was wrong not to tell them the whole thing in the first place. But they'll not blame you for that, and I suppose it really is better for them to know everything we know. But I'd like to know how they found out. . . . I wish I'd had more experience in criminal law. Yet if I hadn't gone to the police, they'd have come to me. And those notes — that man in the house . . ." His mouth set. "No. I was right to tell them. They've got to stop it."

He didn't say, stop another murder. And, as so often it happened, Anne had only a moment alone with him, for Tod came galloping into the library.

"Uncle Brent, Max is home. Cadwallader's asking him about Daisy."

"Send him up here, Tod."

But Max, questioned, knew no more of Daisy than anyone else. "I think this guy she was running around with was a pickup. She said something about that — made his acquaintance in a movie or in the park or somewhere. Must have been in December sometime. I didn't pay much attention; she was always gabbing about him. She did talk about getting married. But honest, Mr. Wystan, that's all I know. I didn't pay much attention. . . . The car took a beating, coming home through the snow. I think I'd better take her around to the garage." Brent nodded.

Shortly after Max left, Dr. Cox telephoned. He was both apologetic and irritated. He was wrong apparently, he said. There seemed to be no Dr. Smith who had responded to Anne's call for Dr. Cox, but how was he to know, he demanded plaintively? He hoped Daphne was all right and that Anne had not had too much of a scare, and what did Brent think was behind all this? Melora's murder and now this maid! There must be some reason for it.

"I don't know," Brent said. "The police are working on it. There's a police guard here and we'll keep one until — well, until we find out who and what is back of this. Anne is well protected."

Lucy came in the middle of the afternoon, arriving by taxi and looking so drawn and tired that she seemed far older than her years rather than, as usual, younger.

By that time Daphne had snatched the newspapers and made for the pantry, where she and Cadwallader were having a long and passionately deductive conversation to which Tod, earning his six bucks by washing dishes, listened and put in a skeptical word now and then. Anne found them all there when she went to get some tea for Lucy. Tod was openly scornful. "They've got it all figured out," he told Anne. "Delayne is a homicidal maniac."

"I'll serve tea at once, madam," Cadwallader said, casting aside his detective role and assuming that of butler. He gave Tod a frosty look.

"And you can carry it upstairs."

"Caddy," Tod wailed. "I've polished the silver and washed the dishes and . . ."

"Six dollars," Cadwallader said firmly.

Daphne sat perched on the table, eyeing a long list of penciled notes she had made on the pad of order blanks for groceries. Anne saw one item in Daphne's scrawl: "Delayne posed as Dr. Smith."

And perhaps he had. Anne went back to the library where Lucy was talking to Brent. "Of course I knew that Melora was lying when she said you'd take her back if you could," Lucy said. "But Melora — you never knew just where you were with Melora. So I gave her what money I had in the house."

"Tell me again what happened," Brent said.

Lucy's lips tightened. "Well, it's just as I told Gary and you. She arrived about ten the night before she was killed. Agnes had gone to bed so I answered the bell and there was Melora."

"Yes," Brent said. There was still no flicker of expression in his face, nothing to show that he had put out his hand longingly for Melora, had spoken her name in his sleep.

Lucy said, "She said she wanted to talk to me. Her slippers and stockings were wet with snow. I didn't want to talk to her but" — she moved her hands in a helpless gesture — "what else could I do? I gave her some hot milk and she asked for some brandy in it so I put some brandy in it. She looked so cold. Then she didn't beat around the

251

bush at all. You know Melora. She said that she'd seen you again, Brent, and she could come back to you any time she wanted to and — she said it would be easy to get rid of Anne." Lucy flashed Anne a warm, altogether reassuring glance. "I said that was not true, and what did she want. So she said flatly that she wanted some money. She wouldn't say why she had to have it. She wouldn't take a check; she wanted cash. But she said I could pay her more later. She didn't say that I — might be able to buy her off, Brent — not in so many words — but it was there just the same, implicit. Like a threat — blackmail, something like that. She took the money, what cash I had in the house and — that was all. I'd have given her anything to get rid of her. She left. But I was frightened, too, Brent. That is" — she looked at him earnestly, leaning forward so her strong profile seemed urgent and determined — "I knew she was lying. But Melora — there was something about her . . ."

"I understand, Aunt Lucy," Brent said again. But he had turned toward the fire; Anne could not see his face.

Lucy said, "You didn't tell the police that I had seen her. You were afraid they'd say I might have quarreled with her — I might have killed her to prevent her coming into your life again."

"I didn't tell them because it had nothing to do with Melora's murder. There's no evidence you could have given them that would be of any help at all."

Lucy thought that over. Finally she sighed. "Well, that's true. Except she wanted money. But they know that." She took a cigarette and said suddenly and somberly, "She was an evil woman. A dangerous woman. I never knew what was going on in her mind or what she was planning to do. I only knew that — somehow — whatever it was — she'd do it."

Tod came in, wrapped again in one of the striped aprons in which Cadwallader cleaned silver, and set the tea tray down with a clatter. Lucy smoothed back her dark crown of curls and smiled a little. "I see you've got a new houseman! For heaven's sake though, Tod, can't you find something besides a tent to wear? How is Daff?"

"In the pantry with Caddy making like a detective."

"She's better then. How is Cassie taking all this?"

Tod hitched up his apron. "Oh, you know Mother. She's like a turtle. Anything she doesn't like, she just draws in her head and waits. Right now she's upstairs writing notes. Says she has to put off a dinner party next week. Uncle Brent — that policeman in the house . . ."

Lucy's black eyebrows arched. "The one who practically demanded my birth certificate at the point of a gun before he'd let me come in the house?"

Tod nodded. "He was having some coffee in the pantry and listening to Daff and Caddy, and he said the motive is revenge and somebody is after Anne . . ." He stopped, with a stricken glance at Anne. "But he said none of us need to worry!" He added quickly, "Said nobody could possibly get into the house now. Don't be scared, Anne. My gosh, the house is full of people. The policeman and Uncle Brent and Caddy and me. We won't let anything happen."

Brent and Lucy had for a second almost exactly the same expression. Both were tense and white, the strong carving of their faces standing out sharply. Lucy's dark, troubled eyes were exactly like Brent's except Brent managed to smile a little, reassuringly. "Get out, Tod," he said shortly. "Anne is all right."

"Okay," Tod said agreeably. "I didn't mean to . . ."

"There's the bell," Lucy said.

Tod whirled around, his ears pricking like a young animal's, and plunged for the stairs. There was a mumbled conversation from below. "The policeman is putting your caller through an inquiry," Lucy said and smiled faintly. "I suppose Daff would say 'grilling him.' "

It was Gary Molloy, and the policeman ushered him from the elevator, one firm hand at Gary's elbow and the other rather suggestively hovering upon the gun strapped to his waist. "Hello, Gary," Brent said and nodded at the policeman. "It's all right."

Gary was purple with indignation. "That young squirt," he said, glaring after the departing policeman. "You'd think I meant to shoot my way into the house. How are you, Lucy, Anne? Any news, Brent?"

Anne listened. Yet still only Brent — only Melora — seemed to have reality.

It was by now a well-worn circle which they traveled. All the bypaths of conjecture had been explored over and over again, yet Gary pursued each one painstakingly again, obliging Brent and Lucy to follow along with him. There was nothing new, nothing that was different, nothing that had not already emerged. In the end Gary said, "There may be no connection at all between the notes and — Melora."

Brent replied, "It can't be coincidence. Daisy's murder — there's got to be some connection."

"Melora didn't even know this maid. She was gone from this house long before you employed her." Gary stared blankly at Brent for a moment and said, "You didn't go to the office today?"

"No." Brent glanced at Gary sharply. "Is that Cadell claimant making himself troublesome?"

Gary nodded. "He was on the phone this morning. Said he'd seen in the papers that you were at home. Wanted to know what happened in France. Says he'll take it to court if you've paid over the money to the other feller."

"He can't get very far. He hasn't got a leg to stand on. We thoroughly satisfied ourselves about the Cadell man in France."

"I know." Gary hitched up his trouser legs and

surveyed his neat, small black Oxfords. "But I'm not so sure you're right, Brent."

It was only yesterday, Anne thought with incredulity, that Gary had come to her and talked to her of the Cadell. case. It seemed now a long time ago, as if Melora's murder — and Daisy's murder — had put a thick barrier of time between yesterday and today.

Gary said in a kind of burst, "See here, Brent, I want to get this thing clear between us. It's not only — well, call it professional ethics but it's friendship, too. You've sent me clients. We've never found ourselves on opposite sides of a legal scrap and I don't want to, My first impulse was to send this feller packing, tell him I couldn't take his case. I'll do that now if you've got any feeling about it."

"Don't be a fool, Gary!" Brent said briskly, smiling. "A case is a case. If you think he's got a case then you owe it to yourself to represent him."

"I don't know," Gary said and sighed. "It's a good enough case in my opinion, but looking at it from your point of view . . . Well, anyway, I felt in duty bound to warn you about it before you paid over the money to the first claimant. Seemed to me that I ought to tell you both in fairness to you and in regard to my client's interests, too. If, that is, I decide to take his case. But I'm violating no professional confidence when I tell you that he's got enough of a case to make some trouble for you."

Brent said, "You told me that he admits he has no papers. He admits he traveled to England under a false name. He admits he has only some letters to back up his claim to being René Cadell."

"I've got photostats of the letters in my office. Looks like a woman's handwriting, signed Lisa Cadell."

"Forged," Brent said briefly. "Or stolen. He's playing a dangerous game — or trying to."

Gary shook his head. "I'm not so sure, Brent. Of course, I've only seen the photostats. He says he's got the letters themselves in a safe-deposit box. Also a passport issued to him under the name of Crayshaw, this English boy whose place he took. How he got that I don't know but it was a time of emergency — bombing, whole families and neighborhoods destroyed. Records, too. In any event he does have proof that he came here as the Crayshaw boy. And the letters are signed Lisa Cadell. If he's heard of this Cadell case — and is trying to pull a fast one, wouldn't he have cooked up something convincing in the way of birth records or a marriage certificate or . . ."

"That's not easy."

Lucy put down her teacup. "What is all this, Brent? Another Cadell claimant? I thought that was settled."

Brent explained briefly. "Young fellow turned up at Gary's office. Says he's Cadell. Of course I'll have to look into it and settle it before we pay the claim to the real Cadell."

257

"Yes, but is he the real Cadell?" Gary said worriedly. "This new feller's got me halfway convinced. I checked by telephone yesterday and a woman by the name of Ellen March did die, three or four years ago. Lived up in Boston. Apparently had no close relatives but I got hold of her lawyer. He said there was no estate — she had an annuity — but she *did* take in a boy who *was* a British refugee and she did keep him after the war. Never adopted him but he lived with her till he was about eighteen or twenty, then drifted away. He was known as John Crayshaw — same as this feller claims. He didn't come back when his foster mother died, but the only thing she had to leave was the contents of her apartment. These were sent to storage and the lawyer said they were claimed by her foster son, Crayshaw, a year or so after her death. Crayshaw — or Cadell — says he didn't happen to look through a box of old letters till sometime this winter. He then found two letters, signed Lisa Cadell and referring to the Controlla Company and the Cadell claim. That set him to investigating. Oh, it's a straight enough story."

"It's a fraud," Brent said, "but it's one we've got to deal with."

"Well, but — there's something else he says he's got. He wouldn't show it to me. He said it was a sentimental object — his words — which he would show us when the time came, didn't want to part with now, but it proves he's the Cadell son. I imagine, from the way he spoke,

258

that it's — oh, maybe a wedding ring, engraved with his parents' names. Something like that. He's very certain of himself, Brent."

Lucy said dryly, "Is this the way cases are settled out of court?"

Brent laughed shortly. Gary replied, "It's put me in an awkward position, Lucy. I had to get things clear with Brent. But as a matter of fact an out-of-court settlement just might be the answer to this."

"How did he happen to come to you, Gary?" Lucy asked. "Did he know you are a friend of Brent's?"

Gary's blue eyes were both canny and troubled. "That struck me, too, Lucy. Made me a little suspicious of his good faith. But when I asked him who referred him to me he said nobody; he'd simply seen my name in connection with the Harrison case — you remember, Brent, last fall — and made a note of it. Of course, it's possible that he wasn't telling the truth and that he nosed around and found out I'm a friend of Brent's. That would imply that he wants an out-of-court settlement but he seems far too sure of his claim for that."

Brent said suddenly, "What does he look like, Gary?"

"Why — like anybody. Young. Nothing special about him."

"Anne," Brent said. "Describe this Dr. Smith for Gary, will you?"

Gary sat up. "You think he's — Brent, you

don't know what you're talking about! Why would Cadell say he's a doctor? Why would he come here and — it's preposterous."

"Describe him, Anne."

She did while Brent and Lucy and Gary all watched and listened. . . . Dark with satiny, smooth black hair. Dressed in a dark suit with a wide pinstripe. Moved gracefully, like a dancer. Polished fingernails. She stopped at last, feeling the inadequacy of her own words. "But I'd know him again."

Gary shook his head slowly. "This Cadell feller's young and — I guess you'd say he's dark. But — no, he's got a crew cut. Sort of bulky-looking — not fat but sort of thick. Tweed suit. No — it's not the same feller."

"Look here, Gary," Brent said slowly. "This is out of order and you'd be within your rights to refuse. You've been overfair about this already. But if it really is all right with you — and if your client doesn't object — I'd like to see him."

"You mean — question him?"

"Oh no. But I'd like to see him and if you and he have no objection, take a look at these letters and the wedding ring or whatever it is. You and he have every right to refuse."

Gary gave Brent a long, astute look. "You think this feller might be the feller that got into this house — maybe the feller that killed Melora. What's the connection?"

"Probably none. I'm grasping at straws, Gary."

"Well, I've got no objection. Fact is, it might be a good idea for you to see him. Clear the air. But I'll have to ask his permission." Gary went to the table and reached for the telephone book. "I've got his address at the office but it's in the book. I looked it up, just to check on him. I suppose I'd better tell him to meet us at my office. Say, in half an hour? Ah, here's the number . . ." He began to dial.

Brent came to Anne. "Nobody can get into the house now, Anne. There's the policeman — everybody. I'll be back in an hour or so. You're not afraid, are you?"

She was afraid. That was unreal, too, in a way, yet it was as if her physical awareness had an independent existence all its own, so she listened in spite of herself, tensed at any unexpected sound, while her mind still utterly rejected murder. It could not touch her, Anne.

But no one could enter the house now in the daylight, with all those people near, protecting her by their very presence. Nobody could do that.

There was something in Brent's eyes, something in his face that suddenly made his errand and the Cadell case seem important, almost as if it might hold some pressing significance. She said, "Do you mean — do you think *he's* the man who — but Brent, why? *He* couldn't have come here and written those notes and — there's no reason for that . . ."

Brent put his hand hard on her own. "I'll see him."

Gary spoke over the telephone. "Mr. Cadell? This is Gary Molloy. I want to tell you that I felt I should speak to Brent Wystan — you know, the lawyer in the case in which you are interested — about your claims. It was a matter of professional ethics, which I assure you can do your case no harm. . . . Thank you. . . . Well, the point is, Mr. Wystan would like to see you, and also the original letters and anything else you can bring. Now if you wish to refuse this you are within your rights. However, it is my opinion that it might be a good thing to do. It's for you to decide. . . . Right. . . . I'm speaking from Mr. Wystan's residence. We can be at my office in half an hour." Covering the mouthpiece of the telephone, he spoke to Brent. "Says everything is in a safe-deposit box and it's too late to get it out but he's willing to see you."

"All right. Tell him we'll be there. I'll take a look at the photostats in the meantime."

Gary turned back to the telephone. "In half an hour then. Right."

Lucy went with them in the taxi. They would drop her at her apartment. It wasn't late really but it was already growing darker. Lights were appearing in the houses across the street. The gray sky seemed lower with the early dusk.

They had been gone for some time when Cassie came down with a stack of small white envelopes in her hand. "I put off the dinner party next week. I don't suppose you even thought of it!"

"No, I didn't."

"Where is Brent?"

"He's gone with Gary to Gary's office. It's about that Cadell business."

"I suppose the policeman is still in the house."

"Yes."

Cassie sighed, sat down, flipped through the glossy little envelopes to check the addresses and said unexpectedly, "Well, at any rate, Melora's dead. She can't come back into this house ever. That's the end of Melora."

NINETEEN

No, Anne thought, that's not the end of Melora. As long as she lives in Brent's being, as long as he speaks her name and puts out his hand seeking her, in his sleep, Melora is alive.

Cassie said with an impatient edge in her voice, "Don't look so shocked. You're a romantic, Anne. I'm a realist. If you knew Melora as I did — the fact is, I was always afraid Brent would want her back. There was something about her — I don't know what it was but everybody seemed to be drawn to her. It was queer really." She looked genuinely perplexed. "She wasn't beautiful. She didn't have any particular wit or charm or — but there was something about her. Why, even Daff and Tod would have done anything she wanted them to do. The servants. Gary Molloy was a fool about her. That's why he doesn't like me. I'm sure Melora complained about me to him — made up some story. Even you felt sorry for her, didn't you? Isn't that why you gave her money on a silly, trumped-up tale? Why did you meet her yesterday morning? I'll tell you why. Simply because she asked you to meet her. No other reason in the world. Well — you see," Cassie said with a kind of triumph, "that was Melora."

She lighted a cigarette. She was as always dressed with the most trim and elegant perfection. Her green wool dress brought out clear,

264

pale gleams of green in her eyes. She wore the great aquamarine and it, too, suffered a sea change and looked pale green instead of blue, glittering against her green dress. She eyed Anne for a moment as if marshaling her thoughts and seemed to make up her mind. "There's so much you don't know, Anne. I'm going to tell you. Why do you think Brent married you?"

"Because he loved me."

Cassie smiled. "It was to get away from Melora. He had to marry someone. He had to put a barrier between himself and Melora. So he married you."

"That's not true." But was it true?

Cassie said, "You poor child! I've watched it all. He was in love with Melora when he married her. I couldn't understand that but I didn't think he'd have married her unless he did love her. The marriage went wrong. . . ." There was a tinge of triumph in her voice, a little complacence, as if she were congratulating herself upon contributing to the breakup of Brent's marriage to Melora. She admitted it with frankness. "I won't say I tried to keep them together. I knew from the moment that woman walked in this house that she wasn't the wife for Brent. And she proved it, over and over again. But no matter what she did he couldn't quite forget her. When he met you and married you it was to lock Melora out of his life."

Distantly, clearly, Melora seemed to laugh — and say, "Cassie wants to marry Brent."

265

Anne locked her hands tight together. "Cassie, I've got to ask you this. Are you in love with Brent?"

The direct question, perhaps the tone in which she spoke, took Cassie by surprise. Something confused and uncertain crossed her face. She leaned back and took a long breath of smoke and said at last, lightly, "What a question! Haven't I been like a sister to him ever since Philip died? Doesn't he love my children as if they were his own? I manage his house. I see to all the social side of his career — and that's important, Anne. You ignore it. You've done nothing. Brent depends upon me in a way he has never depended upon you. Or Melora. He needs me, darling. I don't like to say this but frankly if I were you I'd end this mistaken marriage with Brent before he asks you to end it."

"He'll never ask me to end it," Anne said with unfortunate truth for Cassie seized upon it.

"That's the point, dear. This may seem cruel but it's best to be honest. He'll never ask you to end it. He feels a loyalty to you simply because you're married to him. No other reason. Do you intend to stay here, hold onto the mere fact of marriage, hold onto Brent until . . ." She stopped.

"Until what?"

"Well, if I must say it, until he asks you for a divorce."

"You want to marry Brent."

"I didn't say that."

"Does he love you?"

266

Cassie shrugged. "I've been trying to tell you Brent was in love with Melora. But that's in the past now so . . ."

"So you want to get rid of me," Anne said and felt an incredulous surprise at her own words. "You can't. I love Brent."

Cassie smiled. "All this talk of love, love, love. It's childish." She watched a little blue cloud of smoke from her cigarette for a thoughtful moment. Then she said pleasantly, almost lightly, still smiling, "I'm not afraid to talk to you. I'll be perfectly frank and honest — I'd be a better wife for Brent than you. He's very fond of me. He loves my children. He depends upon me. I've watched, I've catered to every wish, I've made his life comfortable and happy and well organized. He can't do without me! But — I should *be* his wife. Mrs. Brent Wystan. This house really my house. This life really my life. I have a right to it. I've earned it. Can you honestly say that I have no claim upon him? I've given thirteen years of my life to him."

"He's given something to you, Cassie. A home for Tod and Daff. Money."

Cassie put out her cigarette. "Brent has money. Why shouldn't he spend it on a way of living that pleases him?"

"He doesn't need all those servants, this house, bills, bills, bills . . ."

"I haven't noticed you objecting to any of it. It's all new to you. You lap up luxury like a kitten laps up cream."

"Yes, I did. But not any more."

"You've been talking to Aunt Lucy! She always acts as if Brent is working himself to death. He likes giving us — well, anything we want. He likes . . ."

"He does it because he thinks you and Daff and Tod — yes, and I like it, too. But all I want — is time with him. I want Brent."

Cassie rose. "Darling, that's exactly why you're not the wife for him. He's ambitious, he likes work, he likes . . ."

"There's a difference between work and drudgery. You've got enough money, Cassie, to have your own home. . . ."

"I knew it!" Cassie said. "The minute I saw you, the very day you came into this house, I knew you were going to try to get me out of it. Yet I've tried to help you. I've tried to get you to see things Brent's way. . . ."

"Your way," Anne said.

"I've always been a friend to you. I've told you all this in a friendly way, for your sake, even if you can't now see it that way. Now listen. The police know that you saw Melora yesterday, you told us that you went as far as the subway. By tomorrow the newspapers will have it. Mrs. Wystan suspect in subway murder. If it comes to a trial," Cassie said in an unbelievably calm and judicial manner, "I don't think for an instant that there'd be a verdict against you. . . ."

"Cassie . . ."

"I don't think for an instant that even if the

police accuse you of murder and try to prove it, that they *can* prove it! I'm sure I hope not. But people won't forget, everywhere you go, all your life — nobody will forget. And Brent won't forget."

Anne was standing, facing Cassie, her hands clenched together. *"You told the police!"*

Cassie's eyes were perfectly clear and sparkling. "Told them what?"

"You told them." Melora's little shabby figure seemed to move somewhere near, closer, to listen. Anne said, "She said you hated her. She said you hated me."

"I don't know what you're talking about. I don't hate you. I am only telling you the truth — advising you. Tell Brent what I've said if you want to. He'll not believe it. I've been so kind to you, you know, so helpful and friendly. Nothing you tell Brent will change the way he feels about me. He'll only think you're a jealous, hysterical child."

"I believe you lied about that note you burned. I believe Daisy told the truth. Whoever wrote that knew you hated Melora and me and . . ."

"And do you believe that I killed Melora and I tried to kill you?" Cassie laughed. "Tell Brent that, too. I really wish you would, Anne dear. See what Brent says! That will open your eyes."

She dropped the neat stack of notes on the table and walked gracefully and easily out of the room and into the elevator, which murmured and grunted and presently was silent.

She didn't understand Cassie. More accurately, she did not comprehend her tortuous thinking process. She did understand her motive, which she had made abundantly clear. Anne could see, in a kind of shuddering picture, the quicksands that lay ahead of her in that house as Brent's wife; the small traps, the hidden ways in which Cassie would work to undermine her marriage, nothing too small, nothing too trivial. It was to be the ugliest kind of sly guerrilla warfare.

She couldn't fight Cassie like that. She couldn't watch her every word, her every slightest act. She couldn't watch Cassie every hour and every minute, watch out for snares laid for her own unwary feet. Nobody could live like that.

She couldn't attack like that either. She wasn't able to fight Cassie on her own ground. And Brent did depend upon Cassie. She did run the house for him and run it superbly; on that score alone she had earned certain rights. Anne had done nothing.

Cassie wouldn't let me do anything, she thought, and then immediately thought, but I didn't try. I didn't take a firm stand. I didn't once say, but *I'm* Mrs. Wystan. I was afraid of making mistakes, determined not to interfere. I was wrong.

And then, like a blaze of light, she thought, but Cassie doesn't love him and I do. That was important. That was the only important thing.

Strangely, Anne's complete certainty that it was Cassie who somehow (a quick and anonymous telephone call would have been sufficient) had contrived to inform the police of Anne's meeting Melora in the restaurant, following her actually to the subway entrance, did not seem really important. She had already told the police the exact truth. She didn't believe that they suspected her of murder.

But Cassie had been right about one thing. If Anne hurried to Brent with that whole, incredible conversation she would play directly into Cassie's hands. Cassie would only deny it, pleasantly, reasonably, making tolerant excuses for Anne's youth and her mistaken impression.

The house was very quiet, so quiet indeed that she could hear the policeman in the front hall when he walked heavily the full length of it and back again. He must have felt himself free to light a cigarette for a faint fragrance of tobacco smoke drifted up the stairs.

She was sitting beside the telephone, watching the gathering darkness outside the windows, when the telephone rang. She picked it up, swiftly alert to its first tinkle. "Anne," Gary said, "I'm phoning from the office. Brent wants you to come here and take a look at this feller that says he's Cadell. Just in case he *is* Dr. Smith."

"Oh. You mean now?"

"Brent's examining the photostats. I've got to stay here and Brent wants the policeman to stay in the house. So we're sending a young feller from my office. . . . Wait a second. Brent's saying something. . . ." After a few seconds he came back on the telephone. "Brent says not to tell Cassie or anybody where you're going or why. The car will be there, so you just get rid of the policeman and walk out the door. The car will be right there at the curb, watch for it. . . . Yes, Brent?" Again he waited and then said, "Brent says particularly not to let Cassie know you're leaving. I don't know why but he seems to think it's important. Okay, Anne?"

"Yes."

"He ought to be there in about a quarter of an hour. Name's Roberts. He'll bring you right up to my office. You're to stay in the waiting room till — well, he'll tell you." He hung up.

So Brent did believe that Dr. Smith, the Cadell claimant, the man on the stairs with a switchblade knife in his hand could be the same man.

But why would the Cadell claimant attack her? No reason for that, no conceivable answer, yet clearly Brent had discovered something. Why was it important not to tell Cassie where she was going and why? "Cassie killed her and she'll kill you."

Cassie could be deadly cruel — in the most reasonable, deliberate way, smiling all the time. She wouldn't take a knife and plunge it into Melora's heart. She wouldn't creep out of the house and follow Daisy along the street — and then come back and change to a lacy tea gown

272

and drink a cocktail. But Cassie had had time to do that — time! She must hurry. Already minutes had passed while she stood there, thinking, her hand still on the telephone.

She went slowly down the stairs. The policeman was sitting on the lower step and rose, giving her a rather sheepish smile.

How get rid of him? Brent wouldn't have told her to do so, if there hadn't been a reason. "And, particularly, don't let Cassie know you're leaving."

Her heart was pounding so hard that she thought the policeman must hear it. She had to get rid of him somehow. A little blue wisp of smoke drifted betrayingly from behind his blue uniformed back. She said, "I expect you'd like an ash tray. . . ."

"I'm sorry, Mrs. Wystan. I guess I shouldn't be smoking. It — sort of gets dull, you know. Just sitting around waiting . . ."

"No, that's all right. There are ash trays upstairs in the library. . . . I'm just going to tell Cadwallader . . ." Tell him what? She fumbled for a second and said, "Speak to Cadwallader. It's all right about smoking." She hoped that she managed a housewifely and indulgent smile. "But do get an ash tray. Upstairs and turn to the right, you know . . ."

"Why, I — well, of course . . ." He brought his hand around, eyed the cigarette and a little drift of ashes in his palm rather ruefully and smiled. "Thanks, Mrs. Wystan," he said and took the

273

stairs at a youthful but rather too rapid pace.

Too rapid, because he'd be back in a few seconds. She snatched her coat, scooped up overshoes and quietly let herself out the front door. The car should be along at any moment. She had a vague idea that she'd just stand there on the step, close to the house, close to lights and the policeman, who would return in a matter of seconds. He would think merely that she had gone on to the kitchen.

It was cold. She shivered as she pulled on her coat. The car came nearer. She watched it approach as she tugged at overshoes which wouldn't slide onto her feet. The car was almost in front of the house. She gave a final tug to one overshoe and it went on and then the other. She didn't wait to zip them up. She started down the steps and a shadow moved out from the house as if it were a part of it, close and fixed to the wall, except when it moved it took her arm.

Dr. Smith said, "Don't scream. I've got a knife."

TWENTY

He did have a knife, open and pressed against her. She could feel its nudge through her heavy coat. She could see his dark face through the dusk; the distant yellow globe of a street lamp cast a pallid light behind him. If she screamed, the man in the car, the man from Gary's office would hear. She could tug away from the hard grip on her arm, run stumbling over the drifts for the approaching car, scream and wave and — she couldn't. Dr. Smith said, "Come with me," and the car didn't stop but chugged slowly past. Its lights fanned out toward them but were diffuse and dim. If its lights caught them at all they revealed only a man and a woman, walking along together, the man holding the woman's arm closely.

But the car didn't stop. Its red taillight went on toward Fifth Avenue. It wasn't the car Brent had sent for her. She tried to twist around and look back toward Madison in the hope that the right car was coming, that the driver might have been warned, that he might know her, even that he might see them and think there was something strange in the way they walked, so grimly and closely pressed together. There was no car. The lights from the house she had left shone out as if from another, faraway world.

How soon would somebody discover she had gone?

Brent would know; Gary would know. But that would take moments — moments? It would take an hour at the least before Brent's messenger waited and waited and finally went up to the door and rang and asked for her and she would not be there and nobody would know where and how she had gone. And by then she could be anywhere.

They came to the intersection at Fifth Avenue, and the grip on her arm shifted swiftly. Now he had his right arm right around her and the knife in his left hand, still nudging against her.

The light was with them. Traffic had slid to a throbbing stop and now was her chance. He was going to cross Fifth Avenue. He thrust her forward. She walked like a mechanical doll in that terrible embrace. They were going to cross in the full view of lights streaming out through the darkness. She could scream. Would anybody hear it above the throbbing of the motors? She could wrench herself away and run.

She couldn't wrench herself away. As if he guessed her intention he tightened his grip. She couldn't have moved except to keep on walking, walking, one step after the other. She was almost halfway across when she stumbled a little and thought swiftly, if I fall somebody will see, somebody will come, it will give me a chance. As swiftly as it flashed into her mind she let herself fall, down, down, sagging against his arms, and it didn't work. He gathered her up again in what any of those people, sitting, safe in their cars

276

behind headlights which hid their faces, would have thought a tender, loving embrace. He all but carried her to the sidewalk along the park. He made sure she was on her feet and turned her south and she was walking, a doll again, wound up and set in motion but guided by hands of steel. He said, "I wouldn't try that again." He seemed to think about it as they plowed along in a queer, clumsy pace, inexorably held together. "I could have taken this knife to you and got away before anybody so much as knew what had happened. They'd have talked and yelled and somebody would have got a policeman and somebody would have said I went this way and somebody would have said I went that way. . . ." A silent convulsion which was a chuckle shook him. "By that time I'd have lost myself. They'd never have found me."

So this is the way Melora died, she thought. Lost and helpless. This is the way Daisy died, struck out of the night with no warning by a shadow that simply detached itself from other shadows and — she mustn't think of that. She stammered, breathlessly for they were walking faster, "I haven't hurt you. I haven't done anything to you. Who are you? Why . . . ?"

"Keep quiet. I mean it."

The knife pressed harder against her.

A homicidal maniac. Who had said that? Oh yes, Tod. He and Daff and Cadwallader had decided it was a homicidal maniac. But why choose her? Who was he? Delayne?

But if he was Delayne why would he kill Melora? Or Daisy? That could have been a mistake. Daisy was wearing a tailored coat, like Anne's, a beret — like Anne's. . . . In the distance or in terrible haste, he could have mistaken Daisy for Anne. Why hadn't they thought of that?

But they had thought of it. Somebody — Tod? — had said that, too. Perhaps Brent, all of them had thought that. Only Anne herself wouldn't accept it.

She stumbled, yet she kept on walking. They met no one. Nobody would be out a night like that. Once she thought he twisted to glance over his shoulder and then walked faster. He turned her finally into a path that went upward and presently downward, into the park. At once the great, white ghosts of shrubbery, heaped and masked in snow, were between them and the lights of Fifth Avenue. She couldn't breathe. She couldn't walk much farther, but he dragged her along rapidly now, sliding and stumbling in the snow. She slowly realized that he was looking for something which he didn't find. His head jerked from side to side as if scrutinizing the bewildering white shapes that pressed close on both sides, hunting for some special spot or mark. Some special designation, she thought, for her murder!

That pierced her dazed terror. She gave a violent jerk which he wasn't expecting, loosed herself and whirled in the same instant, starting to run back up the slippery incline.

Her escape lasted only a second or two. He swooped upon her, his hand at her throat, cutting off her breath.

This was the moment. This was the instant. But it couldn't happen to her. She fought wildly. There was a roaring in her ears and dancing lights before her eyes and all at once she was standing with only the grip of his hand on her wrist. She was breathless and dizzy and unbelieving, for somewhere, somebody had said, "No! Stop it! I won't let you . . ."

She couldn't have heard that. She imagined it. She shook her head dazedly and put her hand to her face, rubbing at the sharp pain of a blow across her face, so sharp that it dazzled her, and there were sounds in her ears like the pounding of surf.

He said, "I told you to stay away from that house," in a tone of utter, frustrated fury.

So Anne *had* heard a voice, saying, "Stop it," a voice which was never to speak again.

Melora said coolly, "Well, you've done it now. We've got her on our hands."

Perhaps the shock drove away the pain from the blow across her face. Certainly her vision cleared for she was staring through the eerie, amber half-darkness and half-light of the city, which reflected itself against white snowbanks.

Melora stood near her, in the snow. It couldn't be Melora, not Melora living and looking at Anne, and seeming to debate with a kind of annoyance within herself, as if Anne had presented a troublesome problem. But it was Melora all the same. The dim light from some street lamp drew pale gleams from her bare, blond hair. She wore some kind of spotted coat, furry leopard skin. She put a hand to her mouth in an indecisive, childish way and nibbled at the glove on it.

Anne whispered, "They said you were dead. They said it was you. . . ."

The man still held her arm in a steely grip. Melora merely shook her head impatiently, as if she were shaking away a fly.

Dr. Smith — but no, he was Delayne, he had to be Delayne — said sullenly, like a child deprived of a toy, "It's so easy. I'm only looking for a snowdrift. A deep one. By the time they find her . . ."

"No, it won't do!" Melora said, with an air of exasperation. "Come on — hurry." She turned away from them, leading the way up the incline again, and Delayne — he must be Delayne, Anne thought numbly — said sullenly, "I tell you this is the only way. They'll not find her until it doesn't matter."

"No," Melora said nonchalantly over her shoulder. Her little figure plodded resolutely up the slight slope. The spotty coat was vague against the surrounding snow. Bare, black trees arched closely overhead and she passed into the shadow of one of them.

But it was Melora. Anne heard herself crying, "Melora — don't leave me — don't go . . ."

Melora stopped. She seemed to think a moment. Then she turned so there was the pale glimmer of her face and her untidy halo of blond hair. "Come *on,*" she said with impatience. "It's so cold!"

The hard grip on Anne's arm wavered and then tightened and turned her toward the path. They followed Melora, who trudged on ahead of them, seeming to know exactly where she was going, exactly what curve and what thicket of shrubbery to plunge into, exactly what direction to take amid the bewildering, interweaving paths and steps and walks of the great park.

Even in the green summertime and in the sun it was easy to become momentarily confused among those paths. That night in the eerie, glancing light and deep shadows and snow, it was an icy wilderness, filled with humped-up white creatures that were really shrubs and hedges but had no semblance to anything so familiar and earthly. Anne was lost before they had trudged beyond the deep murmur of traffic from Fifth Avenue. It was a strange, slow progression, over slippery snow and treacherous bits of ice, between landmarks which failed to be landmarks, following Melora. But Melora knew where she was going. She had the sure instinct of a cat. She didn't falter once.

Anne was now perfectly sure the man was Delayne. She didn't even question it. Her hope lay with Melora.

Never mind how or why or what had happened, it *was* Melora. She had said, "Stop it." Once they lagged behind and Anne hastened her chilled, numb footsteps, to get closer to the little plodding figure which went on so surely. After a long time, a dull roar of traffic began to grow louder, this time ahead of them.

They came out on Central Park West. There were lights and automobiles passing. A taxi honked near them and went on. Melora said, "We've got to hurry now," and turned to Anne. Anne could see her face quite clearly in the glaring, passing lights. "Just do as you're told," Melora said. "We'll go this way."

Anne felt a kind of resistance on the part of the man who gripped her arm, as if he would draw her back into the park with all its deep, concealing fastnesses of snow. But Melora gave a little nod and went on, along the street, and suddenly across it, all three of them now close together with Anne held between them. There happened to be, just at that moment, no automobiles waiting, their lights trained upon the intersection. Even if there had been cars and lights Anne could have done nothing.

They reached the other side of the street. They had left the park behind them. Anne tried instinctively to orient herself. She tried to catch a glimpse of a street sign, and couldn't discover it. The others, as if by some silently communicated agreement, hastened their steps, pulling her on between them. But Melora *was* there, close beside her.

Melora was dead. She had been murdered, knifed, in the subway entrance — but she hadn't been! And slowly, yet very certainly, too, the sense of unreality which had engulfed Anne all that day began to dissolve. That was because Melora was alive and thus a real woman, who could be fought, and not a tenacious, all-powerful memory.

So everything else was real. It was happening and Anne was cold and exhausted, forcing her muscles to move through the snow and the night, along a street which was endlessly lined with old apartment buildings, high with lighted windows. Once in a while some light glimmered upon an ornate, old-fashioned entrance, and showed marble steps or a lighted, huge doorway.

Melora was out of breath, too. She said, panting, "We've got to risk it. With luck we'll not meet anybody. This time of night. Besides, suppose somebody does see us."

"She'll scream," Delayne said. "This is a mistake."

"Nothing else to do," Melora said. "Come on . . ."

They went on and met nobody and suddenly turned up some wide, snowy and slippery steps. A light from the door ahead of them streamed in their faces. Melora went ahead and peered in the glass of the door. "It's all right. Nobody in the hall."

She opened the door with a key. There was nobody in the hall. It was a lighted, bare space with brown walls, white tiled floor which was grimy with footmarks, and an elevator. It was a self-service elevator. All three of them crowded into it. In the dim light she looked at Melora and the sharp sense of reality became stronger.

This *was* Melora, living, standing there beside her, in a leopard-skin coat, with her light hair tousled and her face pink from the cold. The elevator stopped and they went out, Melora ahead, coolly unlocking another door. She went in first, rubbing her hands together. Anne perforce followed. Delayne closed the door with a thrust of his shoulder. Melora said, "Let her go. She can't get away now," and kicked off her sodden little pumps and left them in the middle of the floor. She then thudded nonchalantly in her stockinged feet across the room and out a door.

It was a living room they had entered. If Anne had not known it to be Melora's apartment she might have guessed its tenant. It was lavishly luxurious and down at heel, shabby and littered. The air was thick with perfume, stale air and cigarette smoke.

Delayne dragged Anne to a sofa and released her. Her body sagged down. It was a velvet sofa, rose-colored and spotted as if wet glasses had stood on its broadly cushioned arms. There were lighted lamps with rose-colored shades. She heard a clatter of something metallic, like a pan being put on a stove, from the open door where Melora had disappeared. There was the sound of running water.

She summoned up the strength to lift her head and look at Delayne.

He had moved from the door to the center of the room and was looking not at her but down at the spotted beige rug. His hat was pulled low over his dark face. There was something brooding about him, something baffled and deeply angry.

Melora came trotting back, her small heels thumping. She had dropped the leopard-skin coat somewhere. She was wearing again a black sweater and a short, too tight black skirt. She looked at Delayne and said, "You'd better go."

He didn't move and didn't look at her. The collar of his dark overcoat was turned up. He wore pigskin gloves and Anne's heart gave a leap as she saw that he held the knife, still open, in one hand and seemed to be looking at it. Melora gave a little sigh, half-exasperated, half-yielding, and padded softly over to a lavishly painted and gilded chest of drawers, a spurious French piece, very large and very ugly. She jerked open one of the drawers and began tumbling things out of it. Crumpled packages of cigarettes, face tissues, newspaper clippings, match folders, a box of candy, an odd glove, all showered to the floor. Melora shoved them out of the way with one small foot and groped deeper into the drawer and still Delayne did not move. But he knew exactly what Melora was doing and why, for all at once he said, "That's no good. This is better."

It was a simple statement, deadly matter-of-fact. Anne's chilled body gave a long tremor. There must be some way out. She looked around the room and found the telephone, standing on a table which was littered with newspapers, magazines and ash trays. How quickly could she dial — not home, that would take too long, but just the single O for operator and scream into the telephone — but where was she exactly? It didn't matter. They could trace the number, couldn't they? They'd have to have time for that.

Delayne said, "Don't try that!"

Her head jerked toward him. He was holding the wickedly sharp knife with its blade open and pointing at her. His wiry dancer's body seemed almost fluid inside that long overcoat. One leap would be swift and conclusive. Anne tried to swallow; her mouth was dry. But all the same, every nerve and vein in her body was alive and leaping. This was real, it was happening, but she was going to get out of Melora's apartment, get out of it all.

Melora said, "Here it is," in a faintly surprised but pleased voice, like a child who has found some lost plaything.

It was not a plaything. It was a gun, a revolver, she held in her hand. She turned it, examining it as if she had never seen it before, her hazy brown eyes interested and pleased. But in fact she knew well enough what to do with it. She looked in a businesslike way into its chamber, squinting to examine it closely, clicked it together again and said, "All right."

286

She turned to Delayne. "You can go now. . . ."

But he wouldn't go. His eyes shifted slowly to the windows. Between elaborate draperies and flounces of pink silk the windows showed long strips of glittering blackness. He crossed the room with lithe steps, which made no sound whatever on the rug, and swished the curtains together. Now I can move, Anne thought, and measured the distance to the door but he sensed that, too, and turned his sullen gaze upon her. He held the knife as if his hand itself might act, happily, as the hands of a pianist rejoice in their certain touch on the piano.

So Anne didn't move. He watched her with a steady unwinking gaze as the curtains whispered across the windows and made a wall of shimmering pink silk, stained at the edges where rain and soot had touched it, draggled along the hems which swept the floor. An eerie, steamy whistle rose from what must be the kitchen. Melora said, "Oh — it's the teakettle," and put down the revolver as casually as if it were a glove or a cigarette and thudded softly out toward the kitchen. The eerie whistle rose higher and stopped.

Delayne moved lightly and gracefully to take up his position before the door again. There was the tinkle of china. Melora came back with a tray in her hands and the homely fragrance of coffee drifted through the stale, thick air.

She put down the tray on the table before the sofa, shoving aside ash trays full of cigarette

287

ends, ornate but empty cigarette boxes, a lighter or two, some tiny china figures of dogs and cats. "I'll see to her," she said, without looking at Delayne. "Come back . . ." She adjusted a cup which spilled and said, "Afterward."

"It's late," he said.

Melora gave Anne a cup of coffee. The cup and saucer shook in Anne's hand. Melora said rather impatiently, "Drink it. You're cold!"

She thudded back to the revolver and took it in her hand again, as nonchalantly as if it were a handkerchief. "I tell you, I'll see to her," she said. She went nearer Delayne and looked up into his dead-still, brooding face. All at once her lifted head, everything about her was all appeal, all supplication, all strength. It was not charm. It was far deeper, far more effective than mere charm. She said, "Trust me. Darling, you *have* made mistakes. We can't make another mistake."

His face in the shadow of that dark, low pulled hat seemed to waver. Melora said in a low, incredibly disarming yet magnetic voice, "It's not too late."

His eyes were held by her face although he seemed to struggle to detach his gaze. "What are we going to do with her?"

"I've been thinking ever since — let's not talk about it now."

"You know what will happen if she gets away."

"Trust me," Melora said and abruptly he turned, black and tall and menacing, and went out. The door closed behind him. Melora took a key from a table beside the door. She must have dropped it there after she unlocked the door and came into the room. There was a big, old-fashioned lock. Melora turned the key in it with a loud click, withdrew the key, seemed to think for a second and then slid it into a pocket of her tight black skirt. There was no sound of Delayne in the hall, no sound of the elevator. Melora gave a faint little sigh. She still held the revolver in one hand. She came to the table, took her cup of coffee and went to a chair, which she seemed to select purposefully, since it stood between Anne and the door. A fancy, gilded table stood beside it. She put the coffee cup on the table, held the revolver in her lap and hunted among the debris on the table for a cigarette.

"Is he Delayne?" Anne asked in a hard, queer voice.

Melora eyed her for a second, her brown eyes very hazy and thoughtful. Then she nodded matter-of-factly and sipped her coffee.

"But he — but you — they said you were killed!"

Melora seemed to think that over, too. "Take off your coat," she said. "You'll get warm faster."

"They said you were murdered. They said it was Mrs. Reginald Delayne. Who *was* killed? She wore your coat! She had a sweet roll and the gold clock in the pocket of the coat. It was in the subway entrance. I followed you that far. . . ."

A flicker of interest came into Melora's face. "Did you?" she said with the interested curiosity of a child. "I didn't know that."

"Who was she?"

Melora sighed and leaned back, savoring her cigarette. "Well, of course, she was Mrs. Reginald Delayne."

TWENTY-ONE

"But I thought — they said *you* had married him!"

A look of exasperation crossed Melora's face again. "Why, how could I? He was already married. Long before I met him. Married and separated from her. But we couldn't get married. She wouldn't give him up."

"Was that . . ." Anne swallowed hard before she could get the words out. "Is that why he killed her?"

Melora's little hand with its short, battered fingernails gripped the revolver. "You'd better drink your coffee before it's cold."

They ought to have known that the dead woman's room — Mrs. Reginald Delayne's room — was not Melora's, could not have been Melora's room, for it was, they said, very neat, clean, nothing that showed that anyone had lived there even for a few weeks. In twelve hours Melora would have left her stamp upon it. It seemed strange now that they had ignored such a revealing description. Anne drank some coffee which was hot and sickeningly sweet and said suddenly, "But Gary identified you — I mean her."

Melora laughed softly. "Really? He couldn't have really looked at her. I expect he just — shut his eyes and said yes as fast as he could and got out."

It was like Gary, giving the dead woman one swift, horrified glance, which contrived to evade just the same, and hustling himself and Brent away. Melora said, "Didn't they ask Brent to identify her?"

"Yes — that is — but he didn't. Gary said he would. She wore your coat. It *was* your coat. And there was the sweet roll — I saw you put it in your pocket — and the little gold clock . . ."

Melora said with a tinge of regret, "I forgot the clock, I was going to sell it," and chuckled. "Was Cassie very upset about that?"

"The clock? Oh yes . . ."

"I thought she would be."

"But it was your coat."

"I had to change coats," Melora said without the least hesitancy. "Hers had initials on the lining. The police would have traced it. So I took hers — that thing over there." She nodded at the leopard-skin coat. "It's too big for me."

"But they *did* trace her. They found out that she was Mrs. Delayne, she was his wife . . ."

"I didn't expect that. She didn't know anybody in New York. Nobody would have missed her. I never thought of that nosy landlady. It was bad luck," Melora said casually, "but it doesn't really matter."

"Melora, you were in the subway. You must have seen her. You must have been there when Delayne — when she was murdered. Or just afterward. Otherwise you wouldn't have — changed the coats." Even as she spoke Anne could not possibly envision the scene, little Melora leaning over a woman who had been knifed, who was dying, who was dead, and swiftly thinking of the betraying initials embroidered on the lining of the leopard-skin coat and exchanging it for her own coat. But then the room seemed stiflingly hot after that cold trek through the park. Anne felt a little dizzy. She couldn't really see anything very clearly. The rosy lamps wavered, Melora's face was like a face in a dream. Anne resisted a sudden temptation to lean back against the sofa and let herself float away into space.

Melora said, "Why don't you just rest for a while?" Her hand released its grip on the gun, which slid to the floor.

This is fantastic, Anne thought. I'm strong. I'll get that gun and then the key — *before Delayne gets back.*

But I'll rest a little now.

Melora said, "Do you like this apartment? It's too big, of course, but I had a chance to sublet it. I have this entire floor. The people upstairs work in a night club. They leave early and don't get home until about four in the morning. The people who live downstairs are away. The fourth floor is empty right now. I've been thinking it all over. Nobody ever pays any attention to what anybody else does. I like that. And right now . . ." Her eyes widened. "It's really almost empty! There's a janitor but he's drunk half the time and all he does is come in two or three times a day and — why, really there's nobody around at all."

With horror Anne realized that her head had sunk back against the sofa. She forced her eyes to focus directly upon Melora. "Melora, let me go."

"You're very sleepy."

"What are you going to do?"

"I don't know exactly. But — I have to keep you here for a while."

"But — Delayne — how did he know I was going to leave the house?"

"Oh, I told him," Melora said simply. "But I didn't want him to go. I was going to meet you." She sighed. "He got there first."

Words were slipping away from Anne. She struggled to ask some important question. "But you — I don't — how did you know?"

"It was my idea, of course. You were in the way. Now just rest and . . ."

"Why does Delayne want to — *kill* me?"

Melora replied to part of the question. "I told him not to go but he did. He got ahead of me. I saw you both, crossing Fifth Avenue. I guessed he was taking you into the park and — he's got a bad temper."

"But you stopped him. You're not afraid of him. You can let me go."

Melora's blond head shook. "Sometimes I can manage him. But he's not very smart, you know. Makes" — she paused and said thoughtfully — "makes mistakes."

"He wrote those notes! He got into the house

— he used your key. . . ."

Melora nodded and smiled in almost a con-
gratulatory way. "I knew somebody would remember my key."

"But — why? Melora, *why?* I've never done
anything that would injure him. Those notes!
Pretending to be a doctor — coming back with a
knife . . . Why?"

"I told you. He's made some blunders. I knew
about his temper. But I thought I could control
him. He never ought to have let you see him."

Talking to Melora was like talking to a rip-
pling, dancing stream which swept questions
away as lightly as if they were leaves fallen upon
it. Talking to Melora was like boxing with an
ever-elusive shadow.

Anne looked at the clock. It was nearly six-
thirty. By now Brent must have returned. By
now certainly Brent would have alarmed the
police. By now everywhere in the city they would
be searching for her. Perhaps somebody, some
strolling patrolman, some traffic policeman
would remember seeing three figures in a close,
too close embrace, trudging along those snowy
streets in the dusk.

Melora knew exactly what she was thinking.
She said, "I wouldn't count on anybody finding
you here. I told you. This is a sublet. My name is
not in the phone book."

"Melora, you can't keep me here! You can't let
Delayne — kill me!"

Melora eyed her judiciously. "I don't want

to," she said and sighed. "I've got to think about it. I had to act quickly. Everything has gone wrong. It seemed so simple in the beginning, so easy. But once something starts rolling it goes on. You can't stop it. And I never know when he's going to blow up into a rage. Almost anything will set him off. Why, I had got plenty of money for . . ." She stopped.

As if a door had opened, letting in light for a second, a flash of understanding drove away Anne's increasing drowsiness. "Money! That was for his wife, wasn't it? You were getting rid of her, paying her — that's why you had to have money, wasn't it? You were getting rid of her, paying her — that's why you had to have money. You were going to give it to his wife. And then she — she would do what? She'd give him a divorce. Is that it?"

"Not at all — I've got to think. Why don't you go to sleep?" Melora said coolly.

It seemed the most natural and inviting suggestion. Anne's drowsiness was overwhelming. Melora said from a great distance, but clearly, too, and with exasperation, "I thought these pills were never going to put you to sleep!"

Anne opened her heavy eyelids. Melora was looking thoughtfully down at the gun. She picked it up and put it on the table. She then lighted a cigarette and sat down, swinging her stockinged foot and staring at the gun with hazy, thoughtful eyes.

A long time later, it seemed to Anne, somebody was shaking her, dragging her out of a peaceful depth, and Anne didn't want to be dragged out of it. She burrowed more deeply, she tried to slide downward into the dark haven into which she had drifted but somebody wouldn't let her.

"Anne — Anne — wake up. . . ."

She opened her eyes. Melora was bending over her. "Sit up. . . . Heavens, you gave me a scare. I thought . . ."

"It would have been an easy way," a sullen, brooding voice said.

Anne's eyes flared widely open. Delayne stood behind Melora.

Melora said impatiently, "Come on now. Wake up. I knew I'd think of what to do! You're going to phone to Brent. Get up."

Anne sat up and everything seemed to move around her.

"What did you put the stuff in?" Delayne said with a kind of detached, weirdly scientific interest.

"The coffee," Melora said and got her hand under Anne's elbow. She brought her face close to Anne and spoke very distinctly as she would to a child. "You do want to phone to Brent, don't you?"

Yes, yes, of course; she must telephone to Brent. She had decided that — at some distant time, she couldn't remember when, but it was imperative. She must telephone to Brent.

Delayne stepped closer and slapped her hard on the face.

The blow thudded through her, rocked her back. She put her hand to her face. Melora said, "That will make a bruise!"

"It'll bring her to her senses. . . . Get up!" He pulled Anne savagely to her feet and across the room. A chair was beside the telephone. He thrust Anne down into it. Melora said, "Now, listen. You're to tell Brent that you went to a hotel. He'll ask which one. You say you won't tell him. He'll say why. You say that you had a quarrel with Cassie. He'll believe that. Tell him you have to think things over and he's not to try to find you. That's all. Do you understand?"

"How did you know I had a quarrel with Cassie?" Anne said vaguely.

The flicker of a smile touched Melora's lips. "It seemed likely. It doesn't matter, Brent will believe it. . . ."

"Don't talk so much!" Delayne said.

Melora nodded and dialed. The little clicks of the telephone were very distinct. She eyed Anne. "You're sure you understand what to say? You've had a quarrel with Cassie. You just walked out of the house and went to a hotel. You want to think things over. Perhaps for several days. You don't want to see Brent, you won't tell him where you are. . . ."

Anne said, "No! No, I won't say that!" Delayne's hand shot out like the leaping thin body of a snake and slapped her again so hard that tears came stinging to her eyes. Melora said mildly, "Now don't lose your temper."

298

"Make her say she'll do it."

"Oh, she'll do it," Melora said, the telephone receiver pressed to her ear. "You've got that knife, haven't you?" Her hazy brown eyes met Anne's. "You *do* see it's better to tell Brent exactly what I told you to say. *Don't you?*"

Delayne's figure moved only slightly but a sharp knife blade seemed to slide from nowhere and danced like ten knife blades just at the edge of Anne's vision. Melora's face grew intent as someone answered the telephone. "It's Brent," she whispered and put the receiver in Anne's hand, clasped her own hand around Anne's and steadied the receiver against her ear. Brent said, "Hello — hello . . ."

It *was* Brent! His voice seemed so close, so near. *"Oh — Brent . . ."* She was going to say — come and help me — it's Melora, Delayne — there's a knife — and just then felt the knife, cold and sharp against the side of her neck. This can't happen, she thought; can't happen, can't happen — I've got to tell Brent.

"Go on," Melora whispered.

Brent shouted, "Anne! Thank God!"

Anne sat up straighter, to avoid the thin, sharp pressure. She held the receiver tightly now, as if she held onto Brent.

"Tell him you quarreled with Cassie," Melora whispered.

"Anne . . . ?" Brent cried. "What happened? *Are you all right? Where are you?* Nobody knew where you'd gone or why. You just walked out the door, nobody saw you. . . . *Anne, where are you?*"

Melora whispered, "I had a quarrel with Cassie . . ."

"No," Anne said and the cold pressure came against her neck, like a sharp thread — which could snap off her life in a second. She turned her head slowly and saw, very near, a terrible kind of smile in Delayne's dark face. His white teeth gleamed. Melora saw it, too, for she put a restraining hand on his arm. But he *wanted* to kill Anne. He longed to kill her then and there. Why, *why?* she thought and Melora whispered, "Hurry . . ."

Anne tried to look away from Delayne and couldn't and said into the telephone, as if she'd learned a lesson and had to recite it, "I quarreled with Cassie — I can't come back. . . ."

Brent said, "Anne, you've got to come back. The police think you — well, they think you tried to get away because you killed Melora. I told them it wasn't true. You didn't kill her. You must come back, Anne, *don't* be afraid. Where *are* you?"

"I went to a hotel. I've got to — got to . . ." What? Melora had told her what to say but she couldn't remember it.

Brent said sharply, "I don't believe you. Is someone with you? Answer yes or no."

"Yes," Anne cried.

The knife pressed harder. Melora's hand hovered over the telephone. From somewhere an odd little phrase, conventional and familiar, surged into Anne's mind. She cried, "I've been unavoidably detained. I can't . . ." Melora's hand came down upon the switch as Anne said "come home," so Brent could not have heard that.

"I told you it was dangerous to let her talk!" Delayne said in cold fury.

TWENTY-TWO

"No!" Melora cried. "*Stop it! Not now.* I think it's all right. She said enough. He'll believe it about Cassie. No, I'm sure it's all right. He'll give Anne a chance to cool off and come home and — I'm sure we can keep it up for several days — as long as we need to. I knew I'd think of the way to do it! First we had to get her out of the house, I knew that, but I really couldn't think of a way to keep Brent quiet for long enough. But this is it. We'll have to phone to him every day and tell him she's all right but she won't come home. . . ."

"I tell you that's too dangerous."

"No, believe me. Brent won't set the police looking for her. He wouldn't want to tell them his wife ran off to stay in some hotel because she quarreled with Cassie! No — it's all right. Take her back to the sofa. She's falling out of that chair."

Anything was better than Delayne's hands touching her. Anne shrank away, somehow she got to her feet and moved, clumsily and uncertainly to the sofa.

Out of another wave of blackness she heard Delayne laugh. "You damn near settled our problem. How much did you give her?"

Anne could hear, she could understand. She had to remove herself from Delayne. She sank down into the sofa and a wave of deep lassitude washed over her again so she leaned over on her side, her cheek against the pink velvet cushion.

After a moment Melora laughed. "She's dead to the world — let her alone."

But they couldn't keep her there; Brent would find her, Anne thought. He had only to look up Melora's address in the telephone book. No — he wouldn't do that, he thought Melora was dead. Besides, Melora had said her name wasn't in the book. But — why yes, he'd find Delayne! From the very beginning he had suspected Delayne. So he'd find them. She didn't wonder how he could find one apartment, hidden away in a great, storm-bound city.

Some time must have passed before she realized that Melora and Delayne were quarreling.

Melora said, "If you'd done what you were supposed to do there wouldn't be any danger."

"If you hadn't gone to see her . . ."

"I had to get some money for your wife, didn't I? And it was lucky I did go to see her. We wouldn't have known about it at all . . ."

Delayne cut in, "*I* left those notes. *You* told me to do that. *You* said the murder threats would scare the life out of her so she'd get Wystan back — call him at the airport, tell him to come home. Did she?"

"No," Melora said with a little sigh. "She didn't. But all the same . . ."

"That kid saw me, too." There was a clink of ice in a glass.

"That will be all right. They'll never think of

303

having Daff identify you."

"It was all your idea from the beginning. *You* said we had to work fast. *You* said everybody would be gone. You gave me your key so I could get in the back way and type those notes in a hurry, so she'd see them right away and get Wystan back from the airport before he left. That didn't work. Then you let her find you there. . . ."

"I thought she'd gone to a movie or something," Melora said. "I thought I had plenty of time to get into the safe. And she did give me some money. And I told you what she told me but I didn't say murder. . . . Don't drink any more!"

Delayne's voice was getting thicker. "You didn't have to say murder. I knew then that we'd have to give up the whole thing or get rid of her."

"But you blundered," Melora said coolly. "You didn't keep your head."

"Don't talk like that to me," Delayne said dangerously.

There was a little pause. Then Melora said softly, "I didn't tell you to say you were a doctor — and give her a chance to get a good look at you. That was your idea. You went back to the house and . . ."

"Of course I went back! I decided she and the kid were alone. I hadn't seen anybody else in the house. I got into the elevator and ran it up and down. I knew she'd come out and the kid was sick, the kid would have to stay in bed, I thought

304

— so I got her chasing the elevator. . . ." Suddenly he gave a whispering kind of chuckle. "That was funny. You should have seen it. There she was running upstairs, running downstairs. Just as soon as she could get near the elevator, I'd send it on to another floor. I had to get her downstairs, away from that kid. And it worked. She followed the elevator. I'd have finished it then but that damn kid came running and the way she screamed . . ."

"You were scared."

"That's a lie. I thought they'd come back. I thought she'd sent for the rest of the family because that kid was sick."

"Daisy told you Brent was going to France. Cassie was going to the country. Tod back to school."

Daisy, Anne thought, Daisy — and her boy friend. Delayne? Delayne, of course. A pickup — on Delayne's part.

Delayne said savagely, "You can plan and plan but I'm the one that gets the dangerous jobs. *I'm* the one . . ."

"You shouldn't have lost your temper when you were talking to your wife. I'd gathered up enough money to get her to leave."

"She said she knew I was onto something! She said, when I sent for her — after I hadn't seen her for years, since I left her — she said, that she knew there was some reason for it. She said, when I told her to bring that box of papers I'd left with her — when I left — she said she knew

305

there was something in the box that I wanted. So as soon as I got it and then told her I'd give her some money if she'd get out — and that was your idea, remember . . ."

"Well, we had to get rid of her somehow, as soon as you'd got the letters. I thought it was better to pay her than — what you did. If you hadn't lost your temper . . ."

"But I tell you she balked. I met her there in the subway and told her I'd have the money, everything I could get just as soon as a friend brought it. She said, the friend's a woman and you're trying to get rid of me again and I won't go! So what could I do?"

Anne understood it, and didn't understand it. The woman in the subway had been Delayne's wife; that was clear. He had sent for her, wherever she had been, after, apparently, he had left her years before. He had had to send for her so she would give him some box of papers, some records which he wanted. That was clear, too. So she'd been there, some weeks, in the clean little room, while certainly Delayne had cajoled, got the box of papers, whatever it was, and then told her he'd give her money to leave. Melora had gathered together the money — from Anne, from Lucy — and would have got some from Tod if murder, and Delayne's fury, had not intervened. Melora had gone to meet them — Delayne and the murdered woman — intending to hand over what money she had. That was clear, too. But Delayne's murderous rage had exploded too soon. So Melora in the hope of preventing identification had suggested switching the coats and had forgotten in their frantic haste the betraying little gold clock — and the sweet roll. All that was horribly clear.

But what records? Why did he — and Melora — have to have them? And what had she, Anne, told Melora that made Delayne consider her own murder imperative? She tried to think back and couldn't and had to listen, for there was another light clink of glass and ice and Melora said, "I told you not to drink. You've had enough."

"I'm tired of taking orders."

"Listen," Melora said. "You've made the mistakes. If you hadn't got scared when that girl Daisy phoned to you and asked if you'd written that last note . . ."

"*You* said to write it! *You* said that since the landlady had said she was Mrs. Reginald Delayne the police would question everybody in the Wystan house and that note would make them suspect the sister-in-law — Cassie, whatever her name is. *You* told me to do that."

Melora sighed gently again. "It seemed a good idea. I thought they'd concentrate on her. I didn't want them to get to hunting around for you. For all I knew the landlady had seen you some time."

"You hate Cassie." He laughed. "So — accuse her of murder!"

"Cassie was too smart for me," Melora said

coolly. "Burning it like that. But you made another mistake there. Daisy . . ."

"Stop that!" Delayne said in a deadly tone. He seemed to make a sudden movement and Melora said, "Put that knife away. . . . You need me, darling."

But there was the faintest, smallest change in her tone and Anne thought, she's afraid of him, too.

Delayne killed Daisy. He was her boy friend, a pickup, because he was casing the house — Daphne had said that; casing the house, getting information from poor, gullible Daisy, so proud of her new boy friend and talking of marriage. And telling Delayne anything he wanted to know, such as when Brent — unexpectedly, sooner than he had intended — was going to France? A shadowy surmise began to establish itself in Anne's mind.

Delayne said, "*You* made me write that last note. . . ."

"I didn't know that Daisy would recognize your handwriting. Why did you ever write to her?"

"I couldn't always be at her beck and call. Sometimes when she'd told me to meet her somewhere I didn't want to — so I'd write her a little note and say I couldn't and . . ."

"You like women," Melora said flatly. "It pleased you because Daisy was so flattered by all your attention. You liked that — but you made another mistake when you . . ."

"I had to!" Delayne's voice rose. "She phoned to me. She said I'd written that note and she knew it and if I didn't meet her right away and explain she'd tell the police so . . ."

"So you met her. That was a mistake, too, but it's done. Now we'll go ahead just as we planned. You didn't see them tonight so you're to see Gary and Brent tomorrow and give them the letters, all that stuff that proves you were the English boy Mrs. March took care of. . . ."

"It's too dangerous now," Delayne said. "Even this way — it doesn't change me enough. Look at me!" he said in the anger of outraged vanity.

As if he had spoken to her, not Melora, Anne took one quick glance at him. He had removed his hat and coat. His glossy black hair was now clipped short in a crew cut. He wore a bulky, ill-fitting tweed suit. He looked strangely different — and was just the same.

Letters, the English boy Mrs. March took care of, he was to see Gary and Brent — he wore a crew cut and a tweed suit, Gary had said. The shadowy surmise sprang into fact. Delayne was the Cadell claimant.

That was the entire answer, wasn't it? Melora would have known of the Cadell case. They had planned together to hoodwink Gary, and through him Brent, into accepting Delayne as the right Cadell, and paying over to Delayne the Cadell money. Melora had sent Delayne to Gary with his convincing story, part of which must be true. There must have been really a Mrs. March who had in fact taken care of an English boy — Delayne! Delayne, of course! A convincing story, Gary had said, because the new claimant had said frankly that he had no birth records, nothing but letters from his mother, Lisa Cadell. Were those the letters which he'd had to have, and for the possession of which he'd been forced to send for his wife? His name was Crayshaw; he'd changed his name to Delayne — Reginald Delayne. And he was not the real Cadell. Letters can be altered, letters can be forged, carefully written, but one cannot forge stamped and post-marked envelopes! There would have been a passport in the name of Crayshaw, perhaps other records in connection with Mrs. March's voluntary guardianship of a refugee English boy. Those records would be convincing, too.

Melora answered, as if Anne had spoken. "I've done everything I could. I wrote those two letters. I put in details that sounded true. I worked in all those references to Cadell and the Controlla Company and the accident. I put them in the envelopes you got from that box Mrs. March kept. Even Gary said they were convincing. The letters signed Lisa Cadell — the details," she laughed. "Warning Mrs. March that you were subject to colds and not let you get a cold! And how she would repay Mrs. March for all her care of you once the Controlla Company made its settlement. If you get the money it'll be because of those letters and what I gave you —

that's the important thing. That will prove your claim!"

"But she knows about it," Delayne said. There was a soft, gliding movement over the rug.

Without opening her eyes, before he spoke, Anne knew that he had approached the sofa and was looking down at her. She controlled the impulse to check her very heartbeat. She must breathe evenly, she must pretend to be asleep. He said, very near, horribly near, "I don't think she's asleep. . . . But it doesn't matter." Delayne laughed deeply and moved away.

It didn't matter. They didn't care what Anne heard or what she made of it. They talked with horrible, matter-of-fact candor and the reason for that candor was clear. Delayne was going to kill her and Melora wasn't going to stop it. Melora had thought it over and made her decision.

Melora said, "I've got it all planned. You were too late to see them today. So see Gary and Brent tomorrow. Give them everything this time. Brent will settle."

"Not till he gets his wife back. He'll put off everything until . . ."

"Dear," Melora said. "If he refuses to settle — well, we've got her! Don't you see? Every man has his price."

There was another long pause. Then Delayne said slowly, "I never thought of that. You are smart. . . . But — what about her?"

And then, just then, with no warning,

someone knocked lightly on the door.

Brent, Anne thought. *Brent!* She almost screamed to him. She almost opened her eyes and scrambled for the door, screaming — and she didn't, for there was a soft rush of movement, a kind of rustle, and Melora whispered, very near, "Take her into the bedroom. Stay there. . . ."

They knew who stood there in the hall and knocked so lightly!

There was no sense of either surprise or fright but they were hurried. She felt Delayne near her. His arms scooped under her and her horror of him was such that she struggled in spite of herself. She writhed away from him, she started to scream and a hand clamped down over her mouth. He dragged her from the sofa, along the floor. His lithe, dancer's body seemed to sense every movement her own drugged muscles could make, as if her intention telegraphed itself to him. Her elbow struck a door casing and the pain tingled through her. She caught at the door casing and he wrenched her away from it, dragged her into and across another room and suddenly let her go, like a sack, so she dropped down on a bed. She opened her eyes then and he wasn't watching her. He had gone across the room again, he was bent over, against a closed door, listening.

The room was full of stale cigarette smoke and stale perfume and rosy lights which danced before Anne's eyes. She mustn't let him see that she was awake. Let him think she had struggled involuntarily, half asleep; make him think that. She shut her eyes quickly.

A man in the next room said, "Did you bring her here? Would she come with you? What have you done with her?"

Anne's world rocked and shivered into pieces like broken glass. But the pieces made a clear pattern of murder.

TWENTY-THREE

Melora said, "I'll show you. She's asleep. I gave her a little pill. She's in here. . . ."

There was not the smallest rustle in the room, no slight whisper of movement, yet Anne knew that Delayne had moved. She opened her eyes cautiously and Delayne was gone and a closet door across the room was barely moving, settling softly into place.

The bedroom door then opened and Anne shut her eyes again. "I wouldn't hurt her," Melora said. "See? She's perfectly all right. I'll just keep her till we get the money. It's easy."

"Not so easy," he said.

"But I told you — we had to get her out of the way somehow."

"Where is Delayne?"

"Oh, he's staying close to the apartment you told him to take, under the name Cadell."

He said abruptly, "We can't go through with it. There wasn't to be murder. Delayne — can't you see that I'm an accessory? You're an accessory!"

"Nobody will ever know if we just keep our heads." Melora's voice was very gentle.

"He's a killer. I didn't expect that."

"I'll protect Anne. We'll get the money, we'll divide it — a third to Delayne and the rest for you and me." Her voice lowered. "Delayne is

314

scared. He'll get out as soon as he's got some money. The police will know he murdered those women. But nobody will connect you or me with it. Besides — I'm supposed to be dead!"

"You'll stick to Delayne."

"No! He is just a — a tool. He is really an English boy, the Crayshaw boy. That can be proved. You made up the story he was to tell and it's solid, it'll stand up in court. . . ."

"No, it can't go to court. There are too many loopholes," he said shortly.

"Well, but it needn't. A settlement out of court. That's the point."

"Things have changed. Those two women — murdered. Daisy and Delayne's wife."

"Why, you're not afraid!"

"I am afraid. Delayne . . ."

"He'll leave, get out of the country, go somewhere as soon as he gets the money. We'll be rid of him. We'll get the money and give him his share and get out and — I love you." Melora's voice was as soft as a light spring breeze, as confiding as the purr of a kitten. And a bell buzzed long and harshly somewhere in the apartment.

"Who is that?"

"I don't know! It's the entrance, downstairs. The bell under the mailbox." This time Melora was frightened and surprised. This summons was not an accustomed and familiar one as the light knock on the door had been.

The bell buzzed again.

"I'm getting out of here. . . ."

315

"Yes — yes, you'd better go," Melora said swiftly. "I'll phone to you later."

Footsteps padded away. The bell buzzed again imperatively. There was the whisper of the closet door opening and Delayne's lithe movement across the floor.

"It's the police!" he whispered sharply.

"It can't be. I'm not going to answer it."

"I heard you. All those promises to him. So you're going to give me a third of the money and then get rid of me. . . ."

"Darling, I didn't mean it! I was terrified. I'd have said anything. . . ."

The doorbell buzzed sharply again. There was a rush of movement in the room and all at once it was empty. Anne knew it was empty but she looked, warily, peering between half-closed eyelids. Delayne had gone. Melora had gone.

But then she heard Melora's footsteps, running back into the room. She shook her arm. "Anne — Anne — you've got to listen. . . ."

But Melora listened, her hand tense. The bell did not buzz again. Melora let out her breath. "They've gone. Now then . . . Anne, listen to me. They may come back. Anne . . ."

Anne opened her eyes. "I heard it all. Delayne wants the Cadell money. You got letters from his wife. . . . He killed Daisy too. . . ."

"I told you he made mistakes. Everything's gone wrong because of him. We weren't quite ready. We thought there was time. But when Daisy told him Brent was leaving so soon we had

316

to do something to bring Brent back before he paid over the money."

"Those notes . . ."

"That day you came home too soon, you talked to me and you told me you'd seen me in the Museum where I was waiting for him. It's near the house and he was seeing Daisy — after that. . . . I tried to tell him murder wasn't the answer."

"You helped him."

"I'm afraid of him. That's why I'm telling you all this. I protected you. Now you've got to help me."

"I didn't recognize him. I didn't even see the face of the man you met at the Museum. Delayne must have known that when he came and said he was Dr. Smith. *Why did he try to kill me?*"

Melora's head was turned; she was listening. She said in a whisper, "Something terrible is going to happen. You've got to come with me. You've got to tell Brent I protected you, I had nothing to do with murder. . . ."

She stopped. Anne heard it, too. A hoarse kind of scream came from somewhere near. It was a cry for help. It broke off, half-uttered.

Melora's eyes met Anne's. She wiped her hand across her face. Then she ran out of the room. Anne got to her feet, she staggered across the room and stopped, clinging to the door of the living room.

Gary Molloy lay half on the floor, half

sprawled against a chair, near the kitchen door. His fine, small hands were over a spreading red blotch at his throat. He gave a kind of fluttering sigh, said, "Melora . . ." and sagged down onto the floor.

Anne couldn't watch, she couldn't hear, the entire world thudded and revolved around her. Yet she knew that Melora and Delayne were talking quickly in whispers. She knew that Delayne had dragged Gary away, back toward the kitchen. A tiny pink rose lay on the floor — the kind of rose Gary always wore in his button-hole.

Anne turned away without knowing it. She stumbled back toward the bed and leaned against it. She was vaguely aware of sounds in the living room. A door had opened, perhaps someone again had knocked, for Melora said suddenly, loudly, "How did you find me? What do you want?"

Brent said, "Where is Anne?"

Brent! And he didn't know that Delayne was there and Delayne had a knife.

Melora said, "Anne? What are you talking about?"

"That's her coat!"

"Brent, what is the matter? Dear Brent, you — you did guess that I hadn't been killed, didn't you, so you came to see me and — and you found me again and — and I want to come back to you, Brent. I want to come back. It was always you I loved. I was so wrong to leave you but —

but that was because of Cassie. It was all her fault. Let me come back to you. . . .”

Anne ran to the door. There was Brent, with Melora clinging to his arm. Brent's white face was hard, blazing with hatred. “If you've hurt her, I'll kill you!” He thrust Melora back, so hard she fell against a chair.

Anne's throat unlocked. “I knew you'd come! I knew it. . . .”

“Anne!” He was across the room at one stride and had her in his arms.

Melora cried, “Anne came to me, Brent. She came for help. She'd quarreled with Cassie. I promised to protect her. I promised . . .”

Across the room the door to the kitchen swung silently open and Delayne stood there, his eyes lethal. Brent felt Anne's body tense and turned. “You're Delayne,” he said. He looked at Melora. “Where is Gary?”

Melora pushed back her untidy, pale hair and cried, “Gary — but this was all Gary's plan, Brent! We couldn't have done it without him. He planned everything. He told us what to do. I didn't . . .”

“Delayne killed Gary,” Anne said. “I heard . . .”

It seemed queer that Brent did not look surprised. He didn't look at Anne at all. He was watching Delayne. He said, “Anne! Get your coat. Get out . . .”

She snatched up her coat. Delayne didn't move. Brent didn't move. But softly, like a scuttling little crab, Melora sidled to the corner of the room near the door. Her hand hovered over the spotted leopard-skin coat. Delayne then lifted his hand. A knife in it caught the light.

Anne flung herself at Brent but Brent caught her and pushed her back toward the door. Something swished like a wire through the air. The door behind Brent opened as if of itself. The knife hung quivering, its point dug into the wall behind Brent.

Anne knew that Melora had slid out of the door and was gone. She didn't try to stop her. Brent flung himself at Delayne, and Delayne fought and writhed and grunted as Brent's fist drove him down in a sprawling huddle on the floor. Brent cried over his shoulder, *"Hurry, Anne. Get out . . ."*

But the huddled, writhing figure was squirming near the table, a hand stealthily groped over the top of it.

"There's a gun!" Anne screamed. "A gun — on the table . . ."

Anne was dimly conscious of sounds through the open door; the elevator rumbling again, the clatter of its door and heavy footsteps pounding along the hall toward her. Brent had seen the gun, too. He had Delayne's writhing, strong wrist in his grip. A tall man brushed past Anne, several men in uniform ran past her, thrusting her out of the way.

A sudden gunshot — several gunshots crashed with such shocking loudness around her that the sounds blanked out everything else.

The silence afterward made the low, terse voices of the men crowding into the room seem clear but remote. Then Brent came to her. "I'll take you home," he said, wrapped her coat around her and took her down in the slow and creaking elevator, down to the ugly, begrimed entrance and out into the stinging, fresh, wonderful cold and snow of the night.

A police car waited for them. But they didn't go home. They went instead to Lucy's where she was waiting for them. She took Anne tight in her arms. There was a fire and the dogs leaped and bounded and Anne sat in a deep chair before the fire with Brent beside her, holding a glass of something hot to her lips, smoothing her hair and touching her face, her hands, as if he had to make sure that she was there.

Brent talked and Anne talked while Lucy listened and asked no questions. But Lieutenant Donovan, who arrived before the milk had cooled in the glass Anne held, asked questions.

"Well," he said at last. "Thanks, Mrs. Wystan. You've filled in almost the whole story. As much as we need to know, at any rate."

"But I don't know why Delayne tried to kill *me!* I didn't recognize him as the man with Melora in the Museum when he came and said he was Dr. Smith. I couldn't have identified him as Delayne or . . ."

"They thought you could. And after he made a bad mistake and showed himself to you as Dr.

Smith, they knew that you could identify him as the Cadell claimant. He made too many mistakes. Trying to govern Delayne was like trying to put a tiger in harness. He blundered from the beginning. Mistake number one was when he showed himself to you and called himself a doctor. Mistake number two, he followed you to the drug store and stupidly aroused the drugstore clerk's suspicion. Mistake number three was his attempt to murder you that very night, when he was frightened by your niece and ran away. Mistake number four, he let himself be carried away by a murderous rage and killed his wife. Mistake number five, he killed the maid, Daisy, for fear she would turn him in as the writer of that last note. He took absurd chances, like coming into the house and typing those first notes — and letting himself be seen by Daphne. Perhaps that was his first mistake."

Lieutenant Donovan rubbed his eyes wearily. "I really can't number his mistakes, they were all of the same pattern. He was not only a tiger, he was a stupid, arrogant and conceited tiger, sure that any idea he had was brilliant. Stupidity, arrogance, not a little spite — and, mainly, I think, greed controlled him to the point where he lost his head not once but several times. I wish," he said with sudden violence, "that we could recognize the utterly amoral and potentially murderous characteristics of a man like this and put him in quarantine like smallpox before he can do any damage! It'd make my job easier." He smiled as if apologizing for his outburst and turned to Anne. "This began it," he said. "And this led to Delayne's determination to kill you." He dived into a pocket, stretched his hand over the table and dropped something on it.

Anne stared. "It's Melora's locket!"

It lay on the table, shining with bright blue turquoises and dark red garnets. Brent said, "You told Melora you had seen her, that she was with a man, and she was wearing a locket. Up to then the notes had been merely threats, designed to frighten you so you'd send for me to come home. Their first efforts were directed toward keeping me from seeing Cadell. The instant Melora told Delayne that you had seen him, and you had seen and described this locket — the pretended murder threats changed to the real thing. You see . . ." He opened the locket and nodded. "We were right, Donovan. Cadell, the real Cadell, sent me this locket as proof of his identity. Here are photographs, inside it. I suppose that is his mother. The other is his father — I've seen his photographs. I'm sure of that."

The pictures in the locket were small and a little faded; a young man, dark, with bright, intelligent eyes and a young woman, dark too, her hair swept up in a pompadour. "Cadell sent this to me," Brent said. "That was when he first got in touch with the Controlla Company and was referred to me. He told me that he was sending photographs. He wrote to me in English; he doesn't write English very well. He didn't say that he had sent the photographs framed in a locket. I presume he sent the locket itself because he thought that the photographs would be more effective as proof since they came to him from his mother, inside the locket. There is undoubtedly something very convincing about an article so clearly an evidence of love and sentiment. However, he wrote only of photographs; he did not mention a locket. So far as I knew the separate photographs never arrived. I concluded that either he had decided not to send them or they had been lost in the mail. He then got a lawyer and although the lawyer did mention photographs, he didn't put much emphasis on them, and he said nothing of a locket. Probably, this lawyer had never seen it. Perhaps he didn't realize its importance. Perhaps he even doubted his client's word for it — I don't know. Certainly by that time the lawyer was engaged in trying to get the right and accurate records assembled, so to him photographs would not be important. If I had actually seen young Cadell, he would have told me about this. That's another reason why they felt that they had to keep me from going to France."

Lieutenant Donovan said, "You see, Mrs. Wystan, as soon as Delayne knew that you had seen him and you had seen and remembered this locket, he must have decided that murder — not merely threats of murder which were only designed to frighten you, but real murder — was his only answer. After he had actually come to the house — stupidly letting you get a good look at him, he *knew* you could identify him — after that, there was no turning back for him. This locket was to be their convincing proof of his claims to the Cadell money. This locket," he said musingly, "and Delayne's real story suggested the whole plan."

Lucy said, "And Melora simply took that locket."

"It must have been in a package," Brent said. "How or why it came to the house I don't know — although sometimes when I was away I'd have the mail brought to the house so I could see it as soon as I returned. Obviously though she opened it. It's pretty so she kept it. Why she didn't remove the pictures inside it I don't know. . . ."

Lucy said shortly, "I do. She just didn't take the trouble. The locket attracted her so she kept it and wore it, that's all."

"It's certain that later when she ran out of money she saw how she could use it."

The locket gleamed in the light as it had against Melora's black sweater in the restaurant. Anne remembered how she had insisted, saying to Melora: "But I saw you. . . . You wore a black sweater." She had described the locket set with turquoises and garnets. "A man came in and sat down with you."

She pushed the locket back to Donovan and he scooped it up. Brent said, "They needed Gary. I didn't suspect him, not even when he produced a claimant to the Cadell money. He did it very adroitly. But when he spoke of something Cadell had of sentimental value, I did remember those lost photographs, which I knew Melora, living in my house at the time, could have got hold of. And it did then occur to me that the Cadell claimant just might be Delayne. But then tonight, when I got back to the house and the Cadell claimant hadn't turned up at Gary's office at all and Anne was gone, I began to wonder about Gary. He'd gone out of his office while I was there. He *could* have phoned to Anne, as he undoubtedly did — at Melora's suggestion, for they had to get Anne out of the way somehow. But I don't think Gary meant murder. He was in the same spot as Melora. They had a born killer for an accomplice and they couldn't control him. And then Anne phoned to me. Cassie began to cry and told me the facts about that note Cassie burned. Daisy had told the truth. It was 'Cassie killed her and she'll kill you.' Cassie said it sounded like Melora and all at once I realized that it was the kind of thing Melora would have done or suggested to Delayne. And Gary had identified the dead woman as Melora. I got hold of you then, Donovan. You took me to the morgue and of course the woman identified as Mrs. Reginald Delayne was not Melora." He put his hand over Anne's. "Daff told us how to find Melora. Daff hadn't told anybody but she'd had a birthday card from Melora — it had a return address and just the street number. Then Daff and Cadwallader re-membered a name Melora had told Cadwallader to use when Delayne used to phone to her. It was Bridges. Melora really knew some woman by that name. There was a Bridges listed at that ad-dress. By then I felt sure that Delayne was our man. The Cadell money supplied a motive which fit the facts we had. If that proved to be right then Melora was clearly back of it and Gary was in it up to his neck. But the main thing was to find you. Melora's apartment was our only lead. Donovan and a police car went with me. The police stayed in the vestibule. I went up to the apartment alone. I was afraid Melora or Delayne would hurt you. I was too late to save Gary but . . ."

"It's just as well from your point of view," Lieutenant Donovan said, "not so good from mine. But Delayne will talk — if he recovers. I can't understand Gary Molloy, a man of his age and standing, letting a woman influence him like that."

Cassie had said Gary was a fool about Melora.

Lucy said in a low voice, "But why did Delayne kill Gary? Surely he didn't need to!"

Lieutenant Donovan gave Lucy a queer glance, half-surprise and half-sympathy. "I know he was an old friend, Miss Wystan. But people change. Gary Molloy may not have meant murder but what he did led to murder. He was an accomplice after the fact, remember. As to why Delayne killed him, Mrs. Wystan told us that. Mrs. — that is, Melora told Gary Molloy that she'd leave Delayne and she and Gary would take most of the money she still hoped to get. Probably she only meant to smooth down Gary, reassure him. He was scared. But Delayne believed it was a double cross. And when Delayne got an idea in that prehistoric skull of his he didn't wait to reason. He acted."

Brent said, "Gary *had* changed, Aunt Lucy. Slowly. Drinking too much. Little by little losing standing. I've been sending him jobs when I could. But I'm sure he needed money."

"And he wanted money. For Melora." Lieutenant Donovan shook his head. "I can't understand it. . . ."

Again Lucy quietly interrupted. "You didn't know Melora."

"No," the lieutenant said, "but we'll find her." He rose.

After he'd gone Lucy said gravely, "They'll not find Melora."

"I don't think she really meant murder," Anne said. "It was Delayne . . ."

"She strung along with Delayne. She helped him," Brent said. It was like the terrible pronouncement of a verdict of guilty. He turned to Anne. "Last night I tried to talk to you about her. I wanted you to know . . ."

"Oh!" Anne said and put her hands into Brent's. "No, you just said Melora and — went to sleep." Her heart said, forgive me.

"Melora wouldn't acknowledge that she

meant murder, not even to herself," Lucy said. "She's a born liar, as Delayne is a born killer. Night and day, year in year out, whenever it suits her to lie. Perhaps she even deceives herself but I doubt it. No — she'll go on like that, lower and lower — well, she can't go much lower than Delayne but . . ." She stirred the fire and said briskly, "She'll never come back. She'll be afraid to. That's the end of Melora."

The dogs barked and bounced. Daff came running in. She had been crying but her eyes were now as bright as jewels. "Anne, Anne," she laughed and sobbed and laughed again. "You're safe and I helped find you. And Mother says we're going to have our own home and not live with you and Uncle Brent any more, but she says I can come to see you whenever I want to and she sends her love. She and Tod are waiting for you but I couldn't wait and — oh, Anne . . ." Daff put her arms tight around Anne.

Lucy said quietly, "Did you have anything to do with this, Brent?"

Brent did not reply. Lucy did not seem to expect it. She said, "But perhaps for everybody, at some time, there's a moment of self-revelation. For Cassie, too." She stopped and put her hand on Daff's black head.

Brent said, "We'll have our own home, Anne. A small house — anything you want." He drew her up, away from Daphne, away from everybody, close and hard in his arms. "You needn't ever go back to that house, Anne."

After a moment she drew back to look at him. He was just the same. He'd never changed. He was the man she'd loved and married. "Take me home now, Brent," she said.

Daff went with them, pink with excitement. Lucy stood in the door, old Brummel under her arm. At the last minute Sister decided to accompany them and frisked out the door but then had a prudent second thought and scampered back to Lucy.